Also by Nicholson Baker

The Mezzanine

Room Temperature

U and I

Vox

The Fermata

The Size of Thoughts

The Everlasting Story of Nory

 Published in the United States by Random House, Inc., New York, and simultaneously in Canada by Random House of Canada Limited, Toronto.

Library of Congress Cataloging-in-Publication Data

Baker, Nicholson.
The everlasting story of Nory / Nicholson Baker. — 1st ed.
p. cm.
I. Title.
PS3552.A4325E94 1998
813'.54—dc21 97-23942

Random House website address: www.randomhouse.com

Printed in the United States of America on acid-free paper

98765432

First Edition

The Everlasting Story of Nory

a novel

Nicholson Baker

Random House New York

For my dear daughter Alice, the informant

The Everlasting Story of Nory

1. What She Liked to Do

Eleanor Winslow was a nine-year-old girl from America with straight brown bangs and brown eyes. She was interested in dentistry or being a paper engineer when she grew up. A paper engineer is an artist who designs pop-up books and pop-up greeting cards, which are extremely important to have easily available in stores because they make people happier in their lives. Lately Nory was in a stage of liking to draw pictures of Chinese girls wearing patchwork Chinese robes with their hair up in a little hat, or held on the side with a pin. She told a constant number of stories to herself in the car while they drove to Stately Homes. She also told them to herself in the bathtub or in the mirror. Sometimes she and her friends made up stories together, but that of course depended heavily on the friend. Another thing Nory liked doing was making up new designs of dolls that she wished you could have the opportunity to buy but you can't and probably never will.

For example, she drew a doll named 'Riena.' Riena had straight hair parted on the side and puffy sleeves. She was not stretched out with a teenagery figure or short with a massive rounded head. Her hands and wrists could bend so she could hold a miniature carton of eggs, and every egg would have a realistic crack in the middle. You would help Riena put the egg down on the saucing pan, and shuffle it around, and after a while the egg would break by itself, because it would be filled with a special substance that expanded when you jostled it. A little folded-up rubbery thing that was an egg would goosh out, probably sunny side up, in the pan. Or you could have the second option of scrambled style, or an omelette. Riena had an apron with a pattern of spoons and forks. Sadly she didn't exist except as a drawing.

Nory was tall for her age, especially in the city of Threll, in England, where she and her mother, her father, and her brother, who was two, were living for a certain amount of time. There were quite a number of girls at her school, the Threll Junior School. She was hoping she would meet a good friend.

2. An Important Building

Threll Cathedral was the biggest thing in the city, by any means. It was an old cathedral that had a tower on it that had the unique ability to look close to you, and yet be very far away. Airplanes can do that, too. They seem close but aren't, unless it isn't your lucky day. Inside the cathedral was almost as beautiful as outside except that there were modern things like wires and plugs that looked as if somebody had made a careless mistake, and modern-day loudspeakers up on the columns looking pretty indistinct. There were also some big tombs carved out of a certain kind of black and red stone that was not precisely frightening but was certainly alarming, because it was so vividly black, and of course there were corpses buried here and there in the walls or in the floor, some of which might be quite mummified. Saint Rufina, a famous woman who had been a very lovely young princess with long black hair who decided to give up her jewelry and become a nun and wear only the roughest clothes, and who died in a terrible way, by being eaten to death by wild dogs that ran through the church in the dead of wintertime, was in a special chapel all to herself, where one arm of her was set aside, that someone had scooped up and saved from the dogs, because everyone had loved her for her kindness and her healing ability. Nearby her chapel was a very tall thin window with pictures of tanks and warships and bombers on it. War pictures didn't seem like a perfect idea for a subject in stained glass in a famously holy cathedral, but on the other hand if you're going to have a stained-glass tank or battleship, this was probably the most beautiful tank you would ever find. The caterpillar treads were made of tiny scribs and scrabs of green and blue glass. The window was in honor of some of the people from the city of Threll who had died at war.

Way, way up in a tower above the stone floor of the Cathedral was the Jasperium. It was a kind of a stained-glass window in the form of a dome, right over where the two pieces of the cross met. A cathedral is usually arranged in the shape of a crucifiction, because Jesus died up on the cross. 'But why,' Nory wondered sometimes, 'do they have to concentrate on the awful way he died? Why not have a cathedral in the shape of a G, for God, a squared-off G with an inner courtyard with a wishing well and herbs growing to make tea for the sick, for instance?' A thousand upon a thousand pieces of green glass were up there in the Jasperium in a little circle—a pretty big circle, actually, but it was little from the distance away you were standing when you looked up at it. When the sun was bright outside, it sent the green light down in a soft green stalk onto the floor of the Cathedral. They had a group of black chairs specially positioned so you could sit in a chair and wait for the green light to come over you like a spotlight on a slug, and supposedly at that moment you could almost think God's thoughts. You were not really thinking God's thoughts, of course, but the thoughts God wanted you to think. If you didn't believe in God, you were thinking what others thought of God, or what they thought God wanted them to think. At least you were thinking the Cathedral's thoughts in some fashion, which was a pretty worthwhile thing to be able to do on its own.

3. A Story About Beetles

The owners of the Threll Cathedral, who were the Anglican Bishops and Deans, had just spent millions of dollars, or pounds, to clean all the glass in the Jasperium and make sure it wasn't going to fall down. But while they were doing that, they had discovered that Death Watch Beetles had chewed through the lead that covered the ends of the beams of wood that attached the Jasperium to the tops of the stone columns. So they had to replace some of the wood, but not all. Death Watch Beetles were called that because in former times, when a person was very sick, if his family heard any of these beetles banging their small heads against the wood of a house—*chk, chk, chk*—it meant the sick person would die soon. Nory, because she wanted to be a dentist, had a specific thought about this, which was: 'Their teeth must be extraordinarily strong to have chewed through lead. They must be hidden away normally and then fold out when they open their mouths.'

Crocodiles grow twenty-four sets of teeth in their lives and they can perform for two years without food. But Nory severely doubted that the Death Watch Beetle had more than one set of teeth. 'It must be a difficult way of life up there,' Nory thought, 'generation after generation of Beetle, trying to find enough to eat in the old, horrible, chewed-over wood. They must be down to the bare gristle.' Near the Cathedral was a very good tea shop that had an extremely good chocolate fudge cake. The cake was served with a little cup of whipped cream, by the way.

Nory didn't like a certain picture in one of the brochures that her parents bought about Threll Cathedral that showed a man wearing a mask putting a metal tube into one of the old pieces of wood under the Jasperium in order to squirt powerful bug-killing foam inside. She had to make up a story about a family of Death Watch Beetles who learned of the approach of a squirt of the poison and packed up their household and made little parachutes out of some candy wrappers one of the bug-killing men had left in the scaffolding and parachuted down, down, down, smuggling through the cool empty air of the inside of the cathedral, swaying, their feelers curled up tight in fear, until they landed in a huge stone land of green light on the cold floor near a little girl with bright eyes and black hair named Mariana.

Mariana was sitting with her eyes closed, waiting to see if she could think the thoughts God wanted her to think. She opened her eyes to see how close the light was to her feet, because she thought that as soon as the light touched her feet she would start to feel the sacred holiness, and she was just creeping her feet a little closer to the light, so that the holiness would get there more quickly, when she thought she noticed something. Yes, she did notice something: four tiny creatures, carefully folding up a chewing-gum wrapper. 'Oh, who are you?' she said, bending toward them and letting them hop onto her palm.

'We're Death Watch Beetles,' said one of them. 'A bad man is squirting our country full of terrible poison.'

'Oh,' said Mariana, 'he isn't a bad man, I'm sure, he just wants to be sure that the Jasperium doesn't fall down. You see, when you eat the wood, the wood becomes weaker and weaker, and finally the whole thing would turn to crumbs and fall. You wouldn't want that to happen to the Cathedral, would you?'

'Well,' grudged the Death Watch Beetle, 'if they'd just explained what the problem was, and given us another piece of wood to live in, we would have left on our own. As it is, look at little Gary, he has gotten sick from chewing on the lead.' And indeed Mariana saw that little Gary was lying on his back and he did not look at all well. He looked as pale as a bug can look, and near death. Mariana gently put all four beetles in her pencil case and walked out to the forest. She knew where a special fallen tree lay. There was a pool of rainwater in a groove of this tree, and she picked a certain kind of flower as she went, singing a mild song, and crushed the petals in the water. It was a special kind of flower that could cure any kind of lead poisoning, and it was called the Montezuma flower, because it could grow in really hot or very cold places, so that it was a great survivor. Then she opened the pencil case. The three healthy Death Watch Beetles carried Gary, the sick one, out. 'Wash him in the water,' said Mariana gently. She was a tall girl with dark brown hair. 'The potion will help him.'

At first the beetles weren't sure, and they sniffed the water and tested it with their feelers and that sort of usual behavior. Then gradually they lost their fears and dipped

Gary freely in, not head-first but gently, tail-first, and they all went in, one by one, and splashed in the water contentedly. They had spent so many centuries cooped up inside the old Norman beams of the Jasperium that they had forgotten that rainwater could be so clean and pure, and they were overjoyed. Gary sat up in the water and said he felt much better. Then all four of them found a place in a spot of sun to dry their bodies and when they were toasty and warm again, they waved goodbye, and began chewing their mazes in the huge tree trunk. 'Lovely layers of wood!' they said. 'Rings and rings and rings! It'll be a long time before we chew up this enormous country! Don't tell anyone you brought us here.'

'I won't,' laughed Mariana. 'Good luck!'

'Thank you, Mariana,' they called, giving a last happy wave. 'Bye! Bye! Bye!'

That was a story she had made about them. In real life Nory had never even seen a Death Watch Beetle. But there were definitely some unusual creatures in Threll. The worst one was a huge spider that her mother spotted in the shower curtain while Nory and Littleguy were in the bathtub setting up a store to sell pretend cappuccinos, with bubble foam. Her mother suddenly jumped up with her magazine and hurried them out and called Nory's father.

'What is it?' said Nory, who hadn't gotten a look because she was shoveled out of the bathroom so quick.

'Don't look,' said Nory's father. 'It's a loathsome Anglo-Saxon bug. It's huge.'

'I won't be disgusted,' said Nory. 'I promise, I won't be.' She peered in, then instantly wailed out in a misery of disgust and hugged her mother. 'Oh, awful!' It was an enormous thing, like a black crab, with the dastardliest hairy legs Nory had ever seen on a spider, and not like a

daddy longlegs's legs, which are quite graceful, but hairy in an ugly thick fearful way. Normally Nory liked all insects, even earwigs, and especially ladybugs, and she did not appreciate any killing, because of the important rule of Do Unto Others, and how would you like it if a huge scrumple of toilet paper came down on you and stole your life away? But this spider in particular was just too hideously hairy-legged to get any empathy from her.

Nory's father came out.

'Is it dead?' they all asked.

Nory's father said that yes, it was dead.

'Good,' said Nory, although immediately she felt a little sad, not to mention embarrassed about shrieking to pieces when she saw it. 'What did you do with it?'

'Flushed it into the depths,' Nory's father said. 'The worst part is I always feel I have to open up the toilet paper to look.'

'Not to dwell,' her mother said.

That was their first adventure in Threll. Nory had some trouble sleeping for two nights, but then she got quickly over it. The only problem was that now she didn't like going to the bathroom in the middle of the night because she sometimes worried that a second-cousin-once-removed of that big black spider was lurching under the seat. But gradually she got over that worry, too. It was a wooden toilet seat—the landlady said that she had bought it for five pounds at an auction from a Stately Home, and that the Duke of Tunaparts, or someone quite obscure like that, had sat on it every day of his life, which was not really a point to its favor.

4. Littleguy Had a Sensible Fear of Owls

Nory was a day student at Threll Junior School, where she used a medium-nib fountain pen with a kind of blue ink that you could make disappear completely from the page with a two-ended instrument called an ink-eradicator. Even when the ink had had a chance to dry for three weeks, the ink-eradicator still had the power to make it disappear. Threll School was started by a kind-looking person with a fur collar whose picture hung on the stairs going up to the dining hall. Pamela Shavers, who was a girl in Nory's class, said he was called Prior Rowland because he lived prior to Henry the Eighth. The dining hall used to be the barn for the monk's cows, another older kid said, but Nory couldn't understand why the monks would have wanted to drag cows up and down stairs twice a day. Then her mother explained that they had built in a second floor when they shipped out the cows. There was still sometimes a slight barny smell about the place, though. The wood had twisting beams, like driftwood, but no Death Watch Beetles that Nory could see; of course she couldn't possibly have heard them banging their heads since kids at lunch make tons and tons of noise.

Prior Rowland began the school to honor the memory of Saint Rufina, something like two thousand years ago, or 'early this morning,' as Nory's brother used to say. Littleguy he was called, although his name was really Frank Wood Winslow. To Littleguy 'long ago' and 'early this morning' meant pretty much the same thing, because his head was still basically a construction site, filled with diggers and dumpers driving around in mushy dirt, and it was hard for him to tell what were the real outlines of his ideas. He knew how to say 'construction site,' and 'traction engine,' and 'coupling,' and 'level crossing,' and 'hundred-ton dump truck,' and 'articulated dump truck' and 'auger driller,' because he loved those sorts of things. But he sometimes held up a very simple object, like a fork or a candle, and said, 'I forgot the word for this.' And he still called a pillow a pibble. But that was a normal thing to expect, Nory thought, because you have to spend your whole life learning more and more about how to draw a difference between one idea and another idea and how to keep them separated out rather than totally dredged together in a sludgy mass. For example, if you say that you're doing something to the honor of someone's memory, say to the honor of Saint Rufina's memory, you don't mean that you're honoring the wonderful memory they might have, as in they can dash off the names of every kid in the class by heart, because they don't have any memories at all, since they're dead. And you don't mean that they have wonderful happy memories of picnics and chicken sandwiches and feeding the ducks that you're honoring, because they don't have those, either. You can't mummify a nice memory in someone's head—no magic herbs will do it. And you don't mean you're honoring any particular other person's memories of the person that is being honored, because the people who are honoring him may not even have known him or met him. Or her, in the case of Saint Rufina. You're just simply honoring the basic idea that this person once lived her life and you're trying to convince the world not to forget her. But any person who remembers her is going to die also, obviously, so you have to keep convincing people from scratch—'Remember this person, remember this person, remember this person.' It isn't easy, but it may be satisfying work.

Littleguy liked having Nory read books to him. However, she had to be careful about certain books. He was not frightened of spiders so much. But owls were a different bowl of fish! To him the nighttime was full of owls rustling and blinking their huge staring eyes. In Nory's house, they couldn't even say 'owl,' they had to spell it out. When Nory read Littleguy a book like *The Country Noisy Book* and they came to the page with an o-w-l sitting in a tree at nighttime, she would bustle to the next page. If she tried to casually cover the owl up with her hand, it never worked, because he knew it was under there. Sometimes Littleguy would try to be brave. 'I like owls very much,' he would say. 'But I don't like just *that* owl.'

Once Nory's mother found Littleguy in the Art Room late at night trying to color over the yellow eyes of a scary owl with a red marker, because he didn't like coming across it in his *Winnie the Pooh* magazine, which he had been flipping through before he fell asleep. Another time he told Nory that two very bad owls were wanting to look in his window, behind the curtain. When Nory heard that, with the frightened seriousness on his face, she also felt a little twizzle of fear down the back of her neck and places like that, because she especially did not like the idea of things waiting outside for her and staring in through blank, black windowpanes at night. The first and one of the few early, early things she remembered about her life was of running down a long hall and stopping at the edge of a window. Then bang: she thought she saw the ugliness of the Tweety Monster with its frown-eyed face, on the other side of the window, and she screamed 'Mommeeeee!' The Tweety Monster was just simply a monster version of Tweety-bird in a *Sylvester and Tweety* tape—Tweety turned into it when he drank a special potion. No reason to be scared of a casual little cartoon. But it *was* scary, and when Nory screamed and dashed away from the window Nory's mother said gently, 'I know, I know, but it's just drawings. There's no Tweety Monster out there, no bad thing, only the gentle night and the squirrels all fluffed up to keep from getting too cold, and the raccoons having a pleasant chew of garbage. Everything's all right.' Her mother's eyes were the most soothing, nicest, softest, deepest eyes that any mother could ever have. They were, to be specific, blue. Sometimes instead of two owls Littleguy had a bad dream about two old, old trucks from the scrapyard with huge tires driving around the living room with their bright lights on. And yet in real life, Littleguy loved trucks more than anything, except trains. One time Littleguy even said he had a nightmare about sitting on the toilet and not having a book to read.

That was one thing that Nory really thought was not quite fair about bad dreams, when they went ahead and took something you loved, like trucks, or mirrors, or your mother, or were proud of, like sitting in the bathroom all by yourself, and made them scary. If Nory had a library, she would not allow any Goosebumps books in the children's department, because just the covers were frightening, never mind the dreadful insides, and kids weren't even aware how frightened they were sometimes until later that evening. There was one book with a picture of an evil doll that she really thought was a bad idea. Why ruin the idea of something nice, like a doll, by making it so horribly scary that you couldn't think about it and couldn't trust it? Your dolls aren't going to do anything bad to you. Your dolls should be trusted to be in your room with you in the middle of the night. Goosebumps books got kids much more scared than they ever wanted to be, or ever expected they would be, and they didn't need that help anyway, since their own dreams would do a superb job of scaring their dits off just on their own. But still, Nory's cousin Anthony and her friend Debbie loved reading Goosebumps books and couldn't think of a funner thing to do. So not everyone had the same reaction.

Nory especially disliked when she had teeth-dreams. Say, for example, a beautiful graceful fluffer-necked duck that was just sitting away the time in the reeds by a river, its feathers being fluttered by the wind, and when you came up to it in the dream to hold out your hand to it to say hello and give it a piece of bread it would suddenly curl back its beaks and show huge fangy teeth. Or a horse with pointy teeth and bug-eyes with white rims would chase her. Or cows with pointed teeth. But those dreams were mostly ones she'd had long ago and gotten adjusted to. Another fairly old dream Nory had was of being chased through various shades of colors by a queen who was determined to cut off her arm for a punishment. Nory dashed away from her, but the Queen came chugging closer, with some of her men, and Nory realized she couldn't escape. So she made them a compromise. She said to the Queen, 'Okay, okay, don't chop off my arm, you can chop off my head.' That way, she wouldn't experience the pain. The Queen said, 'All right!' And *wham,* the ax came circling. 'Ah, how nice,' Nory felt. She didn't have to bow or anything. She didn't even have to put a paper bag over her head.

The moral of the dream was: Better to be dead than armless in agony. It wasn't a perfect moral, though, Nory thought afterward, even for a dream—which isn't too surprising since it's too much to expect of your dreams that they would end up giving off good morals—but really, you can learn to do almost everything you would need to do without arms: play cards with your toes, and that kind of thing. You might hesitate for a moment if your dentist wanted to work on your mouth holding the tools in his toes, true. That might not be the world's most raging success.

5. A Slight Problem After Lunch

At least if Nory had a bad dream she could go into her parents' room and poke at them gently until they woke up enough to comfort her back down. Not every kid had that kind of luck. Some of the kids at Threll School were there all day and all night, twenty-four hours a week. Roger Sharpless was a very short boy with an intelligent face like a detective who cried on the first day in the Cathedral during service during the first week. 'Why are you crying?' Nory asked, in a whisper. 'Sometimes I cry during the day,' he whispered back. Afterward, when they were walking to the Junior School building, he said that he missed his parents horribly. He said that the sight of the little white pillow on his bed in his room reminded him of his old room and that made him cry, because think about it, going away from everything you know, your rugs, your windows, your parents, your driveway, your exact look of street, can be quite a shock to a nine-year-old. He also told her a fact that he said he would never forget in his whole life, because he had gotten it wrong on a test one time: the Greeks wrote by making marks on wax. Nory felt that it was kind of him to tell her, because now she would never forget it either.

The day after that she had a much less good experience. She dropped her tray in the dining hall when it was full of fresh food. Kira, one of her new sort-of friends, said, 'Oh, don't worry, somebody else will get it.' But Nory didn't feel right about leaving the mess in a lavish plop on the floor and walking on. The jacket potato did not look its best. An older girl scooped down to help her, and finally a woman came by with a mop. But by then all the other kids from her class had gone off and were eating merrily along, chew chew chew, getting far ahead of her. Not only that, but the line had gotten very long, because a whole conjugation of older boys had come in. She didn't want to cut in, so she went to the back and waited all over again. The line was so long it even went down a few steps of the stairs, which gave her a chance to look at Prior Rowland's fur collar.

Finally she got a new tray of food, and she sat anonymously down. People in her class were leaving to go back to the Junior School building. One after another they were going. Nory had her eye on them the whole time, except when she was looking down at her plate. She thought, 'Ah, but she's still there, so it's okay.' And then when that girl left, she said to herself, 'Ah, well, *she's* still there, so when worse goes to worse, I can go back with her.' The problem was that the Junior School was far away from the dining hall, across two streets, and Nory had an awful if not atrocious sense of direction and knew she would never find it by herself. So she ate and ate and finished up and whammed out the door of the dining hall, hurrying to be with a girl who was in her class. Dorette was her name. Dorette said, 'Sorry I can't talk, I'm meeting a friend.'

Nory said, 'Oh, okay.' The other girl came up. It was a girl Nory didn't like very much because she had said that Nory had a 'squeegee' accent on one of the first days of school. Nory stood a little way behind and started following them as they went around the buildings toward the old gate.

Dorette turned and said, 'Go away. Why are you following us?'

'Because I don't know the way home,' said Nory.

'Home? Home?' the girls said.

'I mean, the way back to the class,' said Nory.

'Oh, go on, you know the way,' the two girls said. 'You lead us, and we'll follow.'

So Nory started tenderly walking in front of them down the street, not vastly sure she was pointing in the right direction. There was a road curving up a hill that didn't look familiar. There were no crosswalks. She turned around and noticed that the girls weren't behind her. She started to feel scattered and scared. Then the two girls jumped out from behind a bush with red berries and laughed. She started following them again, and they told her to go away. Fortunately just at that point a teacher came out from a door in the building and the two girls said, all nicey-nicey, 'Hello Mr. So-and-so.' They began chatting with him. Nory was worried that they would tell the teacher that she had been following them and she would get in trouble, but they didn't. So she could sneak along, pace by pace, some distance behind, from bush to bush. That was how she was able to get back. Later that day, on the playground, another girl said, 'Hah-hah, you were sent back, you were sent back.' Nory had no idea what the girl was talking about, so she said, 'What are you talking about?'

'For dropping your tray,' the girl said. Nory said, 'I was not. I went to the end of the line because you shouldn't cut in. And I'm from America. We don't say *sent back* in

America to mean what you mean. We don't say *bin* in America, we say trashcan. We don't say *crayons* when we're talking about colored pencils, we skip to the case and say *colored pencils*. Got it?'

The girl made a rabbit-nibbling face and shuffled off to Buffalo.

In history class that day, the teacher was talking about the Crusades, and he suddenly said, in the weirdest cowboy accent you ever heard, 'And they went in, shootin' and hollerin' and plunderin' up tarnation, by golly.' Then he said to Nory, 'I'm sorry. I should have asked your permission first. Do you mind if I make fun of the way Americans talk?'

Nory said, 'If you think that's the way Americans talk, go right ahead.'

The teacher said, 'Thank you. And I give you permission to call us limeys whenever you like.'

'Thank you,' said Nory. 'But why would I want to say that?'

'In the States, that's what you call us, is it not?' said the teacher.

'I don't know, but I don't think so,' said Nory. 'What are limeys?'

'Ah, they're an ancient seafaring people who eat limes on shipboard to keep their teeth from falling out,' said Mr. Blithrenner.

6. *Be Careful About Fluoride*

Besides History, there was I.T., which were the initials of Information Technology, where they were learning the middle row of letters on the keys of the Acorn computers. And there was French, and Geography, and Music, and Netball, and Hockey, and other classes, too. There were a surprising amount of teachers at Threll School all together. Even the headmaster of the Junior School was the teacher of a class called Classics. He started off one class by reading in a deep, roly-poling voice about the trickles of blood of the Trojans mixing with the muddy water that collected in pools at the base of the walls of the ruined city. It turned out to be the story of Hercules. Or, not Hercules precisely, but someone with a name quite a bit like Hercules, although it wasn't Hector either. Anyway, whoever he was, he was dipped in magical waters when he was a baby except for where he was held by his ankle.

A few days after that, the headmaster spoke to the whole Junior School in Hendall Hall, which was the place the whole school got together, except when they went to Cathedral once a week. He told them about a painter who had not believed in himself and had been so hungry that he had squeezed tubes of oil paint into his mouth. The paint had lead in it, and it affected his brain in a negative way, and soon enough he gruesomely shot himself in the chest. Now his paintings were worth millions of dollars, which would probably be billions of yen.

Kids want to eat lead because it tastes sweet, Nory knew, which is also why they want to eat toothpaste. You're only supposed to put a pea-sized amount of toothpaste on your toothbrush but many kids put more. Nory thought that what they should make is a tube of toothpaste that squirts out green until you've squirted out just the right amount, and if you try to squeeze more out after that, the color turns red, meaning stop: Green light, red light. If you eat too much toothpaste, the fluoride in it will turn your teeth gray, but there was a kid at the Junior School who had a bad cavity or some sort of medical thing gone wrong in one of his pointy side teeth, one of the bicuspids maybe, that made it completely gray 'from smokebox to buffer,' as Littleguy would say. You only saw it when his mouth made a malicious laugh, as in 'Hah-hah-hah, hah-hah-hah, I'm going to revenge myself on you for that!' If that boy, who was really a fairly nice boy, had had a sweet tooth and eaten tube after tube of toothpaste, that same tooth would be just as gray as it was now, but he wouldn't have the cavity to worry about, and the rest of his teeth would match the color exactly so it would blend in and wouldn't be so noticeable. Nory's own teeth were sometimes a little yellow, she thought, but then she went on a rampage brushing them individually one by one and got them to look pretty white. They looked white in photographs, anyway, which made her happy.

The moral of the story about the child who was dipped in magical water was: nobody is one hundred percent immortal. Except God, for those who believed in God. The moral of the story about the painter was: you never know who will be famous and talented, so try not to get discouraged, and don't allow handguns. The moral of the story about gray teeth was: sometimes by trying to do a good thing, you do a bad thing instead.

7. Fables in the Car

Aesop's fables were where the idea of having a moral came from, but some of them made no sense whatever. Before bed, Nory's parents read to her in alternation with each other, so one night her mother would read something, the next night her father. That first week of September, while Nory was listening to her mother read *A Hundred and One Dalmations,* she was listening to her father read Aesop's *Fables.* He very often fell asleep a few minutes into reading. You could tell he was beginning a doze because he would start pronouncing the words in a hurrying murmur and then stop. Murmur, then stop, murmur, stop. And phrases would get into the story that had nothing to do with anything. If Nory gave him a nudge in the arm, he would bob awake and squinch his eyes shut very tight and flare them open them very wide and forge off into another page. Then very gradually his voice would fall away into a mutter again. 'Seward's folly hima hima hima cartouche hima hima Barcelona hima hima hima.' Sometimes he read for pages that way, it was really quite remarkable, mixing giblet after giblet of totally unrelated nonsense into the story. 'And the canisters could use some priming,' is something that he said one time, in the middle of the story of the crow and the stones. Nory wrote it down and told them all at breakfast. If the story was good, Nory's father didn't fall asleep nearly as fast as if the story was going through a boring stretch. Then the nudging didn't work and she finally had to say, 'Daddy, you're tired, aren't you?'

'How did you guess that?' Nory's father would ask, from deep in his doze.

'Well, for one thing, the book seemed to be flopping.'

'Was it flopping?'

'Yes, it was.'

And then Nory's father would say, 'Well, I guess that just about wraps it up,' and shut the book and say goodnight. The next time that it was his turn to read, he wouldn't remember any of what he had already read, and he would go through several pages, saying 'Did we read that? Did we read that?' Nory usually could remember because she had a not-too-shabby memory for things that were read to her. It was very rare for Nory's mother to fall asleep reading to Nory. Sometimes Nory almost fell asleep when she was reading to her dolls but almost never when she was being read to.

One night Nory's father managed to read three Aesop's fables in a row that just weren't up to sniff. Aesop had had a very bad fable-writing day. Maybe the wax wasn't smooth enough for him to concentrate. Nory's father fell asleep after about ten minutes of reading and slept until Nory's mother woke him up by coming in to give Nory a K and H and a G of W. That anagram stood for a 'Kiss and a Hug and a Glass of Water.' The next day, they drove to Wisbech to see Peckover House, a Stately Home, and on the way Nory had the idea of getting each one of them to think up a fable, as something to do in the car.

Her mother's fable was about an ivy plant that overdoes himself and stays green year round, even through the freezing snows of winter. First he was evergreen for the pure joy of it, and then he was a little less happy and a little more bitter because the other plants failed to follow his lead of staying green and even made little jokes about the ivy plant and his odd winter habits. Finally the ivy got so upset with the rest of the garden for sleeping through the lonely cold months that his anger made his leaves turn brown at the edges and his tendrils stop uncurling. The gardener, who was used to his being green and healthy all year, pulled him up by the roots and threw him in the compost dump. And the moral was: Stay out of politics.

Nory's father's fable was about a cat who loved tuna catfood in cans and refused to eat the whitefish or the beef or the liver in cans, even though he was starvingly hungry, in order to try to force the girl who cared for him to give him tuna every day. The girl got so worried about the cat's not eating that she took him to the vet. The vet said he was healthy, but he said that she must feed him only dry catfood from now on. And the moral was: He who wants only tuna, may end up with only dry.

Nory's fable was about two Korean girls. Once there were two little Korean girls. Their parents had died in a car accident, because the ambulance had not had the Jaws of Life to use to save them. The Jaws of Life are, as you know, huge scissors that can cut through metal and pull an injured person from a car. So the poor, tired little girls were sent to an orphanage. There they put up signs that said 'Help!' because they were treated very badly. Seeing their signs, a kind woman, who wanted so much to have a little girl, adopted them. They were very grateful. But one day the mother, whose name was Nanelan, had to go to a different country to the Queen's birthday party. She asked the only couple she could get in touch with to watch her children. But she did not know that these were evil people. The first day she was gone they spilled a puddle of water to make the children slip and hurt themselves and go to the hospital, so that they would not have to pay for the children's food. The next night the couple, dancing with evil joy, fell into the puddle. Hearing this, the insurance company refused to pay the hospital, and the couple lost all the money. And the moral is: Do not be selfish or your curse will come back.

They asked Littleguy for a fable, too. He came up with two. His first fable was called 'Bulldozer.' Once upon time was a train. A train on a track. It saw a diesel train coming on the track, too, and they crashed. The two went *kssssh*! All the pieces came off they. The puff-puff broke, and the wheels broke, and the track broke. Everything broke. But they went to the shop and got fixed and they got painted, and went to the station and people came on them and they set off. The end.

Littleguy's second fable was called 'Browned.' Once upon time was a bulldozer, pulling a trailer filled with all kinds of choo-choos, digger-trucks, and auger drillers, and dump trucks. And the other ones that have round things, cement mixers. The bulldozer saw a car pulling a trailer by it. And they didn't crash, they just went right by they. The bulldozer drove and drove and drove and drove and drove and drove and drove. The bulldozer's name was Browned. The end.

Since there were no morals in Littleguy's two fables, Nory added them on. The moral of the first fable was: sometimes when there's a crash, it turns out all right in the end. And the moral of the second one was: sometimes things don't even crash at all.

At Peckover House, Nory got a National Trust eraser from the gift shop after they had tea.

8. About Debbie

Nory was proudly born in Boston, Massachusetts, in America. A lot of houses looked like Peckover House in Boston. Boston was old in a beautiful way and it was especially important to Nory because it was frankly the only city she had ever lived in, except Venice for three weeks when she was three years old, where she was baptized with a surprising splash of water in a huge cold church, holding her own candle, that later got broken and had to be thrown out even though it was wrapped in tissue paper. In Venice she also ate pitch-black spaghetti. The black was squid ink and it was quite good. Long ago, they used to use squid ink to make real ink, for using in Medium Nib fountain pens, but probably it would make a kind of ink that no ink eradicator would eradicate. Ink eradicators were made from pigskin and pig-waste, according to a girl at Threll Junior School, who said her sister once visited an eradicator factory.

Threll was just a town, not a city, and Palo Alto, California, was just a town, too, although it had quite a seedy neighborhood in the way that real cities do. You might imagine a French person going around Palo Alto, California, with an American person. The American would say, 'As you will notice, there are some seedy areas.' The French person would say, in his very strong French accent, 'Oh, is this—city area?' Pronouncing it of course the way the French teacher at the Junior School pronounced it. And the American would misunderstand and say sadly, 'Yes, I'm afraid it is seedy. There's just no getting around it.' Maybe that's how the idea that cities were seedy came about, if it happened quite a number of times. Also when people don't cut their grass, it grows so long that it shoots out a tassel of seeds, which was a sign that the people in that house didn't care about their yard. Maybe they were caring for a sick person who was cooped up in the house, or maybe they were busy giving themselves shots of drugs and alcohol and didn't have the energy to walk out their front door and cut the grass. That's another way the idea that cities were seedy could have come about.

Nory's favorite street in Palo Alto had a number of stores on it, including the toy store. Nory spent half an hour there one Saturday in the summer while Littleguy played with the breakdown train at the Thomas the Tank Engine table. She looked through every one of the Barbie outfits, because her new best friend, Debbie, said she liked Barbies with black hair and blue dresses. Debbie had given Nory a friendship locket to celebrate that they were new best friends, and Nory was extremely happy about that and wanted to give Debbie a Barbie from money she earned selling hand-lettered signs to her parents. She looked and looked, and finally tucked away behind a whole lot of other outfits she found a dark blue Barbie dress with lighter blue sparkles on the front, and she hung it back on the hook as the very first one and went to get her mother. When she came back, though, another girl was there with *her* mother, and the girl was holding the blue dress outfit in her hand. Nory stood there and tried her best to hint by the sad hopeless way she was flopping her arms and looking at the blue dress in the girl's hand that she had just spent a whole half an hour going through every outfit to find it, but the girl and her mother ignored her, or didn't know what she was flopping about, and she didn't want to say anything, because of course the girl had found it all by herself, it's just that the girl wouldn't have had hardly a chance of finding it if Nory hadn't found it and put it on top where it got the special feeling of being the first outfit on display.

They went to another toy store a week later, but there were no blue dresses that were right. Blue was not in fashion at that moment. So Nory got Debbie a tiny glass panda bear posed on a branch, all made of droops of light blue glass, because Debbie was devoted to pandas and had

about thirty of them in her room. Nory wrote Debbie a letter soon after they came to England that said:

> Dear Debbie,
> How ary you? How is your school? I went to the Fitz Willyham museum, where there was a fan room, and there is a fan launguage for things you're not allowed to say in public if you place the fan behind your head it means 'Don't forget me'! There was a fan that I preticularly liked, It is made from coal and mother of peal. I went to Pecover House, but I think it should be famous for its garden more than the house. It has a wunderful statue of a girl and a dog made from stone, and a green house with a fern that will crumple-up when you touch it. I miss you and your dog Sharpy, how is that shoe consuming feind? I hope to be seing you again soon. Love Eleanor PS Please write back.

She drew a picture of a girl holding a fan behind her head at the bottom of the letter.

The best dream Nory had ever had was about Debbie. Nory had died, although she didn't come to that conclusion until a different part of the dream. She whispered in Debbie's ear, 'Debbie, Debbie, it's me.' Debbie recognized Nory's voice and looked up. Debbie had a very wide face, and she could get a look that was kind of still, kind of unnerved. Her mouth looked bigger because her lips were over the wiring of her braces. She made that unnerved look at Nory. She said, 'Nory! Nory! Is that you?' She recognized Nory's voice, even though she couldn't see her.

'Don't worry, Debbie,' said Nory, in a calm gentle voice. 'Don't be scared. I would be too if I were you.' Debbie seemed calmer. Nory showed her the newspaper, which said on the front page ELEANOR DIES IN A FIRE. Not her

family, not anyone else. Later on in the dream Nory said Boo to Garrick, a kid in her class, sort of fakily: 'Garrick? Boooooo!'

Garrick said, 'No way, she can't be a ghost, she's dead already.'

'Oh, yes I can!' said Nory and fumed out in her full ghostiness. Garrick started running out of fear and tripped. That was funny because Garrick was a ten-year-old and usually extremely confident and pleased with himself and made fun of Nory's spelling, which wasn't very good. In fact it was a 'bosaster,' as Littleguy would say. But the wonderful part of the dream was when Debbie looked up, hearing the voice, and knew it was Nory nearby her.

9. A Strange Vegetable

'It's sometimes kind of impressive,' Nory thought, 'to try to envision how many bricks there are in a city.' You could tell a city was old by the colors and crookedness of its bricks. In Boston Nory noticed that usually the bricks were red, but in Threll they were usually, not to be disrespectful, kind of a dirty yellow, and they were even less straight than in Boston. You wouldn't expect dirty yellow crooked bricks to look pretty, but they did, especially where you could see places in the walls where there had been old windows or old doorways that had been stuffed with other bricks and stones and pieces of old buildings.

That was what a certain memory that you had forgotten felt like—you knew that a window had been there but it wasn't now, just an old brick wall, so you couldn't see through it. There was a very tall brick wall around the garden of the Bishop's Palace at Threll, with pointy stones on top, so that the poor people couldn't sneak in at night and steal the cauliflowers, which might have looked tempting in the moonlight to a very hungry mouthwatering person of long ago. At Waitrose, the supermarket, they sold darling little dwarf cauliflowers in the 'Dwarf Food' section. It wouldn't be called dwarf food in America because that would hurt the feelings of a real dwarf, who would feel not too pleased about being compared to a vegetable.

Waitrose also sold a mysteriously pointy green plant, halfway between a cauliflower and a pine tree, called a Romanesco. Nory's mother said that 'Gothico' would be a better name for it. It was intended to be eaten for dinner, but it looked like a screensaver on Nory's mother's computer called 'Permafrost II.' 'Worms' was the neatest of all the screensavers, though.

Nory gave the Romanesco to the Cathedral to be a part of the arrangement that was done by Threll School in the South Door, for the Harvest Festival. Kids had carried in carrots in bunches, and zucchini, which were called courgettes in Threll, and broccoli, apples, and sugar beets. But luckily nobody else in the school had given a Romanesco, which made hers easy to see. Nory's father took three pictures of Nory in her school jacket and tie standing to one side of an open bag of potatoes. The potatoes were shaped just like the stones they put on either side of a lot of the sidewalks in Cambridge to remind your feet in a polite way that you were getting close to the grass. Cambridge was, as you may know, where you go to get a Ph.D. After they went to the Fitzwilliam Museum, in Cambridge, Nory told herself a story in the car, holding one of her dolls.

10. The Story of the Fan

One day, there was a little tiny baby. She was born too early, so she was really, really tiny. She should have gone into an incubator, but her parents weren't rich enough, so she couldn't. They just had to raise her as being a really, really small little person. She had a big soft-spot because she was so early. And her umbilical was too long. And so on. She was, on the whole, too small. Just a tiny little person.

When she was about three weeks old, she could already do her grasping. She couldn't really turn yet, but she could turn her head, ever so slightly. She turned her head ever so slightly. She could almost grasp. She couldn't have handled it yet, because that would be just impossible, so amazing that it would be a fairy tale, which this is, of course, but she seemed to be trying to grab for her mother's fan. And ever since, she seemed to be totally interested in fans. Just completely interested in them. Her parents named her Colander.

When Colander was full grown, she was a midget, because she was just a tiny person. When she was twelve, the tallest she ever was, she was as tall as Frank is. She was really short. So one day—it was really hard for her to go to school and museums and because people might tease her because she was so short—but one day they went to a museum. It had a lot of different things in it, china and armor and sculpture. They wandered here and there. She said: 'I see that dark room. What's in that dark room?'

They went into the dark room she had looked at. And there were the most beautiful fans that she had ever seen. So many different kinds, shapes, sizes. In the corner of each glass case was a little yellow box of some kind of mold killer to keep all the fans from being eaten by a strong fan-eating fungus.

But the fan that really caught her eye was one that was carved from mother-of-pearl, when you opened it up. When you closed it, it had beautiful ivory carvings of children, and then the ivory was put on top of jade. And there was beautiful gold-plating, where the hair of anything would be. For instance, if there was the hair of a mother it was gold-plated, all the hair was true gold plate. And there were also some diamonds put here and there on the fan. There were many other fine fans in the room, but that one was her total favorite.

She wanted most of all in the world to have it. She wanted to start a collection, and she wanted that fan in the centerpiece of it. That was all she wanted. She thought about fans, she drew pictures of the fan, in school she doodled 'fan' on her hand when she'd gotten totally bored with the conversation the teacher was giving to them. It was a long conversation in Latin and she hadn't been studying Latin all that carefully because she was thinking about the fan. The fan was what entertained her.

They went back to the museum on her birthday. Her parents asked, 'Is it possible, you know, to get a model of that fan?'

The museum people said, 'Oh, well, I'm sure we can have a model made.' The owner of the museum was really really nice.

Her parents said, 'Yes, but we don't have much money.'

And the museum man said, 'Oh well, it's only fifteen dollars.'

Colander heard that and said, 'Wait, I have fifteen dollars, I've been saving my allowance to get the real one, but now that you say it's only fifteen dollars, I happen to have fifteen dollars!'

'No, no, that was your allowance,' her parents said.

'No, I want to,' Colander said, 'I'll get the money.'

So she paid the museum the fifteen dollars.

But her parents said, 'No, no, no, little child, you shouldn't be spending your own money, it's your birthday present, we should get it for you as a birthday present.'

'You can get me other things,' said Colander, 'but I'll pay for this.' Because she knew that her parents really didn't have very very much money. She had tried to save up fifteen dollars for ages. She was only given about a nickel each time she completed her work, a nickel or two.

Anyway, Colander forked him the fifteen dollars the next day, and he—the museum owner—said, 'Oh thank you very much, but you should have this. I can see that this is well-earned money. You should have it. I'll give the fan to you free as grass, for your good work.'

Colander said, 'Oh no, you shouldn't. Keep it, keep it.'

Finally, after a lot of persuading, the museum man got Colander to keep the fifteen dollars. So he was actually giving her this wonderful thing free. 'I'll give it as my own birthday present for you,' he said. And so he had a duplicate fan made, in a factory in Bombay, and it was to some people even more beautiful than the first. It was so gorgeous you wouldn't believe it.

The museum owner was exceptionally rich. He was very, very rich. So this was nothing to him. 'Pshaw. Oh, just a thousand dollars, pshaw.' So he spent a ton of money making this one tiny little fan. He put it in a box, wrapped it up, very very nicely, and wrote 'For Colander, from Mr. Harvonsay.' And on her birthday Mr. Harvonsay looked in the phone book and found their address, and said, 'Is this little Miss Colander's house?'

Colander said, 'Yes it is.'

So he gave her the little box.

'Oh, great,' she said. 'Oh, thank you.'

She opened all her parents' presents, and they were excited to see what was in the little box wrapped so neatly, so her mother said, 'Now open the little box.'

Everything she'd gotten up till then was a fan to put in her collection. In the box from Mr. Harvonsay was the fan. Everyone gasped out loud, it was so superb. Then her parents said, 'Oh, and one more present for you.' In her room there was a glass case and little stands to put fans in. She had a whole little mini fan collection of her own.

She was very happy, but the glass case had to be very low, or she'd have to tell her parents where to put everything in it, because she was short. Her parents were relatively short, but they weren't as short as she was. And so, the end.

11. Feeding the Swans

As for the Bishop's Palace garden, across the street from the Cathedral, it was definitely not owned by a Bishop in the Catholic Religion. Nory was a Catholic because her mother was a Catholic, and Nory's mother was a Catholic because her father was a Catholic, and her father was a Catholic because his mother was a Catholic, or had been.

They only went to church on rare times, but they said grace every single night. If it had been a Bishop in the Catholic Religion—which was one of the most popular religions of the world, though Christianity was probably slightly more popular—there wouldn't be a huge garden hidden out of sight, because Catholic bishops would devote all their money to the church and pray the day away, and care for the poor, and wash the poor's wounds with hot rags. No huge grand house, and no greedy high brick wall for a Catholic Bishop.

The way you make bricks is by baking them like brownies in an oven, or pouring the mixture into thousands of small molds and drying the shapes in the sun if you don't expect it to rain terribly much where you live. If it does rain and you haven't baked your bricks, you may end up with drooping walls. The bricks that are used to build a brick oven must get so totally baked into brickness that they almost can't bear it another minute, since they heat up, on one side, that is, every time they bake the bricks inside, hundreds of times over, like a drip of black cheese in the microwave.

Brick is a good word for bricks because it has the sound of the sharp, crunchy edge in it, pulling across. They were looking into Force and Friction in Nory's science class at the Junior School, and finding out that a brick creates a ton of friction. Ricki Ticki Tavi, the mongoose who saved the little boy, got his name from the rick-ticking sounds he made. Near the end, when Ricki Ticki disappears down the hole with Nagaina, the Queen Cobra, with 'his little white teeth clenched into her tail'—animals often had surprisingly white teeth—you're supposed to think that he might be dead. Usually with a story there is a moment at which you're supposed to think some person or animal has died or some other really sad failure has happened—and if you don't know that that's how stories are supposed to work you can become quite upset and have to run out of the room to escape the squeezing feeling in your chest, like at the end of *Lady and the Tramp,* when the movie tries its hardest to make you think the old dog who couldn't smell very well anymore had gotten run over by a carriage-wheel and died.

But the time of worrying that Rikki Tikki is dead didn't last quite long enough, in Nory's opinion. It could have lasted a little longer, and since they're supposed to be having a terrible battle down in the hole you need some sign that something's going on down there, like little faint struggling sounds, or every so often a whiffle of dirt flying out of the hole.

The other small problem with the story—not that there are any real problems with the story, it's a good story by a man who lived in Africa for many years, not an African American man but just a man who lived there, or somewhere like Africa—but it's sad to think of such a likable mongoose eating holes in the baby cobra eggs. The baby cobras hadn't killed anything or frightened anyone. They would when they hatched out, because that's what cobra snakes are designed to do naturally. But a story should not have a small, tiny, curled-up barely alive animal be killed unless it has done a terrible thing, which it can't have done because it hasn't even uncurled itself from the egg. And the story isn't about what cobras do naturally, anyway, since it has the cobras speaking. In real life they don't speak, at least in English. A cobra couldn't call itself 'Nag' or 'Nagaina' because the cobra's tongue is so thin it couldn't make an N sound. A cobra would probably just call itself 'Lah,' if anything.

The swans on the river made a pretty frightening sound when Nory fed them. They came up out of the water and started walking toward her, shrugging up their wings, and no matter how many pieces of bread she threw their way, they kept coming towards her, because they wanted the bigger piece of bread in her hand. When Nory said, 'Hold your horses, back up, back up!' they opened their beaks and made a nasty sound, like a hissing cat. Their necks were like cobra necks, somewhat. Nory's father was alarmed and didn't want to feed them anymore and was shooing them away with his briefcase, but it wasn't fair, Nory thought, that just because a bird was somewhat alarming he should not be fed, whereas the ducks, which weren't alarming, should be fed. There was a group of ducks that were so cute, a mother and about fifteen babies, each with a dear fluff of brown on its head. They crossed the street, just like in *Make Way for Ducklings,* which was the first book Nory ever read. Nory gave them some crackers. A girl at the Junior School, Kira, who was turning out to be a nice friend, said that her parents didn't let her feed the birds any bread, because it wasn't what they would normally eat if they were wild. Nory told her that she fed the birds sesame crackers, at least sometimes, and sesames are seeds and birds eat seeds. But both the ducks and the swans ate grass. There was a lot of grass-eating, which wasn't very natural either, because there didn't used to be so much grass in the world.

There was a lot of attention paid to grass in England. Cows used to keep it short, long ago, but now they used lawn mowers, of course. Sometimes they mowed it very short in a crisscross, so that it looked like a plaid cloth. One large field below the cathedral near Nory's school was totally bare earth, because they were putting in new grass.

One day when she was walking home with her mother they saw five men walking in a row on this field. Each man had a big white plastic thing attached around his waist, like a drum in a marching band in a parade, and they reached into their drums and got handfuls of grass seed and threw it out over the brown field. Nory's mother thought it was a beautiful sight, and it was. There were some interesting holes in one of the fields they used for sports at Junior School, but nobody seemed to know what was inside them. Not cobras and mongooses, but you never know. You don't want to reach your hand down in there. Even if you poke a stick in, sharp teeth could suddenly grab the stick, which would be startling. In some fields, people might have been buried there long ago. For instance near the South Door of the Cathedral it was now all grass, but in the map of the way the Cathedral was during Prior Rowland's lifetime it said 'Monks Graves.' Did they move the monks, or just forget about them?

12. Ladybugs, Butterflies, and a Hurt Thumb

Nory used to not like the idea of burying people terribly much. Now she had come to gripes with it as a fact of life. When she was four she dictated a letter that her father typed out for her:

> To Whom it May Concern:
> Eleanor Winslow does not want to be buried under the ground.
>
> Sincerely,
> Eleanor Winslow.

She scribbled a fake signature, since at the time she had not known how to write, and she put a stamp on the piece of paper and scribbled on the stamp and it looked official. When her hermit crab lost all its claws one by one, very forlornly, and died only a few weeks after they got her, Nory buried her with a grave marker that said:

TO HERMIONE
Soon Gone

She wanted a dog or a rabbit or a kitten, anything warm-blooded, except possibly a cow, but her parents said that they couldn't have one for various reasons.

The field at the school that Nory used for hockey had no holes at all, whatsoever, because it was made of Astroturf. There was lots of sand sprinkled in the Astroturf. Nobody knew why. If you were an animal, digging a hole, and you dug and dug and then dug up to the surface intending to make a South Door for your hole, and you came up under the Astroturf, you would be pretty unhappy about having done all that work for nothing. Maybe there were dead monks under there. Once Nory found a ladybug in the Astroturf and carried it to the edge, and set it on a leaf. That was on a fairly embarrassing day, the second time they played hockey, when Nory's skirt fell off twice. Luckily hockey was all girls. And another girl had the same problem, too. While Nory was carrying the ladybug off the field, she was worried that it would fly off. If it flew off, it might just land in more Astroturf, where it couldn't live.

Nory said to it, very confidentially, 'Don't fly yet, Ladybug. Ladybug, if you try to fly, I'm going to have to confiscate your ability of flying. I can't confiscate you, but I can cup my hand over you and confiscate your ability of flying.' Confiscate was a word she'd learned from a boy who walked back with her from lunch one day. He said that it was a good thing she wasn't in Five-K, because in Five-K the teacher was awful. If you write in pencil and you were supposed to write in pen, or do something of that level of badness, the teacher would confiscate your pencil and tell you she was going to give it back the next day, and then she never gave it back. The boy said he stole his pencil back. He said, 'And rightly stole it!' He opened up the teacher's drawer and had to fumble through it to find his pencil because it was bursting at the gills with confiscated things.

Ladybugs are very useful bugs because they eat aphids. Nory used to think, 'Poor little aphids.' But aphids eat the ladybugs' eggs, so ladybugs have a right to hate them. It was something a little like Rikki Tikki Tavi and the snake. Nory's mother said that when a gardener bought a whole jug of ladybugs they had to let them out at night so they don't know where they are and settle down with those particular aphids as their enemy. Otherwise they might try to escape to the other aphids, which they know better and hate more, because those were the ones who actually ate their eggs. Human beings have an unusual amount of power over the lives of bugs. Kids kill thousands of bugs every day without dropping a hat. Once Nory was looking at a ladybug that was either dead or alive, she couldn't tell, maybe playing dead or just relaxing or sunbathing or burnt in the sun. But then someone came walking along, not thinking about what she was doing, but just walking along, and she smashed the ladybug, without even seeing it. A green spread out. Insects have green blood. Now, if that had been a child who had been squushed, everyone would be tearing their hair out. Even if a small thing happens to a child, she remembers it and talks about it for a long time.

Maybe insects' blood is white or some other color, and only turns green when it is exposed to air. We think human blood is red but it's blue just before it comes out of a cut. The very second it reaches the edge of the cut, it changes, in the twinkling of an eye, because of the air.

They were watching a pianist one night, Nory's mother, Nory's father, and Nory, because when Nory called her friend Kira, Kira said 'You've got to watch this great piano contest.' Littleguy was playing with James the Red Engine. One of the people in the contest played the piano so hard he got a red spot on the back of his thumb. He was from Yugoslaw. Nory saw it and said, 'He's hurt himself.'

'Oh, I think it's just a shadow,' said Nory's father.

But it wasn't. There were little spots of blood on the piano keys. Then the next person had to play. Think of him sitting down and seeing ladybugs of blood all over the piano. He can't wipe them off because the wiping would make an ugly sound and the judges might remember the ugly sound very well, since it was the very first thing he played, and give him a bad result. His eye would be distracted by the blood and he would make more mistakes, maybe. Or he might think, 'Hah hah! I won't bleed, no sir!' It was sad to think of the people in the contest who practiced so hard their whole lives long and still eventfully lost.

That little thing, a bleeding thumb, was a big thing for a person. For an insect or some other small creature it would be minor. One time Nory scrumpled up a leaf to put it on the compost pile in Palo Alto. She didn't know that there was a snail on the other side of the leaf. So she accidentally crunched the snail, and she got snail slime all over her hand. It was awful. She hadn't meant to scrumple the snail. From then on, whenever she picked up a leaf, she turned it over to see if anything was on the other side. Very often there was. Another time she caught a butterfly and was trying to put it in a jar with some grass blades. Its body was in the jar, but its head was accidentally outside, and she didn't know that, while she was turning the lid of the jar. She looked over and there was its head outside the jar. She snatched the lid away and the head was still partly attached. The butterfly flew away. But she felt the guilt of the idea of having done that pull at her horribly.

Nory's father said that feeling guilty was useful because when you felt it you had a piece of useful knowledge: you knew that you didn't want to do that thing, whatever it was, that made you feel guilty, so the guiltiness was a way of teaching yourself what you ought to do in the future. In some cases that was true but Nory felt horribly guilty about having scrumpled the snail and screwed the lid on the butterfly's head even though she hadn't meant to.

But the guiltiness did stay in her mind and make her act differently. For instance, three kids found a butterfly on a tree near the dining hall at Threll School one time, near the beginning of term. They were trying to make it fly, but it wasn't cooperating. One of the girls wanted to put it in her backpack. Immediately, Nory thought, 'If it goes in there, with all the heavy books and notebooks, it will end up like one of the cookies that I put in my backpack that is now just a dust of crumbs. It will be the death of that butterfly.' So she said to the girl, 'Here, take my pencil case and put the butterfly in there.' The girl carelessly took it and put the butterfly in. That meant that Nory was totally without a pencil case. The pencil case had pencils, including a Barbie pencil, her medium nib pen, her ink eradicator, her National Trust eraser, ruler, protractors, everything. She had to borrow pens from kids, and at first they were nice about it, but after a few days they were really mean about it and said, 'Are you going to beg for a pen again? I'll tell you right now you can't have one.'

Of course one of the reasons she'd given the girl her pencil case was not just to protect the butterfly, but probably more because she wanted the girl to be impressed by her generous act of handing over the pencil case. Finally her mother said, 'You *must* get that pencil case back from that girl or you will have to buy another pencil case out of your own allowance.' So Nory asked the girl for the pencil case back and got it at the end of the day, feeling huge relief.

Another story about a pencil case was a more horrible one. Daniella Harding said, and Nory wasn't sure if she was telling the truth, but she said that she got the pointy end of a protractor stuck through her cheek. Kira asked, 'Did you scream?' Daniella said that she'd had to go to the san. She got a little scar on her face. But Nory had had a friend at the International Chinese Montessori School in Palo Alto who was always making things up, and ever since then she was not so quick to believe everything every kid told her, especially if they told the story a certain way. She could have gotten the scar from poking herself with a pencil. Or it just could have been a simple fall-down-and-scrape-your-face.

13. Close Calls with Crying

A lot of Nory's stories used to be about her most beloved stuffed animal, a puppet raccoon called Sarah Laura Maria, who was often being stolen away by a bad witch and helped by a good witch, stuff like that, but lately Nory had begun a whole set of stories about a girl named Mariana who has a very sad but in some ways good life. Coochie, which was Nory's other name for Raccoon, still was in some stories of her own, too. Cooch had recently begun attending a boarding school as a day student in the dresser in the guest room of the house in Threll they were renting. Samantha and Linnea and Vera, other dolls, were going there as well, each in its own drawer. They were full boarders. There were quite a number of flying squirrels at the school, who would climb on the play-structure and fly off in great arches. Coochie tried to do it but she had eaten too many jacket potatoes for lunch and she fell down and got badly scraped and bruised. It wasn't the sort of scrape you get when you scrape your knee on the Astroturf, which makes it completely red, it was more of a real cut. A girl in Nory's class named Jessica—the one who said Nory had a 'squeegee accent' on one of the first days—fell on the Astroturf and got two red knees when they were playing hockey.

'Oh, are you okay?' Nory asked her.

'If I were "okay," would I be sitting down with tears pouring down my face?' Jessica said.

'No,' said Nory. Almost all children were rude sometimes. Nory herself was quite rude from time to time. Once she had told a boy who had said her teeth were too big that his shoes were dusty. He had turned bright red and looked so hurt that she felt bad afterward.

It wasn't a good idea to stop any possibility of liking a person because of one single thing they did. Sometimes people forget themselves. Sometimes, though, what a child did was so bad, so severe, that you lost all your ability to keep up any friendly feelings toward them. Such a thing happened last year at International Chinese Montessori School, when Bernice wrote Nory a folded note that said 'I'm sorry' on the front, after they had an argument, and then inside it said, 'Dear Eleanor, I'm sorry, but I am not going to live with you in a house when we grow up, I'm going to live with my *first* best friend.' That was just the limit, that 'first'—Nory couldn't now detect one tiny scrabjib of friendship for Bernice in her heart when she thought of her. Her best friend now was Debbie, probably, who was shyer and nicer.

Littleguy occasionally said rude things that could hurt your feelings, but he was two and usually it was a question of him just not understanding what he was saying. Once on Saturday afternoon for instance Nory tried to teach Littleguy how to play field hockey, after having spent some of her morning on Astroturf learning the basics. He hurt her feelings when he rejected a hockey stick she especially made for him out of a wooden pole, a toilet-paper tube taped on at an angle, and some green ribbon from her Samantha doll as decoration spiraled around. She had been rather pleased with this homemade stick.

'Littleguy—so do you like it or do you hate it?' she asked him, wanting to jostle him into saying a little thank-you.

'I hate it,' said Littleguy, but in a pleasant, good-natured way. 'I want *that* stick,' meaning Nory's real stick.

'That's not the right way to talk to Nory,' called out Nory's father from inside. 'She made that hockey stick especially for you and used a whole green Samantha ribbon and a toilet-paper tube to decorate it.'

'I'm sorry, Nory, I'm sorry, Nory,' kind little Littleguy said, very nicely, looking up at her with his serious little mouth and hopeful eyes.

Nory said, 'Thank you, Littleguy.' She loved the open feeling you got when someone said I'm sorry to you after you were mad or hurt-feelinged at them—the feeling of the scrumpled paper of the unhappiness going away from your chest. It made you almost burst with generousness toward them. 'But it's really my fault,' she said. 'I'm sorry to *you* for asking the question confusingly in such a way that you couldn't tell which way was the right way to answer for politeness.'

'Me, too,' said Littleguy. 'Do you want to see my gooseneck trailer? It's had a bad mergency. It's stuck in the mud.'

Littleguy of course cried a hundred times a day—he had about eight different kinds of crying, several of them rather ear-gnashing—but Nory almost never cried because she had learned a few years earlier that it more or less ruins your reputation to cry, even if someone says something that makes you want to. It's very embarrassing to cry. Boys especially will like you more if you don't cry, and want to be your friend. Jessica cried when she fell on the Astroturf but it was a pretty bad fall, two knees at the same time. And she said the rude thing to Nory partly just because she was purely a rude girl some of the time, but partly because she was embarrassed, and she was very serious about boys, in almost a teenagery way, or not quite in a teenagery way but in a double-digit kind of way, and she probably worried that her enemy-friend, Daniella Harding, would tell Colin Deat that she had cried on the hockey field. Not as many people cried at this school as at Nory's old school.

There were two times this year so far Nory almost, almost cried. One was when Shelly Quettner found out that Nory kind of liked a boy by the name of Jacob Lewes.

Nory told it to Daniella Harding, who turned out to be Shelly Quettner's sidekick in the whole process. Shelly started saying to Daniella, 'What did she say? What? What? What?' And she squeezed it out of her. Or maybe Daniella wanted to tell her all along, it wasn't so clear. Instantly Shelly Quettner was saying to the class, 'Nory fancies Jacob Lewes!'

Everybody said, 'Is it true? Is it true?' Jacob Lewes immediately turned dead red and stared at his pencil case. Nory was red, too, but only in the places that she got red, which were on the sides of her cheeks, so that her blush turned into long sideburn-things. People said, 'Well? Do you fancy him?' Nory thought seriously about denying it, because honesty may be the best policy at times but it certainly does seem painful at other times. But it's painful the other way, too, because if you say, 'No, I certainly do not fancy Jacob Lewes, whatever for?' then Jacob Lewes's feelings might be a tiny bit hurt, even though he would also act very relieved to hear it, and also you then right away think, 'Oh, I shouldn't have tolden a lie,' and you have to say, 'Well, actually, yes, I mispoke, I do fancy him.' So you have twice as much pain as if you had just gone ahead and admitted it, because you have the pain of feeling the guilt of lying and the pain of admitting that you do fancy him.

So Nory said, 'Well, I do think he's nice.'

Julia Sollen said, 'You're blushing!'

'Yes, I know that,' said Nory. 'Any further questions?' It was all quite terrible and there was a sliver of a moment when Nory thought, 'This is so bad that I have a slight feeling in my lips of wanting to cry, should I cry?'

Luckily one girl came up and said, 'You know you should tell everybody that Shelly Quettner fancies Colin Deat,' because that was what Shelly had told someone, and Nory thought about it and almost did it but then she thought, Do Unto Others. Nory's conclusion was that Daniella Harding was definitely not going to get told any of her secrets anymore.

It turned out that Nory didn't really fancy Jacob Lewes so much as all that. First, he said tiresome things about how he hated Barbie dolls, which is what American boys do, and then especially after he started to make fun of Pamela Shavers. By the way, 'fancy' was the word they used for it in England, and it was an idiotic, dumb, stupid word, *fancy,* but not as horrible as if Shelly had said, 'Nory loves Jacob Lewes.' The good thing about experiencing that horribleness, though, was that because she'd already gone through the 'Nory fancies Somebody' business, she could talk to a boy like Roger Sharpless and nobody would think a thing of it. One time Nory was fighting around with Roger in a playing way and Roger got a little vicious and swopped her in the side of the face with a rolled-up geography booklet. He didn't know it would hurt as much as it did, because when you roll up something like a magazine or a thin floppy book you think it will be kind of soft and springy, like a rolled-up piece of paper, but actually it can feel as hard as a metal pipe, just about. Nory said, laughing, 'Roger, you're going to give me a black eye, now.' And she thought, 'Oh dear, oh dear, they're going to see my eye, it's full of water.' And then she remembered that one time at her old school she'd thought her eyes would look terribly full of water and she went into the bathroom to check and she found out that you couldn't even tell unless you were really looking. So she thought, 'No, I don't think they'll notice.' And Roger didn't seem worried at all. But he did nicely say he was sorry to have swopped her with his geography booklet.

Those were the two times she almost cried so far, but didn't.

14. Fire Safety Tips

Nory left Boston and moved to the Trumpet Hill house in Palo Alto when she was still one year old. So the only reason that she had any memories about Boston and its bricks was that they had been back to visit. That was before she had Cooch, her only daughter from her marriage to Sylvester the Cat, who later sailed away to Africa. It was before she knew almost anything, for instance that long ago sailors threw pigs overboard to see what direction they would swim, because whatever direction they swam in was land. Or that if a cat is bred without a tail he won't be able to feel where he's going to the bathroom, since the tail is their sense of where they're going to the bathroom. Without a tail a cat will just go all over the place, not knowing, like dogs who leave their dog leisures here, there, and everywhere.

Nory didn't even know the word for elbow back then, when she was one. They had a video of her first learning 'elbow' in the yard, much later on. Really almost the only thing she kept with her from Boston was a tiny scar on her nose that she got in the bathtub when she picked up the plastic razor that her mother used to shave her legs and looked at it, and somehow, before she knew it, presto, she had cutten herself with it. Even that tiny scar was gone, almost. And now Littleguy knew the word 'elbow.' He said 'Elbows help you jump!' and he would then jump to demonstrate. He was right, elbows do help you jump, especially if you jumped the way he did, with a lot of arm motion to make it seem like a very high jump.

Littleguy did not seem to know the word 'ankle,' however. Babies learn the words for their feet and toes and fingers quite early because they can hold them close to their faces, and they learn about their eyes and nose and mouth because they are *on* their faces, but for some reason they are never terribly interested in their ankles. The word is weaker in their mind. That might have something to do with the strange myth of dipping Achilles.

It wasn't Hercules who was dipped. Nory learned his proper name in another Classics class—Achilles. Achilles's mother was unhappy that Achilles wasn't completely immortal, so she dipped him head-first into the Watersticks. The Watersticks led from the Alive to the Unalive, in other words to the Dead. She held him by pinching hard on the back part of the foot, above his heel. 'But wouldn't that hurt the baby tremendously?' Nory wondered to herself. 'Wouldn't there be a big chance of it falling right out of your hand?'

She imagined a tiny naked baby hanging by one leg, terribly frightened, bright red in the face from screaming, kicking the other leg wildly. The cold water would make the poor thing gasp desperately and it would pour right up its nostrils, because they would be upside down. Water in your sinuses can be really painful. If the goddess really loved her baby, she would have gotten in the water herself and then gently lifted the baby by its waist from the shore, right side up, one hand on either side, and lowered him in, and where her hands were covering his skin, once he was almost floating, she could just let one hand go for a second, then close, then let the other hand go, then close. You have to be careful to hold up the head, too. The ankle was just not a practical or safe choice of place to hold a newborn child.

But they were much less careful about things like safety in ancient times. Nowadays safety is a major concern but back then the sky was the limit with danger, really. Nory's first school was called Small People, and one of the first things they learned at Small People was the safety tip 'Stop, Drop, and Roll.' That was what you were supposed to do when your clothes caught on fire. If you ran, the flames would flare up, and you would probably get a third-degree burn. A third-degree burn is when the skin is black and charred.

'Should you hide from the fireman?' the teacher asked.

'No,' said the kids.

'If he has a big mask on, should you be frightened into thinking he's a space alien?' asked the teacher.

'No,' said the kids.

'And what do you do if your clothes catch on fire?' asked the teacher.

'Stop, drop, and roll!' the kids shouted.

At first Nory was very happy to know that rhyme, but then she was taught it again at her next school, the Blackwood Early Focus School, where three firemen came by for a visit. That teacher was not in a good state of mind and shouted all the time, because the class was so wild. One kid spent every minute of his day rolling around on the floor, so there wasn't much need to ask him to drop or roll. Stopping might be nice, though.

Nory's parents took her out of that school, which was a public school, when they noticed that Nory had learned to write one more letter in three months, G. One letter in three months was just not acceptable, they said. So they put her in the International Chinese Montessori School, and presto, the alphabet was in her brain in a jiffy and she was learning songs in Chinese about Sung O Kung, the ancient monkey.

And then one day a fireman came in with some blankets and had two kids hold a blanket low to the floor. The blanket stood for the thick, thick smoke that you were supposed to crawl under. Crawling was fun but it also gave you a panicky feeling because you could imagine being in a room and unable to know where the window was because the smoke was so thick, except for a tiny layer just above the floor. How would you possibly know where the windows were? You'd need to tape a card with an arrow on it pointing up at the window, so you'd know that there's where you'd need to take a breath and plunge up into the hot smoke and smash out the window with a pillow. 'And what do you do if your clothes catch on fire?' asked the fireman.

'*Stop, drop, and roll!*' shouted the kids.

That and don't smoke, don't take drugs, don't talk to strangers, and the rainforest is burning to the ground, were the things that it seemed like every kid was taught over and over and over, to an endless limit. You got told them *so* many times, on TV ads as well—wasn't there anything else in the world that kids should know? For instance other safety things, like: Be careful when you play with your little brother because his head is quite hard and it could break your nose. Or, don't run in fancy black shoes because their soles are nine times out of ten extremely slippery. Or, don't try to pull down a wooden Chinese-checker set from a shelf above your head because it can fall straight on your toe and make the toenail turn dark purple and almost completely fall right off. Or, don't chew too wildly or you might bite your tongue, which really hurts.

Or what about things that were not about safety at all, such as for instance salting meat, or about the three layers of the tooth, the inner layer, the middle layer, and the outer layer, called the crown, or the three layers of the coffin in Egyptian times, the layer of gold, the layer of silver, and the layer of something else, like bronze? Everybody's gotten the idea that when somebody died, the Egyptians mummified them. Well, does that mean everybody got to be mummified, or does that mean ten out of a hundred? Why not spend some period of time answering that kind of question, rather than endlessly 'Stop, drop, and roll'?

Long ago they used to preserve meat by stuffing it into a barrel with tons and tons of salt. The salt was so salty that the germs that are dedicated to making meat go bad couldn't do what they were planning to do, because of the gagging taste, and the meat just sat there, month after month, getting saltier by the minute. The history teacher at Threll Junior School told that very interesting thing to the class, and when a boy began talking loudly and interrupting, the teacher said, 'Be quiet, or I'll stuff *you* in a barrel of salt.' The boy turned bright red. Another time the teacher, Mr. Blithrenner, said to Roger Sharpless, 'Roger, if you put your finger any deeper into your nose it'll come out your ear.'

Nory hated added salt, but she loved Parmesan cheese, and when she was littler she used to pour out a big pile of Parmesan cheese on her plate and dab it up with her finger, if nobody was looking. Her cheeks got bright red when they had spaghetti because of a reaction to the cheese crumbs on them, not because she was embarrassed to eat cheese. She had no embarrassment whatever about eating cheese. Pamela Shavers said Parmesan cheese had lots of salt naturally in it. Crisps were naturally quite salty, as well. Once two bothersome boys found an empty package of crisps in a bin, or trash can, and they went up to Pamela Shavers and said, 'Oh, Pamela, would you care for a bag of crisps?' Pamela took the bag and squeezed it and when it went flat they laughed.

But there was something different than Parmesan cheese about pure salt sprinkled around on food—the wicked little crystals—as opposed to mixed *into* food, that Nory really wasn't such a fan of. Also sugar sprinkled in with vegetables—if she didn't know that there was added sugar in a pan of carrots, then it was fine, but if she knew, then she couldn't bear to think about it. Nowadays Littleguy was a tremendous fan of any kind of sprinkleable cheese. He and Nory had their own individual miniature cheese dispensers, labeled 'E' for 'Eleanor' and 'F' for Frank. Littleguy ate the cheese by pouring out a little hill of it on his plate when their parents were talking about something like the history of table manners and not paying any attention, and then he licked his spoon so that it was sticky and rolled it in the cheese so that the little scribbages of the cheese stuck to the spoon.

Well, so far, nothing about 'Stop, Drop, and Roll' at Threll Junior School, not a hint of it, which was a relief. Because really how much use would it be to know that rhyme in a fire? It depended on the kinds of clothes you were wearing whether that would be a good safety tip or not. For instance, say you were trying to dash across some burning piece of wood to escape through the front door, and the hem of your nightgown caught fire. It wouldn't be a good idea to throw yourself on the floor and start rolling around, because the floor might be burning, and if you had on a stretchy soft nightgown, you could pull it off and scamper out of it through the hole in the neck, when if you rolled around with it on, your legs would surely get burned.

They had had two fire drills already at the Junior School—one on purpose, and one by mistake. In a fire, the whole class was supposed to line up in a double row and the person at the front of the line called out the name of each child and checked it off on a piece of paper to make sure they were in line. The problem was that some kids would make a run for it, and the person calling out the names would wonder if those kids were hurt back in the back of the class and couldn't call out, when actually they were already outside, flopped out on the Astroturf gasping in that farm-fresh air. What if there was terrible smoke, would they all line up lying down, and have their names called that way?

Drama class was turning out to be very good at the Junior School. In drama class they were paired off, a boy and a girl together, and they were learning to die in various ways. One person poured boiling oil on the other and the other had to act out what it was like to have boiling oil poured on him. Then they switched off. The drama teacher was very, very good. The first week they learned how to die by being shot, and they practiced fake falls. The teacher said, in a very sweet voice, 'Oh dear, a sad, sad, thing happened to me today. So sad. I forgot my popgun. So I'll just have to shoot you without it, like this.' And she pointed her finger at each kid and said 'Bam! Bam! Bam! Bam!

Bam!' Everybody pretended to get shot and died. To do a fake fall, you begin standing up—of course—and you slide one of your knees down, down, almost touching the ground, then turn your head, and fall on the side, slide your whole arm down, then go still and dead. It's easy to do it slowly, but to do it quickly, as if you're really dropping dead, is not such an easy project. That was why it was so important to learn how in drama class.

In drama they also did a little skit where two people go to a pub, which is a bar, and one asks the other if he or she would like a drink, and then tells him to look somewhere off—'Oh, look at that interesting menu over there, how fascinatingly interesting'—and then, plip, poisons the person's drink by dropping a little tiny red pill into it. Nory poisoned Stefan's drink first, and he writhed around on the floor until she thought he was going to sprain something. (A sprain is worse than a strain—they are two totally different things. A lot of kids didn't realize that.) Then, when it was Nory's turn to be poisoned, she acted the part of a princess who drinks the drink, realizes that it's poison, because so many evildoers are wanting to steal the kingdom from her family, feels the stabbing of pain in her stomach, knows she is going to die within a manner of minutes, puts her hands together in a quiet adjustment on her lap, stretches out on the floor, and dies with the barest flutter of her eyelids.

In drama they never did act out one of Nory's secret ideas of a terrible disaster, though, which was, What would it feel like to be caught in a burning rain? That was just as well, because Nory had already put that idea in one of her Mariana stories. She had become totally emerged in telling it to herself on the way home from Oxburgh Hall, which was more of a Stately Castle than a Stately Home.

15. The Story of the Deadly Rain

When Mariana was only about eight or nine years old, she experienced something that one out of twenty people in India would have experienced. It was The Deadly Rain.

She had gone on trips to the Sahara deserts before, for she went on many different trips, and this was one of them. She had built a shack there for her summer house, or her father and mother had.

But what she had not heard, or that was not known among the people, was that the rain was going to be so hot, so very hot, that with the first touch of it, your finger would be burned black or blackish purple. If she had known this she would have picked a different time to come for sure. But she did not.

She got off a little horrible airplane and stepped with her first step into the orangish yellow sand of the Sahara deserts. The first thing she noticed was the tremendous amount of snakes, lizards, and different animals. She dropped and rolled over in the soft, comfortable sand. And she looked around. It was five minutes after that that the rain started. It rained solidly all night. It was horrible. Burning rain.

The next day, when it was still raining, she wandered, wandered, walking for home, home, all she could think about was getting to her home, out of the Sahara. Now what you may not notice about this, is that she could not just go into her house, or stand under the shade of a tree. She was alone in the desert, with only the wild snakes to accompany her. She stepped into the sand, each step making a mark that would soon vanish because of the heavy marks of the rain. It was not really raining from the sky very hot, but what happened was that the heat wave was so much hotter than the coldness of the rain that when the rain got down to a certain point, it started to boil, sizzling, poppling—sizzling, poppling. Animals scurrying here and there underground. Oh, how she wished she could go underground with them, be sheltered with them. She was too big.

Her slow walk now turned into a fast run. Tears streamed down her cheeks, and her hot face began to sting even worse than it had before. She was noticing that the rain was turning into balls of hot ice.

'But wait,' she thought, she stopped for a moment to look up at the sky. The heat wave was stopping, and huge pieces of hail were coming down from the sky. This made her happy. So she lay down and fell asleep, predicting that the next morning would be just as bad as the first, and took this chance to sleep.

'It might be my only chance,' she thought, lying down on the soft sand once again, this time happily. But just as she was about to shut her eyes, she noticed something—something that she'd never seen before.

It was a little girl, about the age of four. Of course she'd seen many little girls before, but this one was tired and hungry and dirty and blinded by the hot rain and hail. She was stumbling, bumping into sharp cactuses, there was nothing she could do. Mariana thought, 'How could I let her stay here? I've been that sick, I've been that lonely, but I've never been blinded in a hot rain and now hail like this. And, boy, would I have liked somebody to come and help me. I must go and save her,' she thought. 'I must carry her back to my house. I must.'

She got up and picked up the child. The child's heart stopped beating so fast. She calmed down. Her eyes for the first time opened. She looked up at Mariana with such happy eyes, sparkling eyes of pure glee, as if to say, 'You have saved me, Mariana, you have done well.'

Mariana looked back at her, as if to say, 'I've only done what people should have done for me.' She started walking. Each footstep she took now felt heavier and more uncomfortable. But the child was not the burden to her. The only thing that made her upset was the child's tears. The child was crying, not out of pain, but out of happiness. But Mariana had no idea that a child so young could be happy in the midst of something so horrible.

The next day, as she predicted, it was hot rain again. But this time not just boiling like the first, but so hot half of it was turning to steam. Steam only meant hot drips covered her face—both of their faces, rather. Their steps were heavier. The girl was crying, crying with pain, not from herself, but from looking into a face that had so much pain.

But now Mariana had come to a part of the desert where she was not alone. Many other people like herself were suffering, adults. She tried dragging one of them along, but it would not help. She was not strong enough to carry a three-year-old and a sixty-year-old. She found a shawl on a cactus. She took it off and wrapped it around the little girl. The little girl smiled. Then she took another shawl and wrapped it around herself this time. She thought she could walk faster if she had something to protect her from this awful rain, but it seeped through. She thought that this should be her punishment, to suffer this horrible rain, and to carry this heavy little girl, her punishment for being so selfish and taking the best spot she could pick in the year and taking the plane instead of walking.

She knew that she could, of course, because she had done it before. She had walked through places so full of trees and sticks carrying heavy buckets of hard metal for the princess Malina, in India. Finally she tried sticking a hollow stick into one of the cactuses, by cutting with her pocket knife a hole in it. She sucked and it burnt her mouth terribly. For an animal had died, a black-skinned animal, on the cactus, where she had struck in her stick. It was then that she decided that there was no way of getting water, she was stuck, she had to go home.

The little girl spoke for the first time. 'Do not carry me,' she said. 'You have to take care of me and find a place for me when you get home.' And as if she had read Mariana's mind, she said, 'A cactus would be a better burden for you. It would punish you even more, because of the spikes. And you could easily saw one off and carry it home, and then you wouldn't have an extra punishment of taking care of me when you get home.'

But the girl had begun to love her, Mariana, that is, and Mariana was not apt to let the girl go away and die. For she knew she would. She walked on, quicker, quicker now, the hot rain got hotter and hotter. Her face started bubbling it was so hot. Her sweat turned red with blood. The girl cried blood in looking at a face that seemed to have so much pain again. Mariana spoke softly to the girl. 'Do not cry, dear, do not cry, it takes blood from your precious body.' The girl wiped her tears. Mariana, seeing the girl wiping her tears, remembered her own face, and how much it hurt. She touched it. It felt more pain, and what the little girl saw is what you should see in your mind. She saw pain: the face was very swollen and she touched it. The air-filled skin broke, very thin now, because it was full of air, and blood gushed out. It was painful-looking and definitely was painful for Mariana.

She was almost at home now. Of course she couldn't see it, but she had gone two quarters of the way. Only ten miles to go, but her feet were so sore. Her hair was dyed almost red. Walking farther and farther and farther and farther, tired to beat the band. The girl looked up again, like she had done the first time Mariana had picked her up. Now with swollen cheeks but a happier face. She looked wise. 'We are almost home now,' she whispered, 'I can tell by that cactus.' She pointed to the tallest cactus Mariana had ever seen. Mariana stepped back. She forgot about her pain, the heavy child she was holding, and all the hot rain. It reminded her of when she was a baby. She was born under a tall, tall sequoia tree. The tree had been cut down to build a nice beautiful house, but in her mind it was not cut down, but was still standing there, in Australia. The sand was getting more shallow now. It would have hurt more now for me or you but to her it meant home. It meant getting the little child safe, finding her new parents, or finding the old parents, if they had not died, and getting home to her own mother and father out there. In the bottom of her heart she thought they might have died, but I can tell you now that they hadn't. But in her heart she also thought something else. She thought, 'I can adopt her. She can be my own child, I can take care of her.'

The child read her mind once again. 'You are my mother now,' she said. 'My parents have died.' Wisely she said this, not as a three-year-old, not as an old person, but as Mariana's own mother would have said it. Mariana remembered the Australian look of her mother now. Long beautiful black hair, and now she also noticed something else about the child. She, too, was an Australian. Mariana hugged the child tight now, with the child upright in her arms, as she had seen women in Australian doing.

Finally she came to the wooden house. The sight of it was miracly happy-making for her. She lay the child down on the couch on the front porch. Her mother and her father hugged her. Then she fell, her knees bending. They gently took her to her bed. She slept a gentle sleep. It felt like it lasted twenty days and twenty nights. In later years, she raised the child, with her parents' help, and the two of them became best friends.

And that was only one of the stories of the amazing, everlasting Life of Mariana.

16. Something Needs to Fail

The idea of everlasting life came partly from the kinds of things you say in Cathedral, and partly from a movie called *The Neverending Story,* which was an extremely good movie in many ways, one of which was that it was unusually rare to have a two-part movie and have the second part be just as interesting as the first, basically. 'Neverending' and 'everlasting' were good words for the job because they last and last when you say them, like 'forevermore.'

Nory had saved up a few stories from the Everlasting Life of Mariana, and she was wondering how in the world she would remember them, since they were too long to write down. Some were definitely a touch on the gruesome side, but that was what you might expect since if it's a gruesomeness that comes from your own private brain when you're awake it's not the least bit the same as the kind of gruesomeness that somebody else might offer you in a book or a movie. On the other hand, the scary things your brain decides to show you at night are totally different, they can be *very* bothersome, definitely, but the things that you think up on purpose are usually not as bad, because they were just teetering at the exact limit of frighteningness that you wanted them at, and you didn't have to worry that they were going to slip over the limit.

You really need something to fail in a story, because then when it fails it has to get better. The way Nory thought of the burning rain story was that she once noticed that sometimes rain, when it was falling very lightly, would give you pins and needles on your face. Very very light rain, *ting, ting, ting,* could hurt surprisingly. Just tiny, tiny drops of sharp rain, coming down very quickly because they're so small they slide right past the bigger softer raindrops.

Another time, on the way back from Blickling Hall, Nory told a story to her very small Felicity doll. It ended up being about a little brother because her own brother, Littleguy, was right next to her in his car seat, transfixed in his sleep. The story was gruesome, but not *as* gruesome as the story about the burning rain, which was probably the most gruesome one she'd ever told.

17. A Story About a Girl Named Era and Her Brother

There was a little girl named Era. She lived in a beautiful cottage near Blickling Hall with her brother. It was so lovely, everything was perfect. Her mother and father were perfect, they never were angry, and always were nice to them. Era was walking in one day, after playing outside in her favorite place to play. But, ooh, she fell into horrible mud.

'Oh no,' she said, 'I have just spoiled my lovely dress. Oh no.' And she began to cry. She got up out of the ditch and walked over to her mother.

'Oh dear,' said her mother, 'your favorite dress, too. Well, I'll just have to make you a new one, and patch up that one.'

'Thank you, Mother,' Era said, and bowed politely, or curtsied, as you might say. She walked along, putting her school things away in the proper places. 'Mother,' she said, 'is Father out of the hospital yet?'

'Yes, he is, he's in the breakfast room, if you go in there, you'll see him.'

Era walked in, and there was her father. He smiled brightly at her. She played games all morning. But her dress getting mud on it was not the only tragedy of that day. She was walking on the street with her brother, who was eight, coming back from the market with all the goods. She put her brother down, and she, being a thirteen-year-old, went off to do some homework, or prep.

Her mother was making dinner, and went off in another room to get her laundry, and her father stayed in the breakfast room, unable to walk still, because of his injury about a month ago. She walked happily through the living room as she went to her room. There was her brother, taking out the matches slowly one by one.

'Oh no,' she said, 'Help, no!' And she grabbed the matches away from him. But just as she grabbed it away, the match in his hand flung against the matchbox, and a fire started. She dropped the matchbox and called out. But her mother could not hear her. She was covered in laundry from head to toe, bringing it into the kitchen.

'Fire!' screamed Era, pulling her brother out with her. But they tripped over her matchbox and he burned his legs badly. She carried him out, quickly, but she tripped again, falling on him, then picked him up and ran out with him screaming in pain, from fire. She had stepped on a knife that had cut through the back of her shoe. Oh, she was scared, running. It was horrible. They had tripped on the thing where you scrape your shoes, when the snow and dung had been there. 'Oh no,' she thought, 'my poor brother, my mother, my father.'

Her father, unable to walk, and her mother, unable to hear, sadly died in the fire. It was awful, she wiped tears from her face and sobbed. Her brother was bleeding terribly now. She picked him up and got out. He was screaming with pain again. Oh, she could almost feel the pain herself. 'Oh,' she said, 'brother, don't cry, don't cry.' And she wiped his tears. She could see the pain in his face, but he was very obedient, he did whatever his sister would ever wish him to do. He quietly was carried by her. She could see the pain in his face, easily. She could see that he was struggling.

'Oh, brother, you may cry.' She saw a small tear drip across his face, which was wiped back by his shaking hand. He could not resist that tear, she knew, there was no way of helping it.

'Oh, sister, I can walk,' he said.

'You will fall,' she said, because he could only barely walk with his injuries, and tumble over himself. She brought him carefully to the hospital, with blood stained all over her white and now brown dress.

'Oh, no,' she cried, going in the revolving door. She walked slowly over to the desk, carrying her lovable brother. 'Oh, no.' She wiped her tears away and tried to fix her hair, which was horrible now. The curl was coming out, the one that was in the back. It hung almost straight down now. She was scared. Her hair always hung straight down when she was scared. Maybe it was the sweat that pulled it down by getting it wet, dripping. Her brother was horrified. The doctors took him.

And for a while after that you never got to see her clean white prim dress or her nice hairdo, but you saw blood and mud and things like that on her dress. She became very poor, without the tiniest bit of money. She walked to a stone. In the stone, she carved her mother's name, sadly. She couldn't do it, but the stone was covered with mud, so she tried scratching a message in the mud. She walked along, four days she spent without her brother. Finally she went over to the hospital and picked him up. Fortunately he was better. Soon he was well enough to be picking berries and peeling oranges again, and they had lovely suppers together.

She carried him wherever he went. And, the end.

18. A Little About Raccoon

The thing that had failed in Nory's own life was that right now she didn't have a best friend in England. And she honestly missed her best friend from America, Debbie, who hadn't written back. Some kids are not so good about writing letters, though. Another sad and unfair thing was that Nory had only gotten a tinily short time to have Debbie as her best friend, since she'd only met her very recently, in about the past two years.

The great thing that was important to know about Debbie was that she love, love, *loved* telling stories with her dolls. She had four stuffed kitten dolls that made a purring sound when you turned them at an angle, not quite identical in their faces but almost identical, and she had an extraordinary imagination that just went on and on and on to an endless limit. Nory and Debbie played the Samantha game together, which was an everlasting game, in which disaster after disaster happened to Samantha and everybody else who took place in it. One time Samantha was hanged by her foot on the lampshade because a dog named Fur was going to burn her. Fur was actually a very good dog, he was a puppet dog that Debbie loved most of all her animals and slept with. (Debbie loved her pandas, too, but her pandas were more of a collection.) But they had to have a bad creature in the story or it wouldn't have the feeling of something failing, so they had the idea that he had been given a pill by this wandering bad person that made him bad for a short time. So the result was that he was being quite dreadful, temporarily, and wanted to kill the kitties and Samantha. That allowed him to be bad for the sake of the story but not overall bad for the sake of Debbie's dear animal that she slept with. The four adventurous kitties figured out a way to save themselves by pretending there were only two kitties and getting the dog Fur to take a second pill that would make him go to sleep. When he woke he was his old warmhearted self again. Telling those stories with Debbie was so miracly much fun.

Before she knew Debbie, Nory told her stories by herself. It was hard to remember how she began, but it appeared to her now that she might have begun with little snibbets of stories she told in different voices in the bath, or looking in the mirror, because those were some of the most important storytelling situations. She had a rubber raccoon that had hundreds of adventures in the bath. Obviously she couldn't take Cooch herself because Cooch was (speaking of things you shouldn't speak of) *sewn:* she was a cloth puppet and couldn't get wet.

Sarah Laura Maria Raccoon was one when Nory found her, abandoned by her parents lying cold and numb by the road. She and Sylvester had adopted her, and then it turned out that Cooch was their own lost child. A witch had taken away their own child long before. The witch came pouring up from the steam of a grilled cheese sandwich one day, an ugly thing, and stole their dear Coochie away, and their hearts were broken, or 'juken down' as Littleguy would say, since that's how he pronounced broken down. Heartjuken for many long years they lived in their small cottage, until one day they found an older Raccoon cold and abandoned by the road. 'We must adopt her, she looks so much like our own long lost Sarah Laura Maria,' they said. When she revived a little she told them what had happened, that she had been living a perfect life with her two parents when a wicked witch came along and took her, but fortunately she escaped by throwing salt in the witch's eye and dashing out of the witch's boat and jumping overboard, where the mermaids took her to their castle and cared for her and tried to teach her as best they could to be a mermaid raccoon. She had grown very thin when she was with the witch but she grew plumper now, feeding on sea salads. And sometimes—if by chance someone in a boat threw it overboard—a good old potato. She did her best and she wore long flowing dresses made of the finest kinds of seaweed found near Africa, but she was a land-raccoon in her heart and finally she thanked the mermaids with many hugs and waves and swam ashore. There the husband and wife, out on a walk on the beach, found her.

'Darling, do you notice how much this Raccoon looks like our own dear child?' the mother asked.

'Yes, yes I do,' said the husband. 'I wonder if she'll want to play with some of the toys that our dear little child used to play with.' Sadly he went upstairs and got down the box of things. There was a Fisher Price Main Street, with a set of five letters that you could put into a mailbox, and a set of foam numbers that fit together, and many other things.

'I had just that toy,' said Cooch. 'And just that toy.'

'You did?' said the parents, in amazement. 'Could she be . . . ?' they wondered. 'What is your name?'

'Sarah Laura Maria,' she said.

'But that is the name of our own daughter, who was stolen away by a witch many years ago!' said the mother and father.

'I was stolen away by a witch, too,' Coochie told them shyly.

'You're our daughter! Oh, come here, oh my!' And they hugged her and kissed her and were overjoyed forevermore.

19. A Chinese Monk

So Nory did tell stories like that before she met Debbie, to herself, but Debbie was a wonderful friend because she was willing to let the story go where it preferred to go, and she could think up disasters for Samantha that Nory couldn't conveniently think up by herself. Debbie had a very wide, wide face, and long black hair that was shiny and perfect, because her parents were Chinese and Filipino, although she spoke only American, plus the Mandarin Chinese they learned in the International Chinese Montessori School, which was also called ICMS. Neither of them could speak Cantonese, which was a totally different bowl of fish from Mandarin. When the two of them were drawing something together, though, they would sing a song in Mandarin that their Chinese teacher taught them, called 'Namoowami tofo.' The song went something like

Xie er po, mao er po,
Shen shang de jia sha po.

What it meant was basically, 'His shoes are broken, his hat is broken.' Or rather, that was the translation that the teacher gave them. The problem was that their teacher hardly knew a giblet of English. Nory's translation to herself was, 'Shoes are torn, hat is torn, his whole outfit is torn.' The song was about a crazy monk. The best part was just a sound, 'Namoowami tofo,' which was the prayer to the Buddha that the monk used to do his magic. He was born from the Buddha. His name was Ji Gong. He was very free, even though he was a monk.

Nory still sang the song quite often, because some Chinese songs are so great that how can you not sing them? But she was at the point of forgetting a lot of the Chinese characters she used to know, such as

木

which means 'wood,' or

which means 'spill.' She never wrote Chinese now. Nobody in her class now at Threll Junior School was Chinese, even though there were some Chinese kids in the Senior School, and so there was nobody who even understood what a Chinese character was, and what pin yin was, and how you had to memorize the order of the strokes.

Her parents originally thought they might get a Chinese tutor for her in Threll, but Nory had school on Saturday mornings here, and plenty of homework, and that left her only one day off. If a Chinese tutor came on Sunday, Nory wouldn't be exhausted so much as thinking, 'Oh, my poor scrabjib of a weekend!' When would they have time to drive to a castle or a palace, which is what they did every weekend? At Oxburgh Hall, high up in the tower where the princess stayed and sewed, they saw a little brick place where the Catholic priest would have to stuff himself when the government inspectors came sniffing.

So that was just the fact of it: Chinese was going to grow faint in her mind. She hadn't known all the characters in the world, anyway. Four years was how long it took her to learn Chinese, as much of it as she knew, which wasn't all that much compared to what an adult or an older child would know, so she thought that in French it might take her about two years to learn it, because it wasn't as difficult as Chinese. But still, French was nice and hard—nice and hard. *Dix* was a very meaningful word. 'It already means ten, in a sensible way,' Nory thought. When she first heard 'dix,' she thought, 'Oh, puff, that's not like ten.' But very soon it meant ten in quite a sensible way. And *Je* was actually quite a better word for 'I' than 'I.' No language was easy. It was a bad mistake to think so. English was about the most blusteringly hard language you could get. Verbally Chinese was much easier than English.

Certain languages from Africa weren't as complicated in some ways, though, Nory thought. They didn't do 1, 2, 3, 4, 5, 6, 7, 8, 9, 10, drrrrrr, their numbers didn't go for infinity. They went one, two, three—and then 'many.' For instance: 'There were many people at the store.' Well? Does that mean four, or does that mean twenty-five? Their next-door-neighbor in Palo Alto, who spent a whole year in Africa, in Bombay, told Nory that about the numbers. Nory told it to Debbie, who said it couldn't be true, because how could they have phone numbers or know how much things cost? Say you went to see *The Little Mermaid* with your family in Bombay, and the person said, through the little hole in the glass, 'Two adults and two children? That will be many dollars, please.' Or hickles, or gumbobs, or whatever Bombayan dollars are called. Many dollars? How many dollars?

Nory had to agree that her friend Debbie had a worthwhile point. Debbie was very smart and talented at a lot of things, including the piano. She was an all-around wonderful friend, the kind of friend you think finally just *has* to be your best friend, because there is no other choice but to have her be your best friend. Especially when Bernice said she was going to live in a house with her 'real' best friend, which was rude and mean. Bernice had a two-color retainer with a picture of a silver mermaid on it. Debbie had silver writing in her retainer that said 'Debbie.' When Debbie got her retainer, it left Nory as the last girl in the class not to have a retainer. That was one reason she thought, long ago, when people started getting their retainers one after another after another, 'I know! I'll be an orthodontist, and design people's retainers for them.' She would design one with the image of a big teethy smile on it. If Littleguy needed one, she'd do one with a steam train. You could think of the teeth as a train chuffing around the jaw.

In England it would be almost impossible to be a professional orthodontist, because almost nobody in school had retainers to speak of, or rather 'false palates,' as they were known by the select few. Probably the reason nobody had them was exactly because of that awful, queasy-making name, false palates. You might as well call them 'bladder-stones' and get it over with.

20. A Report About the Teeth

The idea of designing people's retainers was part of what first got Nory interested in teeth. Then she found out that the whole subject was more fascinating than you could ever predict. In Ms. Beryl's class at the International Chinese Montessori School she did a report, 'Teeth.' One of the things she wrote about in the report was a two- or three-inch model of a tooth that was carved centuries ago to show the horrible pain of a toothache. There were different pictures on this large ivory tooth, sort of like the different pictures that are in stained glass. Stained glass was invented to tell stories in pictures because so few people could read back then. Now we have to read twenty-five books just to figure out what the stained glass is saying, so it's the opposite of before, when you didn't read but just looked around and thought, Ah, King Solomon, I see. Ivory was a good choice for the model tooth because ivory is the tooth of the elephant. The model showed people throwing skulls in a fire, probably to illustrate the horrible burning pain of a toothache, and a picture of something bad happening to a woman, some drastic tooth operation. It had a hinge. It was a box, which you opened up. 'Maybe if you stored candy in it,' Nory thought, 'you would eat less candy because you would see this horrible carved picture of the skulls going into the fire and think, No, I won't have that lemondrop, not just yet.'

Also in the report—which was probably the best thing she did in Ms. Beryl's class by far—Nory drew a diagram of the layers of the tooth. For years she had thought, 'There must be layers to the tooth, there *must* be, it can't possibly be all the same substance.' It worried her for a very long while, and then, presto, when she drew the diagram, copying from the encyclopedia, she was happy to discover that there were. She liked when things had layers—the earth has layers, the trunk of a tree has layers, the atmosphere has layers. A conker has layers, too. It has a green spiky outer layer and a very shiny wonderful layer which is the conker itself, which is like the finest, smoothest wood in a very precious table or the knob of a chair or something like that, in a great palace like Ickworth House, where the floorboards are curved. (They were somehow bent into curves with the help of steam engines, which pleased Littleguy.) And then inside that there's the growing part of the conker, which is like the nerve of the tooth. Sometimes you can find a double-conker. 'Conker' is the English way of saying horse chestnut, and it's a very good way because they can suddenly conk you on the head. After the sermon in the Cathedral at Harvest Festival they were all crossing the street and Nory spotted tons and tons and tons of freshly fallen conkers. She rushed over and started gathering them. They're very rare in general because as soon as they come off the tree, people come over and get them. Everyone was really happy to find more conkers had fallen, just during the short time they were in the Cathedral. They sang a song in service that went: 'Think of the world without any flowers, think of the world without any trees.' Then it went, 'The farmers spread the good things on the land, but it is God's almighty hand, that waters them, but,' then there was something Nory couldn't remember, 'but more to us as children, he gives our daily bread.' The English way of singing was quite different from the Chinese way of singing. In the English way, you had to hold one note for a very long time, and you didn't woggle the note so much. The English had extremely high singing voices and their songs were meant to be sung in an English accent, so when one child out of dozens was singing them in an American accent it didn't always have a pleasant outcome.

Sometimes when they had sung the flower-gathering song in Chinese class Bernice would sing it with her retainer halfway out of her mouth, which was rude and disgusting, and it made the Chinese teacher furious. Bernice had to go on time-out once for doing that. (Time-out didn't exist in England—they had detention, or DT, instead.) Bernice also talked baby talk with her retainer halfway out. Once she bit it so hard it broke and half of it went up into the part of her nose that connected to the back of her mouth and the doctor had to go in and pull it out, or it would have stayed there forever causing trouble. Debbie would never think of chewing her retainer in half—she was a very sweet girl in many ways. Her braces made her mouth wide and gave her that thinking look that was the most noticeable thing about her besides her hair. Of course her whole face was quite wide. Nory's face was a smashed, squashed, shriveled little thing, she felt. It seemed shriveled partly because she spent her time with Debbie and other Asian kids, who are, you just have to say, the most beautiful type of kids in most ways. Nory would draw a self-portrait and be not perfectly content with it, thinking, 'Well, it's a bit of a squished head on the sides, but all right.' And then she would look at her face in the mirror and think, 'Well, no wonder I drew a squished head.' Her parents said she was a beautiful child and sometimes she did think she looked pretty, but it was not polite to brag that out loud. It was quite all right for parents to tell a child she was beautiful, just as long as they didn't tell her she was beautiful in front of other children. If they announced it in front of other children it would put the other children in an awkward position, because they would be just sitting there, odd man out.

One day at her new school, the Threll Junior School, Mrs. Thirm asked the class to write the first paragraph of a story with each child as the main character. Nory started off with: 'Marielle was a young girl with brown hair and brown eyes who was forty-three inches tall.' But she wasn't entirely happy with this. What she had been tempted to write after the 'who was' was not that she was forty-three inches tall, but something similar to the scene in *The Little Princess,* where the girl is being shown around the school, and she acts as a 'bright-eyed, smart, quiet little girl most of the time.' It wasn't exactly, persistently those words, but at least that was the feeling of the scene. And the girl who played the Little Princess in the movie looked a tiny bit like Nory. Nory really wanted to write that Marielle, who stood for her, was a 'quiet little girl, most of the time, very quiet, and mysterious—or not really mysterious, but if you took a little bit away from the meaning of mysterious, or add a little more to the scene in *The Little Princess,* an almost mysterious girl.' But she wrote none of that because even though Marielle was not her own name, it would be clear that she was writing about herself and it would be kind of bragging to say those things.

21. What You Might Have to Do, Though

The time when Nory most thought about how she looked was, of course, when she looked in the mirror, which was just before bed when she was brushing her teeth. They made a mistake, Nory thought, in advertisements when they showed a long, long stretch of toothpaste starting at the very tip of the toothbrush and going to the other end of the bristles, because that's really not the amount you should have. It's way too much. If you put that much on, it burns your whole mouth, since there are a lot of nerves in the gums, so what happens is that you are desperate to want to spit it out immediately, without brushing your teeth at all. Then you could claim, 'Oh, yes, I brushed my teeth' without really brushing them. Or you do it very quickly and you do a really, really bad job. That was what was so important about the idea of a pea-sized gob.

And always while she brushed she made a toothful smile, because you almost have to, which put her in the mind of pretending to be another person. That was one way she would start telling stories: she would talk to the twin toothbrusher in the mirror, and then she would play a game that there were twins, asking each other questions, and then triplets. She would act out each one's personality, and something sad would have happened to one of them. One time she played a mirror game in which there were five duplicates of her. That was back in America. Each person had strange bracesy things in their mouths that were made shaped like candy, and flavored like candy. So each twin would come on and describe how great her braces were. 'Hi! These are raspberry-flavored braces! They're astonishingly good braces!' 'Mine are apple-cinammon! They're superb!' And so on. They would take turns advertising their braces. And then they would get into a conversation, and that would lead to a story about some trouble one of the twins was having. Then Nory's mother and father would call upstairs, 'Nory? Are you in your night-costume?' Nory would shout back, 'Oops! Sorry! I was dawdling, I'm afraid!'

Nory wanted to work for an advertising campaign, like her grandfather, while she was trying to get her certificate of dentistry, because she loved advertising campaigns. She wanted a Ph.D., though, most of all. Nory's mother told her about Ph.D.s, and she was determined on getting one. She positively *had* to have that Ph.D., because for one thing it makes you feel smart to have one and it's something that basically all people get. She was not going to be kept away from getting one just because she would have to get some strange badge of dentistry. So she would probably need to be something more, like a dental surgeon or a dental botanist, who does research into why teeth grow or get cavities, in order to need to get that Ph.D. But she would still have to go to a dentistry school. That surely would still be a necessity.

Nory wouldn't mind working with a corpse if it meant dentistry. Doctors have to operate on corpses, she had heard, and if you're going to be a dental surgeon, you definitely might have to use a corpse, because dead people have teeth, too, don't they? If you're going to pull the teeth from anyone, it might as well be from a corpse. The school could make a huge plastic figure, like a voodoo doll, and have the students pull teeth from that, but it would be very expensive and you'd have to create all those parts of the body from scratch out of clay or better yet FIMO. The teeth would have to snap in and out somehow. Why not use a dead person, since they're available? Nory wouldn't mind doing it, because she wanted to be a dentist so much. On the other hand, she did get quite disgusted by doing math. Math, math, math. One pencil lead used up, then another, then another. Then you're out of pencil leads and you have to use a regular pencil. Sharpen, sharpen, sharpen. Whole huge erasers used up madly erasing things you did wrong. Her National Trust eraser had no corners left now. It was a pathetic egg of an eraser. The idea of all that math she would have to do in order to be a dentist gave her an extremely carsick feeling.

But: 'Don't count your bad lucks before they happen.' That was a saying that she had made up. It was kind of like 'Don't count your chickens before they hatch,' except the opposite.

22. For Some Reason, People Were Bad to Pamela

In real life there were identical twins at her school. They didn't have braces. At first Nory thought they might become her good friends. But it was hard to be friends with them, because you don't want to talk to both of them at the same time, as if they're one person, because they might not like that, so you talk to one, and then you have to instantly talk to the other, so that you don't seem as if you're ignoring her, which wouldn't be polite. So you ask her a question, and then the other twin asks a question, and you answer that question, and you ask that twin a question about what activities she's going to sign up for, table tennis or French knitting. So then that twin begins talking about activities. Then you have to ask the other twin about her activities. They do mostly the same thing, but not exactly the same thing. And sometimes you can't keep track of which twin you asked what. Even if you didn't want it to be, it was sort of like, 'If I ask you one question, you ask me two questions.' They seemed to have mostly the same friends, and really it didn't matter which one you talked to because they were both equally as nice and equally as interesting, and they both looked pretty much the same, pretty much blond, that is, and sweet-smiling. So you felt just as comfortable talking to one as to the other.

But it didn't turn out that Nory became friends with them. The twins had other friends from last year they relied on heavily. Sometimes, as a matter of fact, they were a bit irritable with Nory and fair-weather-friendish. Once they were even part of a whole gang-up of girls who were bad to Pamela Shavers. Pamela Shavers, for no reason at all, was selected to be that certain someone that everyone should laugh at and say quite sharp, mocking things to. She had skipped ahead one year, so she was in Year Six when really her age was Year Five, which is to say, fourth grade. So? What was bad about that? Pamela lost her prep book in the changing room and was rushing trying to find it and four other girls from one of the older classes started saying they'd used it as loo paper. Not very likely. The twins weren't really a part of that group, though, they were just watching and laughing. Their older sister, though, was one who was saying things like 'Are you sure you didn't bake it in a pie in Kitchen Arts?' Pamela was just on the edge of crying, saying 'I'm going to miss my train!' Nory couldn't stand it and said: 'Stop. You're being horrible to her. Stop it, stop it, stop it.'

'Oh, oh, you're friends with her?' said one of the girls to Nory. 'You don't know better, you're from America, you have no idea how squeegee your accent is.'

'Yes, I am American, I have an American accent,' said Nory. 'Your accent, let me inform you, is dreadful. You bark like a sea lion.'

People giggled a little at that and that made Nory well known and made the girl furious, but the important thing was that Pamela had a chance to look some more for her prep book, which she found.

Another time Pamela lost her jacket, or maybe someone hid it. She was frantically looking, and nobody was willing to help. They just told her rude things. 'Well, we don't know where it is, we gave it to an old drooling man who came to the door who gave it away to Oxfam.'

Pamela kept saying, 'I have to catch my train!' There was the same sound in her voice that seemed to Nory as if she certainly was going to cry, but she didn't. It was just the quality that came into her voice when she was angry—although maybe there was some crying in it. (Nory's own record was still perfect: she had not cried. Had not and would not.) Pamela couldn't leave without her jacket on because Mrs. Derpath stood by the door, totally on the watch-out. She would nip you by the neck, throw you around, toss you back into the classroom, if you did not have your blue blazer on. So Pamela had to find that blazer.

Nory helped her, she rummaged and scrummaged, she found it under a pile of backpacks, and she said, 'Here, Pamela, here's your jacket.' But it was completely trampled over and disgusting. Kids had been practically been doing the Majarajah on it, stamping back and forth without noticing. Nory helped her dust it off. 'Thanks,' said Pamela and she hurried away for her train. She ran in a crouching run, her backpack bouncing like a kangaroo, but her eyes looking down and a little forward on the sidewalk. It was not exactly the way a happy girl would run.

Even Nory's friend Kira, who was turning out to be a good friend in England, didn't want Nory to be nice to Pamela. Pamela had been quite nice to Nory in one of the early days of school, when Nory had forgotten how to get back to the Junior School building from the dining hall, once *again*. Nory had an atrocious sense of direction—about as atrocious as her sense of spelling, she thought sometimes, and maybe the two things were connected, because knowing which way to turn was like when you were trying to spell 'failure' and you didn't know if it was 'faleyer' or 'fayelyor' or something quite else. You didn't know whether to go northeast or southwest at the choices of vowel. Her sense of direction was so horrible that she crashed her plane four times in I.T. They had stopped learning the home row of keys on the keyboard, and they were doing a Flight Imitator, or whatever it was called, and they were supposed to land a plane in the dark according to a map, and Nory simply could not read that map. Her plane shot up toward the stars, and the lights began going around, which meant she was in a death-spin, and she crashed. She crashed so many times that day she had a bad dream about it. So her sense of direction was not at all good. 'You're just a disaster, aren't you?' said the I.T.

teacher, but he said it in a very comforting way that made Nory feel better, in the same kind voice he used when he said, 'Good morning, ladies and jellyfish.' So anyway, Nory lost her sense of direction and got turned around and wasn't sure where she was headed, but Pamela, when Nory asked her for help that early time, wasn't in the least bit surprised that she didn't know the way back, and just treated it as a normal event and very nicely walked with her, having a nice indistinct conversation.

Another time Daniella Harding wanted to scratch 'D H' on the back of her watch, to stand for Daniella Harding—she was a pillish girl in some ways, no question about that, although not always—and she borrowed Nory's compass to use the point for scratching. Nory let her take it because it was flattering to be asked for something and to have it there in your pencil case, and of course, an hour later, the pencil in the compass was totally lost, gone, bye-bye. (Really the compass is called a 'set of compasses' and the things that stick out are called the 'arms of the compass.') And it was the only pencil Nory had just then, because somehow she'd lost the others, including even her mechanical pencil. That time, very nicely, Pamela let Nory borrow one of her pencils and helped her with some of her math. Nory was on the wrong track in her multiplication and was counting up all the numbers to the right of the decimal, including the numbers you add together to get the final number. Pamela showed her that it was much easier than that. You only had to count the number of numbers to the right of the decimal on the two numbers that you're multiplying in order to get the answer.

But even if Pamela had never once been nice to Nory, Nory probably would have said something, she thought, because Pamela had just as much a right as anyone else to go off to school every day and not have her day be made into a state of misery. Her parents were paying hundreds of thousands of dollars to send her there, think about that. Pamela said that she hadn't told her parents about any of it because she hadn't found the time. Nory told her parents about it and they said that it was brave of Nory to defend Pamela. They thought Pamela ought to go right to the teacher. But Pamela didn't want to.

And the thing that was so impossible to figure out, was: Why was this happening? Pamela was never rude or interrupting, she wasn't braggingly pleased with herself, she was perfectly nice to everybody. Was it some chance thing one day that made it happen that one kid decided to pick on her and then everyone else did? Or was it that there was something about the way she acted that made kids get up on the wrong side of the bed with her? Her face was a nice face—maybe a slight roundedness to it in the cheeks, and her teeth were a little bit out of whack in maybe a chipmunkish way. Or rather that was what two boys were saying one time: that she had a rat-faced look, which is a persistently rude and cruel thing to say, but those boys were known for being rude and insulting guttersnakes every chance they got. And her nose did have a pudginess about it. But Daniella's nose had much more pudge to it and nobody took the time to fuss her out. Actually Daniella was one of the most popular kids!

Nory said to Pamela, 'Go to Mrs. Thirm, tell Mrs. Thirm.' But Pamela said she'd gone to Mrs. Thirm last year about something and Mrs. Thirm had said to her that she'd done all kinds of things that she said she hadn't done, so she couldn't go to Mrs. Thirm. Nory said, 'Well, then, go to Mr. Pears.' Mr. Pears was the head of the Junior School and an extremely nice man. He was the one who read them about Hector. The problem with the story about Hector, however—or, not Hector, Achilles—the problem about Achilles, Nory felt, was that he was much more a likable heroine in the beginning, when he was a newborn infant. Later on, in the part about the battle, he takes a downturn and goes bad. The ending should have worked differently. He falls in love with somebody, and he kills hundreds of people, he drags a man around behind his wagon, and he sulks away the time in his tent and says he won't fight anymore. It's just not anywhere near as good. The better part is earlier when a person who was half deer and half human took care of him, and fed him with deerskin. No, the person couldn't have been half a deer, because he wouldn't be feeding him deerskin if he were a deer, that would be cannibalism. The person was half-oxen, half-human. This half-and-half creature fed him deerskin and cream. The deerskin was for good strength, and cream or sugar for good heart or health. Nory had not followed this part exactly, because she'd been inspired by it halfway through to have the idea of a detective story about a Batman ruler and a Barbie pencil. But Achilles was still good when he was having the cream and deerskin diet. He seemed like a much less good person when he got older.

Pamela said, 'Oh no, I can't go to Mr. Pears, because he'll go to Mrs. Thirm.' So she just didn't do anything. And it began to get gradually a little worse and a little worse, time by time. Kira kept saying to Nory, 'Whatever you do, do not speak to Pamela.' She said: 'Every time you speak to Pamela it will make you less popular.' She said, 'Just spend your time with me.' Nory liked Kira and was in the early part of a friendship when you are sort of under a person's spell a little, basically. So for two days she did stay away from Pamela more than she had—not completely, because she sat next to her for one lunch, but she spent most of the time with Kira. But it pulled at her, what she was doing, because she knew she was not helping Pamela and maybe hurting her feelings. Nory told this to her parents. They said that when a group of people decide to not speak to a person and pretend they don't exist it was called the Silent Treatment, and though it wasn't physically bullying in the meaning of punching someone or screaming at them it was a quiet mental torture and awful. They wanted to tell someone at the school about it, but Nory said that Pamela didn't want anyone to know about it. They said that the bad thing about bullying was that people who didn't ever imagine that they would be doing mean things to a person, people like Kira, ended up doing mean things, because it spreads. And the person who's being bullied gets kind of numb and bewildered and doesn't know how to take action.

So next break-time Nory sat on a wall side by side with Pamela. Kira was furious and stomped off. Nory found her later in the music room, with the headphones on, reading a book. Nory said, 'Kira! I've been looking everywhere for you! I've been in a state about it. I looked in the changing room, I looked in the classroom, I looked under the tree, I looked in the bathroom, I didn't even *go* to the bathroom because I was so busy looking for you. I even looked in the front field!'

Kira said, 'Oh, hm, yes.' She was not apologetic in any way and just sat there like a bump on a rug.

It hurt Nory's friendliness toward Kira that Kira had this character flaw of being very possessive and jealous and needing her all to herself. And the thing was, also, that Kira was generally in some ways a rough kind of punching friend—friendly punching. If Kira got mad at something, she would tighten up Nory's tie so afterward for a little while Nory's neck had a sweaty feeling from the itch of the collar. But when Nory went back to being friendly to Pamela, Kira began saying sharp sarcastic things, that were half-jokes, half not-jokes, like: 'Nory, do you like torturing people?' Nory was confused for a second because her parents had used that word and she thought Kira was talking about Pamela. She said, 'Um—do you?'

'No,' said Kira. 'But evidently you do, because that's what dentists do.'

'Kira!' said Nory, laughing, but not feeling particularly good. Her feelings were still hurt later when she thought about it. She could have said, still jokingly, but meaning what she was saying, 'How dare you insult the poor dentists, who are just trying to help. It's your fault. You got your own cavities. You should have brushed your teeth. Then the dentist would only have to put good old paste inside of your mouth, spread it around, and Mr. Thirsty would suck out all the saliva that gathered into a little puddle in your lower mouth.' Nory liked the feeling of Mr. Thirsty thirsting out the saliva, the hollow bubbling sound he made. Mr. Thirsty was just a name dentists gave to a certain little bended piece of suction tube, to make it seem friendlier to kids. And it worked. If you you kept it in too long, you might completely dry out your mouth, which would be an interesting experiment. Probably a dental researcher has tried it. Nory used to try to dry her tongue completely by sticking it out for a long time. If you lie there on your bed with your tongue out for long enough it will get so totally dry that it glues itself to your mouth when you pull it back in. But it's probably not good to do that too much. In one of her books about Egypt there was a horrible picture of a mummy curled up on its side with its tongue sticking out. They'd found the tongue in five pieces, dried up of course, and they'd carefully glued it back together. It was black and completely disgusting.

23. Pot-stickers Are Not an Easy Thing to Make

One boy, one of the three boys named Colin that Nory knew of—there was Colin Sharings, Colin Deat, and Colin Ryseman—started coming up to Nory after she was spending time with Pamela. He started saying, in a smeary little high voice, 'Oh, ho, Pamela's friend, oh? Pamela's *friend.*' Nory had saved up a little list of things that she could say back to this kind of person. Such as: 'Calling all police, calling all police, there's a grub in the classroom. Take it away, take it away.' There were lots of grubs in the yard of the Trumpet Hill house. They were white little wigglers, not very attractive, and if somebody stepped on them, they went all red.

If it was outside that Colin came up and said something unpleasant, then Nory could say that she had no idea that earthworms could talk.

Nory tried the earthworm one out on him one afternoon. 'My goodness, I simply had no idea earthworms could talk! Boy, did you prove me wrong.' Colin kicked some leaves and said, 'So you didn't know earthworms could talk, Pamela's *friend*? You don't know very much, do you, Pamela's friend?' Then he walked drearily away, chin on parade. It was sort of a tie. It's difficult because of the golden rule, you shouldn't ever say anything that's extremely rude, but you get angry, and you have to come up with comebacks that are not bad words, and not *too* insulting, not so insulting that it's really mean to bring them up. So for example you couldn't ever bring up Arthur's problem with the cavity in his bicuspid, because that's too true to make fun of. Colin Sharings had a pink mole on his ear, but you couldn't make fun of that, either. You had to come up with whatever you're going to say very quickly, too, because there you are, and there's the person who's said the rude thing to you, smirkingly looking pleased with himself, and the longer the rude thing is out on its own the more chance there is that people will laugh against you.

The first time Colin came up and mocked her for being Pamela's friend Nory wasn't prepared for it. She just said, 'Yes, I'm Pamela's friend. Is there a problem?' That worked quite well, except that Nory was standing with Kira when Colin said it, so Colin then said to Kira, because he was a fiend of badness, 'And you like Pamela, too-hoo,' using the grossest kind of mocking singing voice. Kira didn't say anything, so Nory said, 'No, as a matter of fact Kira doesn't like Pamela. So that shows how much you know about the whole kitten caboodle.'

But Pamela herself was nearby and probably heard Nory say that, and Nory worried afterward that that would hurt her feelings to have said that Kira didn't like her to Colin. Pamela didn't mention it next time they talked, though. After that crude awakening, Nory began saving up the comebacks so she wouldn't get tricked into saying something she wouldn't want to have said.

But the other problem, which was a bigger problem, was that some of why Nory wanted to be friendly with Pamela was because she thought Pamela truly deserved to have some friends who stuck with her, and she knew that if she was friendly with her it might be just that tiny straw that broke the camel's back of the habit that the kids had of ganging up on her. But Nory also had an idea that probably Pamela would never be a really close true friend, a dear friend, because they were quite different in certain ways. Other people were being bad to Pamela, and so Nory was feeling she ought to do her best to forfeit her obligation and be more of a friend than she would have been naturally, in real life, which made her feel a little artificial. When she walked back to the Junior School with Pamela they had all-right conversations but they weren't the kind of conversations about things that she would have had with Debbie, where they talked about how much fun it was to put Barbie shoes on 'My Little Pony' horses and dress up their manes with flower petals. Debbie loved those 'My Little Pony' horses, and you had to admit, seeing them all set up in a row, they looked pretty fancy in high-heeled shoes, with their puffy manes. And it wasn't the kind of wild-laughter conversations that Nory sometimes had with Kira or Janet or Tobi, at the Junior School, where somebody would keep trying to say something over and over and couldn't because it was so heroriously funny they couldn't finish the sentence. Pamela told Nory about everyone in her family. Very interesting: her uncles, her aunts, her cousins, her second cousins, what they did, what they looked like, what they watched on TV. Nory told Pamela about her family, but not in as much detail because it wasn't as impressive a family, since she only had four first cousins and a lot of her great-aunts and people like that had already died. They both agreed that chutney was fairly disgusting, but when Nory said that the thing she liked least in the world, par none, was fried chicken, Pamela said she liked fried chicken and that her Dad went out and bought fried chicken from Captain Chicken USA at least once a week. (Captain Chicken was a place that was trying to trick you into thinking it was Kentucky Fried Chicken, with the same red letters, and figuring that, 'Oh, you're English, you won't be able to draw a difference.') Nory hurried on to explain that probably she disliked fried chicken for a particular reason, which was that she'd had it so much at her old school, the International Chinese Montessori School, where it was piled up in large foil pans and got cold and was extremely dark-meatedly greasy. Nory had eaten too much Chinese fried chicken in her life for her to be able to stand another drumstick. The rest of the food had been pretty good, though, she said. No jacket potatoes, of course, because the Chinese are basically less interested in potatoes than America and England is. The jacket potato is a European dish. One time, Nory told Pamela, her whole class at the International Chinese Montessori School learned to make pot-stickers, which are difficult because sometimes you make the wrapping small and there's too much of the meat, or the filling, in the pot sticker, and sometimes you do too little filling. There are many problems and things that can go wrong. It's really difficult, and you have to seal it with egg.

Pamela asked what pot-stickers were, and Nory said they were a Chinese food filled with meat that can burn your mouth when you bite in on them. At her old school, they also learned to write in Chinese characters, Nory said.

Pamela laughed and said, 'In Chinese! You learned to write in Chinese?'

'Yes,' said Nory, feeling a little proud of being able to do that fairly unusual thing. 'We had to, because it was the International Chinese Montessori School. We spent half the day on Chinese, we did our multiplication tables in Chinese, lots of things. Would you like me to write something for you?'

Pamela said okay, so Nory got a piece of paper out of her backpack and sat down on the sidewalk and wrote her the character for 'hao.' Hao was made up of two parts. Half of it was part of the character for mother, and half of it was part of 'child,' because the Chinese think that mother plus child equals good. It's a good thing for a child to have a mother near her and a mother to have a child near her. So, sensibly, *hao* means good. In Chinese it looked like this:

好

Nory gave the paper to Pamela. Pamela looked at it and nodded. She said, 'How would you say six times seven in Chinese?' Nory said 'Liu cheng qi den yu si shi er. So six times seven is forty-two.'

'Oh,' said Pamela.

'If you know your numbers, it's really easy,' said Nory. 'Would you like me to show you how the Chinese character for two could have turned into our American-English number 2, and how the Chinese three could have become our 3?'

'Yes, but maybe another time,' said Pamela, 'because I think we have to go in.'

'Okay,' said Nory. 'Well, bye.'

'Bye,' said Pamela.

24. What You Do and Don't Remember

That afternoon Nory tried to reinstruct every tiny detail of the International Chinese School in her mind. Talking about it to Pamela showed her how much she was already forgetting. It was a lovely school, where the kids were nice, most of them. When she first started in Upper Elementary one of the kids, Carl, who should remain nameless, told her in detail how he was going to kill her by throwing her in a swimming pool filled with poisonous insects. Carl was a warped older boy who left after that year.

A number of kids ganged up on her in the very beginning of that year, which was just about the only time anything that an adult would call being bullied ever happened to her. It was distressing enough that she could connect it to what Pamela might be feeling. But then she tried to think, 'Honestly, was it a terrible thing that that boy, Carl, said all that mean stuff to me, and other kids mocked me?' In her memory it wasn't so unbearably bad because it was a very very long time ago. But that might be because it hadn't gone on and gone on. You remember things better that happen over and over again, like Stop, Drop, and Roll. Except when they happen so many times that you don't notice them whatsoever. Some parts of *Neverending Story,* the movie, she remembered very well, like the stone giant, and the flying dog that the boy meets. There's a girl in the movie who is a princess who is important in a way because she's going to die, but she's minor, actually: the heroine is the boy. Nory thought she must have seen *The Neverending Story* recently in an advertisement, maybe a preview before another movie that her mother rented for her, because parts of it she had in her mind very clearly and colorfully and parts of it were fogged in. At the beginning some bullies throw the boy into the garbage, and he comes back at the end and he throws them into the garbage, all three of them. And someone loses his horse, because it sinks into the swamp and dies. That could be in *Neverending Story II*. There was a story similar to that part in a booklet that Nory's father bought for her at the Cathedral shop. A man asks another man if he's seen a hat floating in a very muddy road. The other man says, 'Golly, no, I haven't, why?' And the first man says, 'Well, I suspect there may be a man sitting on a horse underneath the hat.'

At the time they were mean to her, Nory had told Ms. Fisker about the boys in her class. Ms. Fisker was the upper elementary teacher who taught in English, in the afternoon. (Bai Lao Shi taught in Chinese, in the morning.) But Ms. Fisker said Nory had to learn how to handle the older boys and work matters out for herself. 'Oh, Nory, I can see you're developing a long tail, I can see it growing'—that's what Ms. Fisker would say, because she was strongly not in favor of tattletales. The rule was: 'Don't be a tattletale for little things, do be a tattletale for big things.' Say if someone has broken someone's thumb in the door. Something major. But Nory's parents thought that Ms. Fisker probably should have ordered the older boys not to gang up on Nory. At some point the boys just stopped, though. And now it was just in her memory.

When Carl said that he would kill her by tossing her in the swimming pool with the insects she just disgustedly said, 'Carl, you're fat.'

Carl said, 'Well, not as fat as your butt.'

When Carl said that, Nory couldn't help giggling. Then he pointed at her and said, 'Haw, haw! You think it's funny! Haw, haw! I made you laugh!' So Carl won that battle face down, because it's really dumb-seeming to giggle at times. Carl just hated Nory, for some reason. And Nory hated Carl.

But a lot of what happened that year she couldn't remember nearly as well as that bit. 'That bit' is how they would say it in England, and if you asked your friend to come over, they would say that you asked her to 'come round.' These days Nory couldn't remember the order she had learned things at the ICMS or all the works she did—they called them 'works,' the little projects, like the number pyramid or a geography puzzle that they did. She couldn't even remember all the kids in the class. She remembered one very nice girl named Steffie who left later on, who had a birthday party at her swimming pool where Nory had floundered into the deep end and had gotten about a gallon and a half of water in her lung and thrown up a tiny bit on the grass. She gave Steffie a pair of tiny glass slippers, wrapped up in probably the best wrapping paper she had ever drawn, with a picture of a girl in a rowboat near a willow tree on it. She still thought about those glass slippers. They were paperweights that a glassblower made, but they worked as real doll shoes. She wished she had those glass slippers, they were amazingly wonderful. But Steffie's parents moved away to Lafayette and she started going to a different school. So that was the last birthday with Steffie.

It disturbed Nory very much to think that all she was going to know about what happened in her life was not very much at all. You only can really remember the things that happened when you were an older child and the things that happened to you now—that is, yesterday, or the day before yesterday, or late last week. You live your life always in the present. And even in the present, this day, dozens and hundreds of little tiny things happen, so many that by the end of the day you can't make a list of them. You lose track of them unless something reminds you. Say someone says, 'Remember when you dropped your ruler this morning?' And you do remember. But then that is lost in the tangle.

Now, some things you can just accept that you're not going to have the slightest chance of remembering. It would be nice, but you know that it would be basically impossible. For instance, being in your mother's womb, as it's called. Some people thought babies could remember that. Nory one morning asked Littleguy if he could remember being tucked away in Mommy's belly, long ago, and he said, 'Yes. It had all things there, in she's tummy. It had things that were called *steam trains.* It was filled with they. Filled with steam trains, City of Truro, Lord of the Isles, the Mallard. Pictures with steam trains, and toy ones, and jumping things, all. Filled, filled with they.' Well, of course there weren't toy trains in Nory's mother's womb, unless maybe he was remembering the small intestine chuffing around. Maybe he was remembering a freight train of food being digested going around and around him. But probably not.

Still, Nory thought it would be nice if you could think back at least to the age of three. It shouldn't be impossible. Three was older than Littleguy, and Littleguy could understand an amazing number of things. But Nory couldn't go back that far, really, except for a few scribs and scrabs. She remembered being eight, and back into being seven, and she went pretty much back to five, and then—it teetered a little bit. She only remembered her fourth birthday party, a Mermaid party, because she had watched the tape of it a number of times on TV.

One thing, though, she made a point of remembering and passing on to her older self. Every year that she got a year older she said to her parents, 'Remember when I was five, I said I was five going on six? Remember when I was six I said six going on seven? When I was seven I'd be going seven on eight? Then going eight on nine? Well, now I'm going nine on ten.' So each year the list of years got a little longer, but she remembered the earlier times that way, by saying the list over. Being thirteen would be very nice, because you're in your teens when you're thirteen, and you don't have to read a big sign that says, 'Children under the age of twelve cannot attend to this.' Another thing she made sure to bring along every year with her for a long time was the memory that there were many many little amounts of money that she hadn't paid back to her parents. Little collections of change she had found in the car and thought could be hers but maybe not, or times her parents had bought her a doll outfit or something when she told them she would reimburse them later when they got home from her own money, or gifts she bought other people with her own money, but borrowing it from her parents since she'd forgotten her purse. She would skip a week, not thinking of it, then still remember it and bring it into the next week, then skip a week, then bring it over. Finally she couldn't keep the amount in her head because it had been added onto and subtracted from so much, and it began to pull at her, and she thought, 'I know, I'll pay them a hundred dollars when I grow up, and that will surely make up for anything I borrowed along the way.' Then she didn't have to keep track of that.

25. The Last Straw

Ms. Fisker was a very good teacher with a humongously good memory. She could keep in the front-runners of her brain what each child knew and what they hadn't learned yet. And she could persistently keep the whole class quiet and doing their own work, privately. That's something you almost had to do as a teacher in a Montessori school because each kid is at a different level, learning some different scribbet of a thing, and there are lots of different ages of kids in a class. So for instance in Nory's class there were kids who were seven and kids who were eleven. Some were doing 'six plus five' kinds of things, some were doing 'numbers of seconds it takes a flicker of light to spark to the earth divided by the speed of light' kinds of things, and Ms. Fisker had to be totally on her toes about that. Some were learning how to break up words into syllables and some were learning that a noun was a large black triangle and a verb, which is an action, was a large red circle, and the reason why is because it's a red rolling ball, moving. And a proper noun was a long purple triangle, if Nory wasn't mistaken, and the the articles, like 'an,' 'a,' and 'the,' were either a short light blue or a short *dark* blue triangle. The adjectives were either short light blue or short dark blue, depending on what the articles were. The adverb is a smaller orange circle. Each of these things had to be learned, one by one, by coloring in the shapes over the sentences, and some kids were at the black-triangle stage and some were at the small-orange-circle stage. And there were keyholes and green half-moons, and on and on— Nory had never learned grammar out that far. Nobody at the Junior School knew about these grammar shapes because they were specially designed as part of the Montessori system, so all that time she had spent thinking about why a black triangle was like a noun, because it had a wide base and just sat there steadily being whatever noun it was, was just time that could have gone 'poof' away, as far as her teachers now were concerned. But she liked knowing that a red circle stood for a verb because it rolled. You could use it for other things you learned later, for instance you could say to yourself, 'Mass is a blue triangle, energy is a red circle.'

So each kid in Ms. Fisker's class had a different number of these shapes and math skills scrummaging around in their head, and Ms. Fisker had everything that they had in their heads in *her* head, at just the level that they had it, each of them, which was part of why she was such a good teacher. After Carl luckily left, Nory got used to the class and Ms. Fisker started to like her and told her things. The most amazing thing Ms. Fisker told her was that she was getting married and going to a different city. It was really amazing to think of Ms. Fisker, one of the proudest teachers, getting married, but she did. Of course, she had been married once before and had a son who was eighteen, but the class hadn't really taken that in. They didn't really know that very much. Ms. Fisker had a mischevious cat, and she would wake up, and the cat would prance around on her, and knock down her bottles. Her cat was a mischievous little thing. One time her son had had an operation on his knee and the cat jumped up on his leg and she said he almost went through the ceiling. If you were designing a teacher from scrap, you couldn't design a teacher better than Ms. Fisker. But Ms. Fisker's last day at the school was at the teacher-appreciation dinner at the end of the year. The main dish at the teacher-appreciation dinner was a huge fried pig. Its head was there on the big pan in the middle of the table. The head of a pig was not in Nory's opinion a good menu choice for a teacher-appreciation dinner since there were a lot of younger kids who might be very bothered by the sight of that head, not to mention older kids such as Nory herself who might be revolted as well. You could see its closed eyes. To be polite, she ate a taste of the pig, but only a taste. And that was the last she saw of Ms. Fisker for quite a while.

The teacher who came in place of Ms. Fisker was Ms. Beryl, who was good but totally different. She liked talking about herself a lot, whereas Ms. Fisker only told them a few careful things, such as about her cat in the morning. Ms. Beryl gave out extremely hard spelling lists with words like 'dicotyledon' and 'pinnate' and 'microeconomics' because she was probably more interested in the much older kids, the eleven-year-olds, and wanted them to be getting ready to go to college. It kind of slipped Ms. Beryl's mind that the younger kids were still trying to get it into their heads how to spell 'really' and 'tomorrow' and 'would' and 'unknown.' Nory had a custom of spelling 'tomorrow' as 'tomaro.' The math suddenly turned into a jostle of cube roots and algebra kinds of things, with x's and y's and breaking things down into their factories, when Nory was still trudging away with her times tables. As her friend Bernice said, 'When you wear a bra, you study algebra, not before.'

So Nory got exceedingly distracted, looking at the days of the week on the wall calendar and thinking 'SuMTWTHFRS, hmm, that could almost spell *smothers with furs,*' and from time to time she got into a state of click-laughing with Bernice, who was an easy person to get into a state of click-laughing. They positively could not stop, even though they were almost on the edge of crying, begging each other with their eyes not to start out on another huge laugh, and Ms. Beryl would get furious. Click-laughing is just when you laugh so heroriously that you only make little tiny sounds at the back of your throat. It set Ms. Beryl on fire, and one time, she wrote a note in Nory's booklet that said that Nory must make a more asserted effort on her concentration skills, because her constantly wanting to know what others were doing around her and her constantly being unable to resist distracting them from what they were working on by giggling was her FATAL FLAW. Ms. Beryl read her note to Nory's mother and underlined FATAL FLAW three times while she read. Nory was standing a short distance away, pretending to be thinking over other things or nothing, but she heard it near and clear. On the other hand, she wasn't exactly sure what a fatal flaw meant. But now that she had been going to Classics class at the Junior School and had learned about heroines like Achilles, she knew.

The fatal flaw was quite similar in what it means to the last straw, and the last straw was the straw that broke the camel's back. The last straw was NOT, REPEAT NOT the last straw in the machine at a restaurant that when it was taken meant the machine was empty and you would have to drink your milkshake sadly without a straw. Kids find out rather quickly that it is less fun to drink the normal way, with your mouth, because with a straw it's as if you have magical powers and are telling telling the drink, 'Kazam, kazaw, now climb the straw!'

Nory suspected that the straw that broke that camel's back was an unsensible idea anyway, because first of all, stop and think of that poor camel. How could it happen? Doesn't he have something to say about the situation? Also, camels' backs are pretty strong things. If you've ridden on them, you know that they can support at least two people, if not three. And if they are able to support two or three people, they should be able to support a lot, a lot, a lot of hay, because hay doesn't weigh very much at all, and some people weigh quite a bit. One single straw might weigh a thousandth of a gram, so two straws would weigh two thousandths of a gram, and three straws three thousandths of a gram, and so on, and so on. If they got enough straws together to weigh a very large amount of pounds, a massive knob of straw or a rectangle of straw like the ones that are out in the middle of the fields you see when you drive for what seems like hours and hours to Stately Homes, the huge shape would plop off before they got it all strapped on. Just stuffing the last straw under the strap of rope that was tying it all together, ever so gently, would make the huge heaviness start to tilt, and the straps under the camel's stomach would slip, which might give him an Indian burn, and the whole thing would thump to the side on the ground, unless they somehow had a machine that condensed every single bit of straw together into tiny blocks the size of sugar cubes that were so heavy you could barely lift them without a pulley and you put them all over the camel's back somehow. But that would be quite unusual.

And the other main point was, a camel is a mammal and a mammal is a sensible animal. He's not just going to freeze in place there. As soon as the load felt like it was getting uncontrollably heavy, he would fold his knees under him the way they do. He wouldn't stand there and have a major injury. When camels get cross they do something about it. They squirt large amounts of spit from their mouths, for one thing. That happened to Captain Haddock in Tintin one time. He was tickling the camel under the chin, and then suddenly, pshooo, his head is gone and a huge splash of camel saliva is in its place. So if you are the one in charge of putting the last straw on the camel's back, watch out for that risk. And also, if Nory was anywhere near by, watch out for Nory, too, because she had seen the camels at the zoo, which had hurt-looking gray places on their knees from having kneeled down on rough gravel all the time rather than soft sand, and she had cut her knee on a rock once while she was swimming, and then the cut had opened again and bled, leaving a bigger scar than she had expected, so she knew what it was like to have sore knees. She had enough empathy for camels that if she saw a camel in the desert that was being loaded up so much that its back might be broken she would walk out in front of the people who were doing it and she would just say, 'Stop, there is a fatal flaw in what you're doing. You're going to hurt the camel.'

Fatal flaw indeed! How dare Ms. Beryl say that? She was definitely a little chatty from time to time, but she had been chatty at every school she had ever been to, it was in her deepest nature to be chatty, and other kids were tons chattier, they actually shouted or threw things, and she was only eight at that time, eight going on nine. In Chinese class in the morning she did not have nearly so much of a problem with the 'fatal flaw,' but there too she sometimes did forget herself and talk a little to Bernice or Debbie. The Chinese teacher was much more strict, and a few times she got furious at Bernice and shouted in Chinese, because Bernice made fun of her sometimes by saying slangy things very softly in English that the teacher couldn't understand, but Bai Lao Shi was much calmer than Ms. Beryl. Every morning the kids stood on the field next to the school and did Chinese exercises, shouting out the numbers—yi, er, san—while Bai Lao Shi blew puffs on a silver whistle. Sometimes she held the whistle in her teeth. She had one silver tooth.

26. A Bad Dream That Joe, the Baby-sitter's Son, Once Had

Nory's parents were not completely happy about Ms. Beryl as a teacher, especially after she wrote them the note about the fatal flaw, and at the dinner table they had discussion after discussion after discussion about what they should do for the next year. The result of the discussions was they rented over their house, and presto, 'We don't mind if we do go to England!' The good thing about being in England was that there were lots of teachers at the Threll Junior School, and each one had things they did well and things they did less well. So you never got that feeling of too much Ms. Beryl. Each morning Nory's mother would take her and Littleguy to the school, Littleguy in his miniature uniform, which was very cute, and Nory in her jacket and tie and gray skirt and backpack, and each afternoon Nory's father or mother would pick her up and take her to tea at the tea place near the cathedral, where she had peppermint tea and a piece of chocolate cake with a little dopple of whipped cream next to it, while Littleguy slept in his stroller if they were lucky. Sometimes they read and sometimes they talked about the subject of the day, whatever it was.

Each person contributes something in this world. Some people make bricks, for example, and some make chocolate cakes. Some invent a new kind of powerful glue or maybe a marionette that works by magnets. Or they put the little ball bearings inside whistles that twirl around. Of course some people contribute more than others. Nory's contribution was going to be that she would be a dentist and help people with their teeth. Nory's mother's contribution was teaching Nory and Littleguy about everything, and how it's important to be honest and not hurt people's feelings. Nory's father's contribution was writing books that help people go to sleep. The books that Nory read to help her go to sleep were: Garfield comics, Tintin books, and sometimes a chapter book like *The Wreck of the Zanzibar*, although there was a description in that book of a cow lying on his back with his feet and arms extended in the air, cold and dead because it had been drowned in the water, that was not too pleasant. When she was just dozing off she liked something cheerful, with hand-lettered words, in capitals, nothing scary. Tintin was very popular in England, Garfield not quite as popular as in America. There was a Garfield cartoon in which Garfield has amnesia. He's talking about how he's upset that he's lost his memory, and how John is upset, and Garfield lies back on the table and turns his head back and puts his hand over like he's swimming backwards, just one hand, and he puts his finger up, and he takes a bit of the frosting of the cake off and says, 'Well, I remember being hungry.' Or no, maybe it was, 'Do I remember being hungry?'

You needed to give yourself the best chance of not having a bad dream by dozing off reading something cartoonish and happy, basically. But even then a bad dream can launch itself off in your head. It could just be something from a movie you saw. In Palo Alto, there was a girl in Girl Scouts whose mother was very big on letting kids see grownup scary movies. There was one movie about a mother who turns out to be evil, with yellow fangs and eyes with nothing but white. Nory had to be very careful not even to think about not thinking about that movie, because it could clamp onto her and she then would not be able to help thinking about it, and the only way to escape thinking about it would be to tempt herself by thinking up something even scarier, and the only way to escape from that was to think about sometime even scarier than that, until you were swamped with scariness and couldn't escape until morning.

Sometimes a movie isn't frightening at all, except for in one pacific spot, when you don't dream of expecting it, like that very good movie about a kid who's being flown over Canada in a plane, but the man who's flying him has a heart attack, so they crash, and the heroine has to survive by himself in the wild until he's rescued. All that is just fine. But nobody warned Nory that there was a scene in the movie in which the kid has to swim out to the plane, which is in the middle of the pond, to get something he needs, and dive under the water, and the dead man's horrible light purple staring face suddenly floats into the picture, with fear-music. Oh! It should say on the box, THIS MOVIE IS REALLY GOOD EXCEPT FOR ONE SCENE THAT WILL SCARE YOU OUT OF YOUR SHOES FOR THE REST OF YOUR LIFE NO MATTER HOW HARD YOU TRY TO KEEP FROM THINKING ABOUT IT. (ALSO ONE SCENE THAT IS DISGUSTING BECAUSE YOU SEE HIM EAT A GRUB.) The movie came back to her much less often nowadays, though. When you spend time in another country like England, there is so much new stuff coming pouring in that it even changes your nightmares. There was another movie about a boy who goes on a dogsled race. Everything's going along just fine, until for some reason the movie gets it into its head to have a corpse slide down on a dogsled at night. The corpse hits a bump and sits up, and there's his blank dead face, sheet-white, staring backwards at you.

Probably one thing that some kids do is that they watch the particular movie over and over until they go kind of numb and it doesn't scare them, because you're not supposed to be scared. Your brain toughens up, like the knees of the camels. But you have to stop at a point being tough, because there is definitely such a thing as being much too tough. There are other things you can do to help the situation, though. If you have a bad dream, and you wake up really frightened, and it's still dark, don't just lie there unhappy. You can finish the dream off in a good way. You tell yourself, 'This is my dream, it came from my own brain, I control it, and I have a chance now that I'm awake to make a few small, shall we say, adjustments to it.' Nory told this tip to Joe, who was Ruth the baby-sitter's son, when Joe told her a bad nightmare he'd had. Joe was Ethiopian, from the country of Africa, where he spoke a completely different African-American language, or rather African-African language, and he had learned to speak English quite well in only one short year in Palo Alto. His bad dream was that he and his dad were walking along, when a man jumped down from a tree and said 'Mfoya, mfoya!'—something like that—which means, 'Dead, dead!' The man pointed to some bones. Joe's dad thought the man was just Joe's friend, or just being kind of friendly. Then when his dad turned away the man bit Joe deep in the neck. Joe said 'Gah!' His dad turned around in surprise, and then he and the man fought, and his dad finally killed the guy by strangling him and hitting his head on a rock. But the guy's wife came out and she was very very angry. They were carnibels, or they seemed to be, anyway. The guy's wife ate Joe, finished him up, tooth and nail. So in the end Joe was only bones in the grass by the roadside.

Nory said to Joe, 'Okay, that's scary, I admit, but now you can finish it. Try this. Your dad sees your bones and thinks, "Gosh, I have to act fast, I have to get Joe to a hospital." He puts the bones in a bag and goes off. "Please could you help him get better?" your dad asks.'

Joe said: 'At the hospital they're going to say, "Sure, we'll do it, but you have to give us two thousand dollars." '

'Right,' said Nory, 'and your father just won the lottery, so he pulls out his wallet and he says, "This is your lucky day!" '

'And they put me in a machine that sticks all my parts back on me, arms, legs, a built-in heart, a built-in liver,' said Joe. 'And I wake up and I see my dad, and I say, "Dad? Dad? What happened?" '

27. Nory's Museum

That was back at the Palo Alto house, while Nory's parents were out for dinner and Ruth was there baby-sitting. Later on that night, Nory asked Joe if they had fake food in Africa, fake Japanese food, the beautiful kind that was in the window of Japanese restaurants, and he said they didn't. Japan wasn't important in Africa. Nory asked Joe if he liked fake Japanese food. He said he did. Nory told him her idea for a museum of fake food from all different lands. She would take very beautiful china plates, and place the food on them. It would be a small one-room museum, full of glass cupboards. She would go to all the Japanese restaurants, and call all the toy stores. There would be a children's area and a gift shop. And she would sell fake foods, for good prices, if she had duplicates, because thousands of toy stores would be sending her fake food at the same time. There would mostly be fruits and vegetables, and Japanese food, such as the one of seaweed shaped in a cornucopia, with rice tucked into it and crabmeat sprinkled over the rice. The children's area would have plastic plates, but beautifully painted also. 'Does that sound like a good idea for a museum?' Nory asked.

'Sure, yeah,' said Joe. He said a lady came into his school to do a nutrition demonstration, and she had tons of fake food. The chocolate chip cookie looked so real, Joe thought it was real at first. The meat was cool also, he said. It was red, but you could see light coming through it.

'Ah, the meat was translucent,' said Nory. 'Transparent is when you can see clearly through it, but translucent is when you can only see the glow of light but nothing in particular.' Joe nodded. It was amazing how much English he knew. You couldn't even tell he had ever not known English. Joe knew a huge amount more English than Nory knew Chinese, and she'd been studying it for four years. But they both had the same trouble with the multiplication table. Nory's parents gave their little red car to Ruth when they moved to England, and Ruth wrote a letter telling them that the car was running very well except for the fact that it needed a new engine.

28. Problems with Rabbits

So at night you could read Garfield or think about something happy-making, like a plan of having a fake-food museum, and arranging the fake loaves of bread on tiny plates, in order to try to be sure not to have a bad dream. But still they sometimes happened, and there was nothing you could do. Clang! Bad image. Fright. Run, wake up, lie in bed, panting. Nory's latest bad dream came after they went for a walk one day and saw hundreds of rabbits poking their heads out of holes. How could you get a bad dream out of something nice like that? And also, why would you want to? It had to do with the place that was just grass now, near the Cathedral, that said 'Monk's Burial Ground' on the map. So the monks were probably still under there even though their gravestones were totally and completely gone. In the dream she was a monk at first, who went out every day to feed the rabbits, wearing her hood. She fed them celery from a big white barrel. They were quite happy. But then a disease hit the rabbit families, a bilbonic plague with sores around their eyes. They started dying, even though Nory tried to care for them. She found the antidote, some yellow flowers in the forest, but then she died and was buried as a monk, in the monk's cemetery, under the grass. The rabbits got better and grew back after some time and they started digging tunnels. Nory was a rabbit in this part of the dream, nibbling her way through the ground. All of a sudden she came to a different kind of thing she nibbled through. What is this white crumbly stuff? Ugh! Bone is what it was. The earth trickled away and she was in a humongous underground tomb, where she saw that she'd just nibbled straight through the chest bones of a dead body that turned out to be the corpse of the monk. They had to cover over the corpse, because it was shrunken and awful to the eye. Plus it was starting to shiver or tremble. Then Nory was flying overhead in an airplane, but the airplane ran out of gas, and she couldn't find northeast. It went into a spiral, and she jumped out in a parachute and fell and was knocked out. The rabbits saw the parachute spread itself out on the ground and thought, 'Aha! Perfect material for covering the corpse of the dead monk!' So they took hold of the parachute in their teeth and started pulling it down, down, which of course dragged Nory down, too, into the hole, since all the parachute strings were still harnessed to her, and she woke up underground, with rabbits all bustled around her and with something lumpy and unnerving next to her hidden under her parachute. She pulled the parachute away and there was a dead shrivelly face whose eyes and mouth immediately opened, all together, and a tongue popped out that was totally black. That was where she woke up in real life.

Now that was not a particularly good spot to be in when you wake up from a dream and Nory was not in the least bit happy. She got up, tottled to the bathroom, which was also not a perfect experience because the lightbulb that was usually on over the mirror had burned out, so the only light was from the streetlight, and then she went into her mother and father's room and said: 'I had a frightening dream.' Her mother reached her hand out and squeezed her arm and hand and said in her murmury sleepy voice, 'I'm so sorry, my baby girl, try not to think about it, everything is all right, goodnight, my baby, love you.' She made kissing sounds with her lips.

'Goodnight, love you,' said Nory, and she stumbled back to her room, but she still had the fright living in her chest and when she saw the covers of her bed she thought, 'No, I definitely can't get back in there by myself,' and she turned around and went back to her parents' room and said: 'Can I sleep in your bed? I'm still scared.' But her parents almost never let her sleep in their bed, although they used to let Littleguy sleep in their bed until he was over two, which wasn't totally fair. Sometimes they let Nory come in in the morning and snuggle in, however. 'Tuck in, tuck in,' her mother would say then, lifting a corner of blanket, and that made her feel so happy.

Her father got up and said, 'I'll tuck you in.' He tucked her in her bed and stroked her head and said, 'Nothing is bad, everything's okay, pick something to think about with bright sunlight in it, Splash Mountain or having tea at the museum with the fan room or looking out from Oxburgh Hall over the fields. Or playing in the sprinkler with Debbie.'

'But I'm still quite scared,' Nory said. 'Can I read?'

'It's the middle of the night,' said her father. 'If you absolutely have to read to get your mind going in a different direction, go ahead and read. Goodnight, sweetie pie.'

'Goodnight,' said Nory. She clicked her light on and read a tiny amount of a book she was reading for the Readathon, which was a competition at the Junior School that gave money to leukemia depending on how many books you read. She was reading a book she liked about a hen who went on different vehicles, and with each vehicle she went on there was some disaster, and then the disaster was solved. For instance, the hen got stuck in a new road of tar and was almost rolled over by one of machines that press it flat. And whenever a person rescued her, the hen politely laid an egg for them, to say thank you. One time she laid an egg in someone's crash helmet. The book was called *The Hen Who Wouldn't Give Up*.

Nory was so frazzledly tired that she didn't want to read, even about this friendly hen, but she had to read, because she had to stay awake, since the thing was that if you wake up in the middle of an awful dream that is quite powerful and you go back to sleep too soon, the dream will heal over the cut you made in it and will finish itself. If you are very, very, very, very, very capable, and very determined, you'll be able to stay awake, just twelve, thirteen more minutes, and the bad dream will melt away, and you will have somewhat of a good dream instead, because the brain forgets and says, 'Hmm, that file is taking forever to finish, let's go on to the next file, ah, yes, fake food, very interesting, let's think about fake food.'

Nory struggled, but finally she couldn't read for one more second—couldn't read, and couldn't go to sleep. So what she decided to herself was: 'I won't read, and I won't go to sleep, I'll just think, because in reading you think and in dreaming you think, so that's exactly what I'll do—I'll think. And if the scary things come into my thoughts, fine, I'll change them.' What a bad dream does is turn something nice in your life, a simple plain event, like seeing some rabbits (including one dead one that was lying on the grass), or seeing a map of the Cathedral, into something dreadful. So all you have to do in going against the bad dream is turn it back into something nice again, since that's what it began from anyway. So she started up with her thinking, and of course, presto, the dead person from the dream came into her mind, but she said to herself, 'Stay calm, stay seated, let's figure this out.'

She went back into the dream a little bit and looked around. Ah, yes, she saw her mistake. It turned out that the dead monk was not really dead—it was just sleeping deeply, wearing a frightening mask. Really the monk was a girl, a princess of some kind, with skin as white as cream and lips as bright as boysenberries and long flowing golden hair, and she had only worn the frightening mask and the awful raggedy rotten clothes so that everyone would be scared away while she slept—everyone, that is, except for Nory who was brave enough to come and help her take off her mask. Nory turned the mask over and saw that it was molded plastic. The black tongue was made of paper mâché and had a little spring that made it pop out. The princess had waited there all those centuries until Nory came down, so that together they could help sick animals. 'I'm sorry for frightening you, my child,' the princess said. 'It was the only way.' Out of the rabbits' tunnel they climbed together, and over the next few months Nory learned many things about caring for animals from the princess. There was a dog with a broken leg, but they wrapped its leg in a special white cloth, and the next morning it was completely healed. There are three kinds of broken bones—simple, compound, and green stick. The princess knew all about them, because she was an expert in first aid. A green-stick fracture is when it bends like a flexible stick and makes a smuggled noise but doesn't break apart. A simple break is when it breaks in two, so that you can see two ends of bone if you look on an X-ray. A compound fracture is when some of the bone tears out of the skin. Compound is really bad, and grotesque to look at even for a doctor, probably. Jason from Nory's old school had gotten a simple fracture from jumping off one of the climbing structures. Flying squirels jump from the climbing structures, but Raccoon is more careful.

Somewhere along the way of these ideas, luckily, Nory's thinking turned into good-dreaming.

29. Why Not Make a Quilt?

After that busy brainwash of a night you might think Nory would wake up terribly tired and alarmed, but no. Her eyes came easily open and she immediately wanted to work on a project in the Art Room—something like make a popup book of an airplane, which would have the little tables you could open and close, or make a teacup out of clay with the steam twirling up in spirals of rolled clay—since Littleguy squushed the last teacup she made—or tell a long story to her dolls while she changed their outfits, or draw a comic strip called 'The Two Bacteria' about the many adventures of two bacteria, French and Germ. She got the idea for the comic from a book about teeth which had a picture of some bacteria standing on a tooth. One of them says, 'Hey, hey, this looks like a perfect spot to dig for dentin.'

She lay under the covers moving her fingers and thinking about the things she could do that day, drawings, inventions, projects. She could make a booklet for Littleguy full of puzzles using things he liked, for instance a maze that would say: 'See if you can drive Solomon the Steam Shovel back through the mud to the construction site.' With her cousin Irene in Burlington, Vermont, she was working on a book of projects for kids. One of the projects Nory had already written down was: 'Make a Tree. Make a tree, every time you do something good hang a card on a branch saying what you did. It may make you happier.' Nory had never made a tree like that and hung cards on it, but it seemed like a good sort of a project. Another project was to make a ruler.

Make a Ruler:

What you will need:
cardboard
a Ruler
A pen & pencil
A Pair of scissors (For thin cardbord)
for thick cardboard: knife (ASK FOR HELP)
A clear space
A piece of paper & Tape
An Adult who is willing to help you out.

1. Take a thin or thick piece of cardboard and cut it
so it is about 4.7 in. Long and about 1.1 in. wide
2. Trace your cardboard
out on the pice of paper with a pencil & cut
along the side in in. and/or cm. and/or
m.m and Make a mark each time you
come to another one. and number it.
DON'T FORGET TO SAY IF IT'S
M.M OR I.N OR C.M.

Nory hadn't made a ruler herself, unless you count the one she had drawn on the paper to illustrate how to make a ruler in the project. Another project was a quilt: 'If you have any rags, why not make a quilt? You could embroider it. It would be very hard but worth a try.' Another project was:

WRITE A STORY!

Why NOT Write a story. It's very satisfying.

Here's some of mine: 'It was a cold icy freezie day in Autumn. A poor girl dressed in rags shiverd, she was huddled bythe side-walk.'

The project book was going at a slug's pace, though, because Irene was in Burlington, Vermont, and Nory hadn't sent off any of the pages she had made so far. Irene had a wonderful dog named Simone.

30. The Rest of the Story About the Icy, Freezie Day in Autumn

The story about the icy, freezie day in Autumn was quite different from Nory's other stories because she had written it down at Junior School, as an assignment for Mrs. Thirm, rather than just telling it aloud to one of her dolls. So unless she lost the notebook that it was in she couldn't possibly forget it. The story so far was:

> *Event One and Intorduction of Characters.* It was a cold icy freezie day in Autumn. A poor girl dressed in rags shiverd, she was huddled by the side-walk. Long brown hair swept across her face, and tangeled though it was, if it had been brushed and combed it would be lovely hair. She could hear barking in the distance, she sighed, how nice it would be to have a dog to play with to always be at your side. 'Oh Well it probably already belongs to someone,' she thought. She blew the hair out of her face. The barking seemed to be geting closer by the minet. She lisened very cearfully and heard the raket came from a Sealyham she new alot about dogs they were her favorit thing in the world she used to get around at night by listening to the barking of the dogs now the barking was so close so could almost hear the padding of the dogs foot hit the ground. She turned in the direction she thought the barking was coming from there was a small black figure who seemed very pleased inded for making the

loudest noise anyone could hear for miles, with no leash no person behind him only people trying to soo him away this what at the bottom of her heart she was wishing for. she couden't control her self she ran as fast as she could to him and throgh her self around his neack. and It was nice to feel his warm breath on her hands, and his soft fur on her face. The dog stoped barking, and looked at her out of his lovely black yees. He was a large dog for a Sealyham, he was also quite strong. She gathered her self and knelled by the dog. She smiled at him, What is your name? The dog looked content, then he barcked three times quickly, and it sounded like rour ran roph. Since he looked so content she figured he had sucsessfully told her his name was Ranrof. She sayed 'Ranrof is a lovely name.' She looked round her self and every one seemed to be staring so she and the dog slowly walked away. Mines Marielle she sayed how old are you she asked the dog, rine barked the dog. Which Marielle thout was nine, 'I'm nine too' she sayed. 'It's time we get somthing to eat' she sayed agin. They had come to a bush full of ripe berrys, they almost were more berrys than bush, and they had a lovely dinner of berrys.

Event two: the complecation. Marielle woke up from a long sleep to find that Ranrof was gone, she was upset 'Perhaps it was only a dream' she thought. how she longed for Ranrof, his beautiful black eyes, his soft fur and his warm breath 'I wish dreams came true' she sayed. 'It coulden't hurt calling for him' So she stood up and called ranrof again and again but nothing happened. So she sat down and looked for traces of him to, prove he wasn't a drea. there were footprints but it could have been something else. She fell back and was going to relas, When she notesed the ground was very soft in one part she sat up and saw that a trace of a what seemed dogs foot-print. but It seemed to be thear on purpose. Not just a dog was ramdomly walking and happened to step there, but really worked hard to make a deep foot-print. Mayby its a sort of signiture to say it was that dogs property but, maybe just maybe it was tring to take place of a card in which case there might be a present inside a sort of goodby persent. And she decided that it would be better to open it and have it not be hers, than it be hers and not open it because of corse if it wasen't herse she could cover it back up agin, and any way she wanted all the eviedence she could get to prove Ranrof wasn't a dream and if it was from any dog it might be as well from Ranrof.

Then she heard strage issing noises very cloes. She looked behind her and there were two large cats hissing and meowing at eachother they seemed to be arguing, hey hey she sayed dont argue but they kept on so she had to sit inbittween them so they couden't go on. Now now she sayed slowly for theas cats were sort of fritening becase they were so lage. The cats looked embarassed, and gave Marielle the look of 'what do you want.' So she ansered there look of 'what do you want,' with a look of 'you know perfectly well.' Then the cats seemed to be wispering at eachother. In fact they were wispering so quietly that she could almost hear her heart beeting, for it was beeting rather louwdly because of the size of these cats. Then a thout struck her mind, wouden't It be best to become friends with these cats maybe somehow they could tell her, somehow if they had seen Ranrof, and besides they were huge things. Itwas then that she deicided she should look at them becaus she hade been looking at the sky this whole time. They were onely showing off. They had their tails lifted high in the air (as they say) and where swaing while walking slowly cicleling her. They where going in oppisite directions so when they bumped noses, they would turn around at the same time and start off in the other direcion So they realy looked as if one was in the miore. She stood there for a few minutes just staring, and sometimes realy did beleve that one was a riflection in a mior. Oh! because I forgot to tell you they where totaly idenical and I bet they could trick people as to wich one they were. After staring at them for about 5 minets her eyes got tired and she glased away for a minut, they sat down and curruld up as if that was what they were wating for in wich case she wondered what would happen if she had stared all night just then she felt something lick her with their tounge.

Event Three. . . . TO BE CONTINUED.

31. Oatmeal

Nory liked writing 'TO BE CONTINUED' at the end of stories, and of course she could go right ahead and continue them. But she had very old stories that she'd written when she was seven and eight that had that in big letters at the end, and when she came across them stuffed in her desk in Palo Alto she thought, 'Wow, I haven't exactly done what I said I would do, have I?' Basically, when she wrote 'To Be Continued' at the end of a story it almost always meant 'To Never Be Continued,' that is, 'To Be Dropped Like a Hot Potato.' This made her a little sad when she realized it. She had gotten the idea of 'To Be Continued' from the movie *Back to the Future,* which ends with those words in huge letters. *Back to the Future* was another movie where the second movie, *Back to the Future II,* was equally as good as *Back to the Future I,* like *Neverending Story* and *Neverending Story II.*

So probably she wouldn't write any more of the story of Ranrof, because by the time she got around to it she would have become a little older and she would think some of it was kiddish and she would be on to other unexceptional things. Also everyone had to read their stories aloud in class and when she she read hers some of the boys made low gurgles and snickers when she read the part about the girl throwing herself around the dog's neck. They thought it was girlish and sweetsy-cue, which didn't matter one bit because Nory liked the story. But it was true that after they gurgled she stopped working on it.

Her mother came in while Nory was still dozily under the covers thinking of what project she should do that morning and she said it was time for Nory to hop to. A few minutes after that her father came popping in and said, 'Let's go, kiddo, let's go, let's go.' So it was a school day, was it? Well well! How fair was that? Nory chatted to herself for not a very long time in the mirror, pretending to be surprised by her toothbrush flying in from the side, and trying out different surprised expressions. Then she tucked in all her dolls for the day, which took a good amount of time. She had only been able to take eleven dolls to England from America, not including Raccoon. By then her mother was calling out, 'Urgent call for Nory!' and her father was calling out, 'Extreme two-minute warning!' So she bustled on her school outfit and tied her tie and tucked the ends of it in her skirt, since they were always much too long to be becoming since basically the tie was too big for a child her age, and she went downstairs to have oatmeal.

The bowl was hot enough to burn your fingers from the microwave but the cold milk cooled its heels. Nory's father sometimes hummed to the sound of the microwave, because the microwave was extraordinarily loud, much louder than the one they had in America, which is named after Amerigo Raspucci, who made a map of America that was not terribly accurate because the technology that they had available in those times was not good, and the microwave sounded like the humming note of a bagpipe. He hummed a hymn that Nory liked from her school hymnbook, 'And did those feet, in ancient times.' Sometimes he hummed songs he made up, like 'Snort-victims on parade, exchanging glances.' But he had gotten into a very bad habit of also making a strange little humming sound when he put a spoonful of oatmeal in his mouth. He said the warmness of the oatmeal made him simply have to make that strange noise, but Nory's mother said she wasn't very fond of hearing that sort of moaning at the breakfast table before there was time for the coffee to work, and once Nory had to say to both of them, 'Fee, Fie, Fo, Fum, I smell the blood of an argument.' That was the way Nory got them to stop when they were going up the stages of having a fight, although it didn't work every single time. However, they didn't fight nearly as much as some of her friends' parents.

In America Nory ate cornflakes or frozen waffles with maple syrup. The cap of the syrup got congested with scrabs of dried syrup, which turned to pure sugar, so that you could barely get it on or off. But in England, no frozen waffles. In America Littleguy had Cheerios with bubanda, which was what he called banana. But here everyone ate oatmeal, everyone in her family, that is, and were quite content eating oatmeal in fact, and they quite happily sang hymns to the sound of the microwave while it cooked their breakfast. In the International Chinese Montessori School Nory wouldn't have dreamed of having a hymnbook. Yet here she had a prep book, a hymnbook, a reading logbook, and six or seven subject notebooks each of a different color. Her favorite was the 'English - Stories' notebook because it was a soft blue color, and she had sort of gotten used to the idea that she had made a mess-up and written 'Engish' first and had to quietly sneak in the 'l.' That was the notebook where she wrote down her stories for Mrs. Thirm, for instance the one about a girl who finds a dog.

Nory's family liked being in Threll because it made them do things not too differently but a little differently. Here Nory had tons more religion in her life than in America, since they never went to church in America except on Christmas and Easter, and maybe one or two other times when her grandmother visited, since she liked to go. But here the whole Threll School had a service at Cathedral once a week, on Monday usually. There was a great joke Nory knew about Friday. What is the fish's least favorite day? Fryday. That joke was probably invented in England, because England was a place that loved things swamped in hot grease. One day when they went out for breakfast and Nory's father ordered bacon and eggs and the bacon came out all clenched up in a little shape like a lettuce, and he said 'Jesus Christ, they deep-fat-fried it!' That was the day Nory had the idea of making a doll that would have an egg she would cook in a pan. It was not good to take the Lord's name in vain, or shoot the bird at anyone, for that manner, no matter what they do.

Every night they all said grace. They also said grace in America, but in America Nory always said the same thing, meal after meal, which was: 'Thank you, God, for this delicious dinner, bless the food on the table, Father, Son, Holy Ghost amen.' Nory's father didn't believe in God but he said that he liked the idea that other people did, and Nory's mother believed in the idea that God was the goodness in human beings but not that there necessarily was a certain particular god who knew everything everyone was thinking and worked us all like magnetic marionettes.

But Nory really believed in God as a thoughtful and extremely supreme person, and Littleguy believed that God was the driver of a steam train and the devil drove a diesel. And they all liked saying grace because it was just a calm and holy thing to do before you start munching away at your first bite, no matter what you thought about religion.

And here in England Nory was starting to say different graces, because she went to the Cathedral so much and had R.S., which is Religious Studies. 'Thank you God for this delicious dinner, and bless the Pope and the Bishop and all the people in the church, and Mr. Pears, and all the people who are sick in their minds or their bodies, and everything else, Father, Son, Holy Ghost amen.' Or, 'Thank you dear Lord for this delicious dinner, and thank everyone who was worked so hard in their lives and is still working hard now, and bless our lord and your son who we cruelly murdered amongst ourselves, and bless the Pope and the Dean and the Bishop and the Archbishop and all the chaplains, and everyone else in the church, please forgive these humble words of prayer, Father, Son, Holy Ghost, amen.' A different one every night, sometimes with little silent parts in the middle while Nory was thinking out what she wanted to say. And now Littleguy was coming in at the end saying, 'Now me: Holy Ghost, everyone in the church, amen!' When he said it he touched his chest in a dear way.

Then Nory's parents would nod and say 'Thank you, very nice,' and they would start eating. If before dinner they had been shouting at Nory to come right *now* to the table, the grace stopped any scolding of her by building a little wall between what had happened before dinner and what happened at dinner. No singing was allowed during the actual main part of the dinner but you could sing in between dinner and dessert, or if you had to demonstrate something you learned in drama class or something a kid did that you had to show by standing up, you could do that between dinner and dessert, as well. For instance, Roger Sharpless and Nory had had a pretend fight in which he had pretended to swop her in the face and she had ducked so that each time his fist would clong into the wall. That sort of event happened in Tintin a fair amount. Roger and she had Tintin in common, and they also both liked 99 Flake. 99 Flake is a candybar that you can't get all that easily in America. Actually 99 Flake is the name if you're talking about the ice cream made with the candy bar, and Flake is the name if you're just talking about the candybar.

32. Don't Forget Your Pencil Case

But back to the morning after the dream about the rabbits and the corpse. After breakfast there was a catastrophe of a broken mug that was holding apple juice, which was Littleguy's favorite drink. And Nory couldn't find the pledge sheet for Readathon, which she was supposed to have brought in ages ago. So they spent a lot of time dabbling up apple juice and looking in piles of paper for the Readathon sheet. Finally her mother found it tucked in the phone book. The apple juice had hurdled itself amazingly far away from the main place that the cup smacked into the floor. It was like a solar flare of apple juice. So they drove instead of walking, so as not to be late, since Nory's father had to go in to London anyway to look something up. Nory saw Pamela from the car hurrying up from the train station in her usual leaning-forward, staring-forward way. 'Pamela! Pamela!' Nory called out, but

Pamela didn't hear her, since they went past too fast for Nory to roll her window down, plus it was getting pretty cold these days for wide-open car windows.

Nory's father asked how things were going with Pamela.

'Mezzo-mezzo,' said Nory.

'Are people treating her a little better?'

'Not perfectly, no,' said Nory.

'Shouldn't we talk to Mr. Pears about it?'

'I think Pamela really doesn't want that,' said Nory. 'Please not yet.'

'Okay,' said Nory's father. 'I'm very sorry you had that awful night last night.'

'Oh, thanks,' said Nory. 'I was just agitated. Bye Littleguy! Bye! Love you!'

'Bye Nory! Kisses and hugs! Now off to *my* school,' said Littleguy.

Nory was a tiny bit late when she got there, and the office, where you go to be ticked off when you're late, had nobody in it, and Nory had a total brainwash and couldn't find the list for her house, Lord Lamper. There were five houses in Junior School, Bledingsteale, Beaston, Morris-Sirrer, Lord Hivle, and Lord Lamper. The sheet for the Lord Lamper kids had slid under Morris-Sirrer, and Nory, spinning around trying to find it, went out of the office, back in, out, in, thinking, I'm going to be horribly late, until finally she saw Betty in the hall, who was always nice to her. Betty said, 'The list is in the office.' Which was not all that helpful, but what can you do? Then a woman who sometimes helped Nory with spelling sorted her out, as they say, and she went to the classroom, but on her way she saw Mrs. Thirm talking to Shelly Quettner. Mrs. Thirm gave her the nicest, nicest smile. Why in the world did

Pamela not like Mrs. Thirm? Mrs. Thirm was a really nice housemistress. Shelly, who was not always the greatest of kids, called out, 'Tutoring is in Mrs. Hant's classroom today, I'll show you where it is.' Nory couldn't resist that offer, even though, yes by all means she knew that there was maths tutoring and yes also knew where Mrs. Hant's class was, because it's always pleasanter to arrive at a slightly out of the ordinary classroom with someone you know, even with Shelly, who was the girl out of all the girls at that school probably who did the worst thing that anyone had done to Nory so far, which was when she told the class, 'Nory fancies Jacob Lewes.'

But that didn't turn out to be so much of a bad thing anyway. A few weeks after Shelly had said that she had said 'Nory bad-worded Belge Coleman.' Using the most horrible bad word there is. Nory said, 'I did not!' She did not say, 'At least, I don't think I did.' For a tiny second she thought about saying, 'Well, maybe I did, but I don't think I did,' because you forget so many tons of things in your life and you don't want to tell a lie about a thing you mistakenly forgot, but then she thought, 'No, in this case, I know for sure,' and she just said, 'I did not!' Only a few girls heard it, none of the boys, and basically nobody believed Shelly anyway, in this case, because think about it: Shelly was obviously the one who fancied Belge Coleman in real life and nobody else would stand a chance of fancying him because he was one of the two kids in the class who were kind of thought of by the whole class as pests. Belge Coleman that same day had plucked away Nory's snack, which was a wonderful Flake, and said, 'Oh, thank you,' in a Vampire accent and squeezed it and squeezed it. Nory struggled it from his hand, and it fell on the ground. It was broken in half. The good thing was that Nory gave the other half to Kira, because it was broken in half so conveniently. But still, it wasn't so nice of Belge Coleman and nobody if they knew could understand why Shelly would ever like someone as idiotic a nitwit as him, but she did, and Nory knew it because Shelly even told her straightaway, 'Some days I go mad over boys.' And she told her, 'I really fancy Belge Coleman and I just go mad about him some days.' Shelly was saying that Nory had horrible-bad-worded Belge Coleman because she was bothered that he was paying attention to Nory by stealing away the snack from her and using typical Vampire behavior. She was jealous, basically. The thing about Shelly was that she was from New Zealand and it could be that nine-year-olds were more teenagery in New Zealand. You could know very easily that Shelly was a jealous kind of person because her sidekick, Tessy Harding, one time told Nory a story about how she was showing off and Shelly climbed a tree and started throwing chairs at her! Nory was shocked that anyone would bully someone by throwing chairs at her, since that could really injure you if the chair fell on you a certain way, or even kill you, if, say, one of the legs of the chair hit you in the soft spot on the side of your head next to your eye, which was like an Achilles heel of your head. Later she found out that it was just cherries, that Shelly had thrown, not chairs. But still.

So Shelly wasn't a complete and utter delight as a person, but never mind, Nory was happy to go with her to maths tutoring. Shelly said, 'Wait, I just have to go get something.' Nory said quickly, not to interrupt her with Mrs. Thirm, 'Okay, I'll meet you right here.' Shelly came back and they started going to the class and suddenly Shelly said, 'Your pencil case! You need your pencil case!'

Nory froze and said, 'Oh, gosh, my pencil case! You mean, we need *our* pencil case.' Because Shelly seemed to be totally empty, nothing on her. But no, Shelly said that hers was already in the class. So Nory said 'Wait for me here, all right?' And Shelly said okay. Then Nory rushed to the other classroom to get her pencil case but when she was leaving Mrs. Copleston said, 'Nory, where are you going? You're supposed to be in here.'

Nory said, 'Oh, right, okay,' and sat down.

Then Mrs. Copleston looked at her book and said, 'I'm sorry, you're right, go to Mrs. Hant's class, my mistake.'

So Nory went partway to Mrs. Hant's class. Then she remembered she was supposed to be meeting Shelly. So she went where Shelly had been. But Shelly was gone by this time. So she went to Mrs. Hant's class. Mrs. Hant hadn't gotten there yet and Shelly wasn't there. 'Is this Mrs. Hant's tutoring class?' Nory asked.

'Yes, you're not supposed to be in here,' said one of the kids.

'Yes, I believe I am,' said Nory. Then she looked around and realized that true, she had her pencil case but in her brainwash she'd forgotten her notebook, so she popped up and said, 'Oh no, I forgot something!'

'You're an Americayan,' people started saying in an exaggerated accent.

Nory said, 'Yes, and I'm glad of it, but first, excuse me, I have to get something,' and she shot out the door. In the hall Mrs. Thirm said, 'Are you getting things sorted out?' Nory said she was just going back for her notebook.

'And then you'll be going to Mrs. Copleston's class?' said Mrs. Thirm.

Nory said, 'Ah, no, I think I'm supposed to be in Mrs. Hant's class.'

'Oh yes, yes, you're right,' said Mrs. Thirm, waving. 'And I believe I'm your last port of call today.'

When Nory got back to Mrs. Hant's class, Mrs. Hant was there. 'She's not supposed to be here,' said one of the kids.

'Are you sure you're supposed to be in here?' said Mrs. Hant.

'I'm not completely positive, but I think so,' said Nory.

But then Mrs. Hant said, 'Ah, yes, I see, you'll be spending the class with me, yes.' So finally Nory was in the right class with the pencil case and the notebook. And then Shelly came storming in and sat down. So everything was settled, and they did maths for ages and ages of time. And then it was over and they went to English class.

English class was devoted to Readathon because the school wanted the kids to read as many books as possible for Leukemia, and that night was the end of the time period for the Readathon. Kira was in Nory's English class and she was a passionate reader. Every spare second, Kira was there nonstop, reading, reading, whistling through book after book. Her father had pledged twenty pounds per book, she said, and she wasn't like Shelly Quettner or Bernice from last year where when they tell you something you never know what's true and what isn't. Shelly Quettner brought in a book about simultaneous human combustion that had a picture of a bloody piece of leg where a man had blown up for no reason, and she expected everyone to believe that it had happened, and everybody did, for a while, until they began thinking about how simple it would be to fake it. But when Kira said something had happened, it had happened. Nothing bothered her while she read, she just read like a hot butterknife, totally emerged in the page, because she wanted to have read more books for

Readathon than anyone else in fifth year, and she had a good chance of doing it, too. She never talked about what she read, she just read. Nory couldn't read that fast and when she read one book like *The Wreck of the Zanzibar* in a day she had a staring wobbling sensation as if she'd been playing too long with the screensavers on the computer.

The English class read their Readathon books pretty well for a while, although there had to be *some* chatting. Absolutely no chatting was a little bit hard to ask. Then the teacher went out of the room, and the chatting turned to a muttering and a chittering and a smattering and a fluttering in every direction, because when the teacher goes out, let the rumpus begin. The two main chitter-chatterers for most of the time were Paul and Ovaltine, who was called that because his first name was Oliver, and he liked Ovaltine—or maybe he was just a good sport and said he liked Ovaltine, since basically everyone liked Ovaltine and you wouldn't normally make a big thing out of liking it and, for instance, stand up on a chair and say, 'Hi, everybody, I like Ovaltine!'—and his last name was Dean, and his face was oval, and maybe another reason that Nory couldn't remember, but that covered most of it. Paul and Ovaltine were friends but they couldn't stop talking and arguing, on and on and on and on. As soon as the teacher was gone they started fighting, and they actually drew on each other's cheeks.

Then the teacher came back in and everybody dove headfirst back to the Readathon. And then the bell rang and it was time for the next lesson, which was Classics. But unfortunately Classics was totally devoted to Readathon, too, so no chance for Nory to ask her questions about Achilles.

33. Unexplained Mysteries

Her questions were: The only place that Achilles wasn't immortal was in the back of his ankle, in what's known as his heel, because his mother did less than a perfect and less than a gentle job of dipping him. So, Nory felt, the only place he absolutely has to wear armour was around his ankles. He could fight in whatever strange underwear they had back in ancient times except for two huge gold and silver dust-ruffles around his ankles. Nory knew a little about ancient underwear because of the movie, *Ji Gong,* about the crazy monk. In it a rich, rich, rich man got naked in clothes that he would have worn very long ago. If you were rich in China your underclothes would be little shorts and a huge apron over your chest that tied in the back.

It would not matter how many times Achilles was stabbed in the neck or the heart—those parts were totally immortal. He would never have to fight back with Hector, he could just stand there with his hands at his sides and let Hector stab and jab the day away. But then you would miss the good part later, when they fight so fast and were so good at swordfighting that the crashing together of the swords made sparks, and the light of the sparks could be seen for miles in the night sky. But probably that wasn't true. It was probably two stumbling men, swamped with blood, shouting bad words at each other and fighting in the mud until one slumped down. Nory hated when people said that oh yes, so-and-so 'bit the dust,' because what it meant was that the person lost his balance and fell at a point of being so faintingly weak and near dying that he couldn't even put his hands out to stop himself when he fell, and so his teeth hit and dug a little way into the mud or dust or dirt, which was sad and a little disgusting to think about. But say a young child had been crouching in a doorway watching, a frightened young thing. She would have seen the fight, and then seen everyone else stab each other and die off, and when she was older her child would ask her, 'Mommy, tell a story of a bad thing that happened to you as a child,' just the way Nory herself always used to ask her mother and father that same question, so many times. 'Tell me a bad thing that happened to you as a child.' Nory asked it, year after year, and her mother and father told their stories of getting stitches in their thumb or getting hit by a car while running after a paper airplane or being kicked under the sinks in the school bathroom or mocked for long hair or falling one floor down and getting a concussion and then having to stay awake all night hearing *Winnie the Pooh* so they wouldn't doze into a coma (this last bad thing happened to Nory's mother when she was four), until her parents ran dry of bad things and had to start all over again with one of the early ones.

The girl who saw Hector get stabbed to death would say to her young child that she saw Hector and Achilles fight and Hector die, and the child would say, 'What did they look like fighting?' The mother wouldn't want to say what it really looked like when a sword puncture-wounded deep into someone's body, since it was a plain basic gruesome thing like the sight of the butterfly's little head when she made the mistake with the lid, and she would think around for something else, and would have an instinct to say ah, that she saw the swords sparkling each time they smashed together, something nice like that, because maybe there was a poem already in Latin or some African-American language that people spoke in those days, or ancient Chinese, about swords sparkling. When you're asked to say how you saw something you almost have to give up the idea of doing it exactly, since whatever bad thing happened had a happy ending because here you are, an everlasting grownup, happily holding a child.

'But all right,' Nory thought, 'let's say that the story is obviously made up in certain aspects, the way that legends so very often are.' Myths were totally made up from scrap, according to Mr. Pears, but legends were a combination of made up and true-to-life. Even still, just to have it be a working legend, you need to know the kind of way that Achilles was immortal, and the story doesn't provide you with that. Say Hector tried to stab him in the chest. There were three possibilities of what could happen. The sword could just not be able to go into Achilles at all, even an eighty-sixth of an inch, because his skin would be incredibly durable and unable to be cut in a good, sensible immortal way. Or the sword could go in just as deep as it would be in a normal human and hurt him very badly, so badly that he would have to be in the hospital, since you can be severely badly injured and be under intensive care in the hospital and still not die. Or the sword would swish completely through the chest as if it was the chest of a realistic ghost and Achilles would only feel a little sense of tickling inside, like when you swallow a very cold, pure, sour glass of cran-blackberry juice and feel it pouring down your ribcage in a waterfall.

But that's not really even the difficult part of the question. Achilles is definitely killed by a poison arrow. Mr.

Pears stressed that they had to remember that it was a *poison* arrow. The arrow goes into the mortal part of him, his heel, making a nasty puncture wound. But if the poison killed only his heel, he would survive just fine, since you can survive losing your whole foot or even your whole leg. If your head dies, you die. If your heart dies, you die. If your liver dies, even, you die. But if your ankle dies? It would hurt, no question about that, it would not be a comfortable or cozy experience at all, at all, because you would probably have to have your foot chopped off above the ankle so there wouldn't be any gangrene. Gangrene was a situation that Nory knew about from Debbie, who said mountain climbers usually got it. Debbie made up a pretty funny joke about it. When you had gangrene, the doctors all crowded around your foot, if it was your foot that had it, and shook their heads and said, 'It's green, gang,' and then, *chop*, off goes the foot, in the trash, two points. Debbie had a tape of an expedition to climb a very difficult-to-climb mountain, Mount Everlast. One guy fell and his foot broke so that it bent back against his leg in not a natural way, and it got badly infested, because the bone was projecting out, and they ran out of antibiotics, so they had to put plastic tubes all through the injury at his ankle, so water was pouring through his ankle every second. But he was all right once he got back to civilization.

So Achilles would not be able to kill as many people after they had to cut off his foot, since he would have to fight hopping to and fro, or rolling around in a wheelchair, or a wheelchariot, going 'Charge! Rip, slash, stab, rip,' at people and then frantically pushing the wheels. But he wouldn't die. He would not die and be buried underground because the immortality wouldn't let him. So you have to assume that it's the poison spreading that does it. But this can't be exactly correct because remember, if you're Achilles, every cell in the rest of your body is immortal. Totally immortal. If you looked through an electronic microscope on the highest power, each molecule of the poison would be there with a little sword of stabbing chemicals pointing harshly at each cell, and each cell would be fighting harshly back, and you could see the sparks for millimeters around, but each cell would win each fight. The cells wouldn't die. And then you have to think of this as well: in real life, your cells do die, and you get a whole new crop of cells every year, or every five years. The old cells get dissolved and get sent down by your blood to your bladder, and your bladder takes it from there. If you were Achilles, no cell would die, so you would get bigger, and bigger, and bigger, since your bones would be adding cells on, and no cells would be leaving, and your muscles, same thing, and your skin, same thing, every part of you would be growing in size and expanding like the expanding universe so after a little while you would be this absolutely huge monstrous thing just because you were immortal.

34. Things to Rem

So those were the basic questions that Nory wanted to ask Mr. Pears but couldn't, and instead of asking them, she finished her book about the hen who wouldn't give up. She wrote down on her Readathon sheet that she'd finished the book, and she saw her plain old ruler in her pencil case, which was made of plain clear and red plastic, and she listed through all the fancy rulers she had back in Palo

Alto. She had a whole collection—two Lisa Frank rulers, a Pompeii ruler, a Little Mermaid ruler, a ruler that had liquid in it that fishes slowly swam through, and the Hello Kitty rulers from the Sanrio store in Japan Center, and on and on, maybe twenty feet worth of rulers, and all of that was *plus* a whole separate collection of erasers. Maybe this wasn't quite as good as having a collection of fake food but it was something that Nory thought she should really be more pleased about. She kept her erasers in a blue ice-cube tray, not in the freezer of course, but it was a way of keeping them neatly in place, one eraser per ice place.

One time she was trying to earn some money to buy Underwater Barbie. Underwater Barbie, as many may know, kicked her legs in the bathtub. It was pretty good when she got it although the problem with it was that its motor made a massive amount of noise, so you couldn't tell a story about something that happened to Underwater Barbie while you had her kicking gently along under the water, which was what ahead of time Nory expected she would be doing. But she was really desperate for Underwater Barbie, and she had almost enough, and to earn the last bit of money she did a lot of different things. One of them was to set up a poster-making store with different styles of lettering for sale and different kinds of pictures to go along with them, but the customers, who were of course Nory's mother and father, mainly, chose what they wanted it to be a poster of. Nory's father asked for a poster of five important sayings or mottoes, which could be sayings or mottoes that other people had said or sayings that Nory herself said. So Nory wrote a poster titled 'Things to Rem.' She ran out of space for the rest of *Remember* so she made a thought-cloud and had the *Rem* remembering the *ember* part as if it was a contented memory. She only charged for ten headline letters because of that mess-up—three cents for each letter. The sayings were:

A Home Made Gift is Worth More than a Pot of Gold

Things May Not Be How You Rember Them

Things That You Take for Granted others May Treasure

Some Thing That you Think is Good
Another pearson Will think is bad

She only did four sayings, not five, because she was almost out of room and couldn't think of any more, but Nory's father liked the poster and wanted to pay extra for the border design but Nory said that was included free, and the total was 84 cents for the sayings at 2 cents per word and 30 cents for the headline, which came to $1.14. The saying Nory liked best was 'Things That You Take for Granted others May Treasure' because that might be true of something like her eraser collection or her ruler collection, especially her ruler collection, which even she took for granted up to now and didn't even bother to think of as a collection except that now at the Junior School she only had this one plain red ruler that said, 'Helix.' Rulers were useful for drawing the cubicles of a cartoon properly.

Nory drew a face on her fingernail and then smeared it away, trying to figure out how you would draw a cartoon picture of a girl thinking about clouds. You'd have to draw the thought-cloud with the usual three puffs leading promptly down from it to the girl's head, and then in the cloud you'd draw a cloud, and you'd have to shade the background of the thought-cloud with a different color, maybe, to draw the clear distinction between it and the real cloud that the girl was thinking about—but anything's possible with a pencil and paper, just about. Nory had in general two favorite types of clouds. One was the low flat steamy gray ones that you can walk right up to, and the other kind was the fat puffy ones that seem to have no end.

35. Break

Then the bell rang and Classics was over and Nory went to her break. She had been spending a lot of breaks with Kira, so to balance things out this break she spent with Pamela, who gave her some prawn chips which have a very dry feeling on your tongue, as if they're pulling out all the water from the tastebobs completely, but being infinitely delicious at the same time. They didn't have that awful glittery added-salt taste. Kira stopped by where they were sitting, under a conker tree, and said to Nory, 'Come on, let's go.'

'Take a seat and join us, Kira,' said Nory. 'We're having our break here.'

Kira said, 'I'll be back in a bit.' That was what she said when she wanted to go away but didn't want to say so. She didn't want kids to see her near Pamela. Pamela was quiet. Pamela didn't like Kira, because Kira didn't like Pamela, and Kira didn't like Pamela because nobody else liked Pamela.

Colin Sharings came up and said to Pamela, 'Have you ever gone bungee jumping?'

'No,' Pamela said.

'Good,' said Colin, 'because you'd probably break the cord and make a mess on the rocks.'

'That is an idiotic, nitwitted, dumb, and very stupid thing to say,' said Nory.

'Are you *friends* with Pamela?' Colin asked, pretending to be amazed.

'Yes, I am,' said Nory. 'And you are quite attractive. For a dead monkfish.'

'Oh, thank you, little American girl,' said Colin, who had a curly little mouth. 'Little Americayan. Take care that your *friend* Pamela doesn't get on any boats. They'll sink to the bottom as soon as she goes aboard. And as you may know, we dead monkfishes are quite hungry.' Having finished up with his insults for the day, he walked off with his nose aimed high.

'Colin Sharings is just awful,' said Nory.

'With a knob of butter and some parsley on his head,' said Pamela, 'he would look quite fishy.' She held out the bag of prawn chips for Nory to have another.

'These are infinitely delicious prawn chips,' said Nory. 'Where do you get them?'

'My mum gets them from Tesco,' said Pamela.

'We go to Tesco, too,' said Nory.

'It's quite a popular place to shop,' said Pamela. 'I think we probably should go in now.'

36. A Bird Problem

After break it was on to the next event, because each school day was packed with tons and tons and tons of events—good events, bad events, mezzo-mezzo events, confusing events, alarming events. The next event was I.T., where the class was trying to land their airplanes on an island. Nory mostly taxied around the airport, which was quite enjoyable. Finally she got her plane to take off down the runway, but then she started having some trouble. She pressed on one of the arrow keys, and if you held on to it for too long (which she was desperately doing to steer her plane back in a straighter direction) the plane went into an acute turn, which is the opposite of an obtuse turn, and would not ever turn back, it would just crash. So she crashed, as usual, but this time she not only crashed her own plane, she somehow curled persistently all the way around and crashed the plane that was following along behind her. Mr. Stone, the teacher, shook his head and said: 'Millions of pounds of expensive technology, sinking to the bottom of the ocean.'

Mr. Stone was a very nice teacher and probably the only teacher Nory had who hadn't yet said shutup to the class. All the teachers said shutup, even Mr. Blithrenner, the history teacher, who was a delight and knew every strange fact you could imagine. No grownup would have said shutup at the International Chinese Montessori School, but here, boy oh boy, the word was all over the place. Mr. Blithrenner was explaining, half jokingly, that there simply had to be bloodshed in the Aztec religion each and every day because the sunsets and sunrises were much redder and darker in America, and the Aztec religion was a religion of the sun. So blood had to be shed every day or the sun would become angry and simply refuse to rise, which would be a disaster. That explained the confusion. But two of the boys were being very disruptive and chitter-chatting about human sacrifices, and finally Mr. Blithrenner reached his limit and said, 'Colin, Jacob! Just—shut—*up!*' And they did.

Mrs. Thirm said shutup, too. The first time she did she put her hand up to her mouth, and the class was in shock, thinking, 'Wait just a tiny minute, teachers don't say that.' But now they'd gotten used to hearing it: 'Shut *up!* Shut *up!*' Not that often, though. At least the teachers didn't say, 'Shut your trap,' which was something Nory sometimes said to other kids, even though she knew she shouldn't. Sometimes she was noisy and interrupting in class, too, and then she felt guilty and when one of her parents picked her up at the end of the day she said, 'I can't have tea because I was not particularly good today. I talked a lot and laughed a lot and drew madly on my fingernail.'

But Mr. Stone, the I.T. teacher, never said shutup. Nory one time called the little rectangle that was in the middle of the screen the Bermuda Rectangle, because inside it were five little green blobs that were islands and on one of the five islands was the little landing strip—and Mr. Stone liked that name for it and started calling it that, too, which made Nory feel proud. If you can imagine trying to land a huge airplane on a popsicle stick, that's what it felt like to approach the Bermuda Rectangle. There was a ninety-percent guarantee that they would crash. Nory liked the old unit of I.T. better, when they were doing touch-typing, where if you make a mistake and typed a j for a k it just made a fly-buzzing sound and said 'Try again.' The next unit would be good, though: they were going to put on black hats with visors that plugged in and do Virgil Reality using the four new computers that were set up especially for multi-mediorite.

Then all the fifth-year kids went to lunch. No jacket potato for Nory this time, sadly enough, because Nory's mother was quite firm about how Nory had to have something meaty from time to time. Fortunately they didn't have the ham on display as a possibility. 'Oh, the ham,' Nory thought, 'the salty ham of last week.' She wanted to make an 'ulll' sound in her throat when that ham sprang to mind. It was a flat round thing with a narrow border of fat almost all the way around it, a capital G shape of fat, and it was dead cold and pale red. Actually it started out hot but got cold later. Nory was going to put it away and not eat it after one tiny bite. One of the people serving the food had said, 'Ham?' and given Nory such a nice tender smile that Nory said, 'Yes, please.' She should definitely have said, 'No, thank you.' But she felt that the person serving the ham might have her feelings hurt, so she said, 'Yes, please.' Also there didn't seem much like anything else she would like that day, so she got the flap of ham. But one taste and she was salted off her rocker. The music teacher came by and said, 'You should eat more of that delicious *ham,* what a waste.' Nory ate it and ate it. The teacher came by again and said, 'You should eat a little more.' So Nory ate a lot more, chewing endlessly, about two thousand and one chews of ham. Kira was whispering advice the whole time. 'Hide some of it, Nory, hide it in here,' she said, pointing to Nory's pencil case. Nory said no way could she hide the ham in her pencil case, not after all she'd been through with that pencil case. Finally she finished most of it. Maybe it was Danish ham. Mr. Blithrenner told his class one day that he didn't buy Danish ham these days because Danish people keep the young hams locked up in tiny lockers when they're alive and don't let them get any light or fresh air. Or rather, the young pigs. That was when he was talking about salting meats. The important thing people should know about the tip of finding the right direction to sail to shore by throwing the pig overboard is that you had to pull the pig back onto the ship very fast, because pigs have sharp what's-known-as trotters and could injure their face by desperately swimming. Pigs can smell mushrooms underground very well, amazingly well, in fact, so maybe even way out on the ocean they are smelling the underground mushrooms and that's why sailors can use them as compasses. Trotters are the things they trot on, sort of like hooves.

Fingernails are our hooves. Littleguy had a problem with his fingernails when he was a tiny newborn child—he would wave his arms around so clutchingly that he would scratch his face with his fingernails. Nory's mother and father had to be careful to cut his nails all the time so there wouldn't be too much scratching, but, poor little man, he sometimes scratched himself anyway. Nory's fingernails got to be a problem for her at the International Chinese Montessori school, an opposite sort of problem, because Bernice had a total habit of biting her nails until they were bare round nubs, and then nibbling off the skin of her tips of her fingers, too. Since Nory was best-friends with Bernice at that time, Nory began biting her nails as well, out of friendship, because when you're friends you start doing many of the same things. Now that she wasn't best-friends with Bernice anymore, presto, her nails were just their usual length, if not longer. Same thing with Kira. Kira had the habit of always jumping the last three steps of any stairs she went down, for instance the stairs in the dining hall, and now that Nory was becoming better and better friends with Kira, Nory had gotten in the habit of jumping down the last three steps, too, and she was starting to find she couldn't stop jumping, just like with biting her nails: she got near the bottom of the stairs, and before she had time to think about it, she was in the air and landing. Nory's mother had told her strongly to stop, because her landing made a huge thud of a noise at home, but usually she would forge ahead without thinking, and then have to call out, 'Sorry, I forgot myself!'

Debbie she hadn't been best-friends with for long enough for that to happen, or maybe Debbie just didn't have any weird habits like that. Another habit Nory's brain got into was writing a letter 'e' after words that of course had no 'e'—like 'had' or 'sad.' Before she would be able to remember to tell herself 'Stop, all systems stop, don't curl the little curl,' she would curl the curl. This was very maddening because she'd have to use the ink eradicator. 'Said,' however, was not spelled 'sayed' as she had been under the impression it was, until Mrs. Thirm wrote it on the markerboard, but with an 'i.'

One time just before she went to sleep, there was a bad thing that wouldn't stop thinking itself. She started in a perfectly ordinary way going out in a rocket into the universe, and landed at the edge, on some grass, and kept on walking. She walked over the field with cows and squishy places, and came to the Great Wall that was at the far edge of the universe, and naturally she climbed that wall, and at the top, she saw another field with more cows, lighter brown this time, and grass that was a little different, too. She crossed that field, and came to a moat, and another Great Wall, climbed that wall, saw another field with more cows, black and white spotted cows this time, and she kept walking and climbing, climbing and walking, getting more and more bothered by the infinity of it. She looked behind her and there was a crowd of angry cows. They knew a way through the walls. Some of them had a look as if they were about to pull back their lips and show their teeth. Finally she went downstairs and found her mother and father talking in the kitchen in the quiet casual way that grownups talk after kids are in bed, and she said 'A bad thing is in my head and I just can't get it to stop. It's like a bad screensaver.' Nory's mother took her back upstairs and put Cooch close to her cheek and told her not to worry, when you're sleepy your brain sometimes repeats things for no reason. She said when she had trouble like that she sometimes thought about how she would furnish a dollhouse, going from room to room, because your brain needs a simple problem to give it something to work with. That helped enormously. She thought about the fake food in the cabinets of the dollhouse, the tiny boxes of oatmeal, with tiny packets inside, the tiny roast hams.

But fortunately, no ham whatsoever today for lunch! Instead there was a wonderful piece of some kind of brown meat, totally soft, so that you could use it as a piece of bread and just wobble it all around. Nory said, 'Jennifer, it's really good, taste it,' and when Jennifer bit into it she said, 'Mmmmm, that is delicious.' Jennifer was just a girl who was amazingly gifted at drawing horses. So it was a good lunch, and after that came after-lunch break, which Nory spent with Kira because she'd spent the whole first break and some of lunch with Pamela and she thought it was hurting Kira, although, honestly, it wasn't fair that Kira wouldn't be with Nory when Nory was with Pamela. That break was when the bad thing happened. It was almost the worst thing that happened that whole day, except for a worse thing that happened later on. They were making a conker-pile, and Kira started saying—again—that whenever Nory was with Pamela it made her unpopular, which Nory was sick as a dog of hearing. Suddenly Nory wanted passionately to climb a tree, so she went over to the one that she'd been looking at that looked like the perfect tree-climbing tree, and started to try to climb it, even though a skirt and tie wasn't the ideal outfit for doing that. She looked up, happily, and suddenly there was a discreet thud on her face. She thought, 'Boy, quite a pinecone, oh dear.' It felt hard, because things that are really light can feel really hard when they fall from a distance. 'Oh, my, what a pinecone,' Nory thought, 'and what a lot of sap, too.' And then she wiped with her finger and took a look at it. 'This is *not* good looking sap,' she thought. 'This is not the kind of sap I'm used to. This is brown sap with a berry-skin in it.' Then she realized what it was and said, 'Kira! A disgusting bird took its leisure on me!'

Kira came running over and looked at her. 'Oh, Nory,' she said. 'Oh, dear. Oh, yuck. Come on inside.' Nory held her face out so that the rest of the bird leisure wouldn't drip on her jacket and Kira led her to the bathroom. They spent quite a good amount of time cleaning up.

'Smell my hand, does it smell okay?' said Nory.

Kira smelled it. 'It just smells like soap.' Then she thought for a moment. 'Wait, let me sniff it again.' She sniffed it again. 'You're fine, just soap.'

They were a tiny bit late for French class, but when they explained to the teacher what had happened, she said, 'Fine, fine.' The French teacher was a young, short-haired, dark-haired, short-bodied, stylish-dressed person. She had a wonderful way of saying 'superb' and she said it a lot, probably too much for some people's taste.

37. Pig Bladders

Then there was drama class, where they were doing sword fighting. Sword fighting is useful to know because you never know when you might be in a play in which there was sword fighting. Although that was as if a student said, 'I.T. is useful because you never know when you might need to spend the morning taxiing all over the airport in an airplane.' The drama teacher warned them again that you have to be very very careful with sword fighting, because even though the swords aren't sharp, they're heavy. And they were heavy, they weighed about five hundred grams, Nory thought. The teacher told a story about going to see a play by Shakespeare where a man had a rib broken by a wooden sword because he was supposed to take three steps one way and he forgot and took three steps in the opposite way by mistake and wound up in exactly the wrong place. A wooden sword plunged through a curtain, for some reason in the play, and slammed right into his ribcage and he had to go out on a stretcher, not as an actor but sincerely as an injured person. Shakespeare was famous for writing plays. Boy were they ever plays, and boy were they ever long. Nory's aunt and uncle took her to a Shakespeare play outside in a park one time, *Romeo and Juliet*. It might have been very interesting for a twelve-year-old, but for an eight-year-old, which was how old she had been when she went, it was impossible to understand, too long, and extremely boring. Thank goodness for the Inman Toffees that Nory's aunt brought along—Nory ate quite a number of them and thought about what it was like to chew them. Sometimes you think when the candy sticks to your teeth that maybe your teeth will be plucked right out, but they're stuck into the gums pretty strongly.

Shakespeare's name was probably William R. Blistersnoo but he thought he needed a preferable name in order to be famous, and since there was tons of stabbing and spearing of people with swords in his plays he thought, 'Let's see, William Swordjab, no. William Fight? No. William Killeveryone? No. William Stabmyself? No. Aha! William Shakespeare! Yes, that will be just the thing.' In Shakespeare's plays what they would do, according to the drama teacher at the Junior School, is they would have an outfit on and they would sew a pig's bladder in a little tiny place under the outfit that would have a little mark on it so that the person knew right where to stab. The guy would go *king!*—stabbing lightly right at that particular spot, and blood would instantly coosh out from the pig's bladder.

'But wouldn't they run out of pigs quite quickly?' Nory thought to herself. 'And therefore run out of pig's bladders, and therefore could not do another play?' Shakespeare would have to go on stage before the play and say, 'As you may know, we cannot do any of the blood we were going to do tonight, because we have run out of our lovely pig's bladders. We checked in the cupboard this morning, but due to good business, and a number of highly gruesome plays, we have run out. Please enjoy the show. You can have your ticket refunded if you would rather not see the show without blood, since early next week we will have more fresh pig's bladders shipped to us. We are also going to be getting some big, fat, juicy cow bladders in stock that we will be using for some extremely disgusting effects in a play I will be finishing soon. So please, dear friends, sit back, and enjoy the show.' And say if somebody was in too much of a rush and forgot to empty out the urine and pour in the blood? In the big swordfight Shakespeare would stab the guy. 'Die like a filthy scoundrel, you midget!' And then, *pssshooo,* oh dear, that blood's a bit on the yellow side, hm. 'Oh, yellow blood, is it?' Shakespeare would say. 'You monstrous, yellow-blooded confendio master! Hah-hah! Return to your imperial distinctive land!' Hack, chop. And a little later he would take a smug giggle and walk off the screen.

After drama there was Sciences. They looked through microscopes at different kinds of line—pencil line, crayon line, colored pencil line, medium-nib fountain pen line, and one other line. Biro line, they call it. A Biro is just a normal kind of everyday pen that you would use next to the phone to write out a phone message. In class they used an eraser on the lines to see what happens when you erase. The amazing thing was that the pencil left big gaps of white paper in its line, sort of the way an eraser will jump in a rubbery way in little tiny bounces if you pull it lightly over the paper, and the eraser left twisted shapes like something an insect would leave behind. One kid, Peter Wilton, was still in a state from drama class and was fidgeting all over the place. He was obviously in a Shakespeare mood of wanting to chop something up, and so he looked down at his desk and thought, 'Here's something.' He had a whole nice beautiful green pen in front of him. He sawed a quarter of it off, using his ruler, and then another quarter, and then a whole half of it. Nory shouldn't have smiled but it was quite cute, this tiny shrub of a pen, just enough for the cartridge to fit in, which he tried to write with. Then he got carried away and took the cartridge and sawed that in half. Now that was not a brilliant idea. As you can imagine, the cartridge went *plume,* everywhere. He said, 'Mrs.

Hoadley, my pen leaked.' But Jessica—who was sitting right next to him and rather exasperated by this point since it's very hard to look in a microscope even when things are calm and peaceful because your head moves and you push the thing the wrong direction and lose what you're looking at, or the light gets boffled up—so Jessica had lost her patience and she said to the teacher, 'Yes, it leaked because, ahem, he was sawing it into a-tiny a-little a-pieces.' The science teacher got steamingly angry when she got the picture and breathed through her nose in a furious way after everything she said. She said, 'Peter, that is unacceptable behavior, bup bup bup bup bup bup bup bup bup.'

'May I go wash my hands?' he asked.

'No, you may never wash your hands,' said the teacher. 'Your hands will stay blotched for the rest of your life.'

Which was a little joke by Mrs. Hoadley, although in fact she didn't let him wash his hands. But it was really nice to see the pencil lines and to think how many adventures happen to a pencil line while you're just writing a simple word.

38. More Things That Happened to Pamela

The next thing in the order of the day was that they were supposed to go to music class, and that's what Nory was in the process of doing, but she went by a place near the auditorium where there were some wooden boxes, because she took the wrong turn in the hall, and she found some boys crowding around saying 'Feeding time, Pamela.' Pamela was shoved back behind one of the boxes and she was hiding there. It was just after the sixth year kids' drama class. Nory couldn't understand exactly what was happening except that Pamela couldn't come out and wouldn't come out, and the boys were saying stuff about 'Eat,' and saying 'Are you hungry, Pamela?' One of them said: 'Feed the monster.'

Nory said, 'Let Pamela out! Stop it, let her out!' But they wouldn't. Then the French teacher walked by and the boys went into a quick flutter. They said, 'Sssh, don't let her see.'

'Pamela, please come on out,' said Nory, while the teacher could hear, so she would notice the situation. The boys were all pretending to be doing something else. The teacher said, 'Pamela? Are you there? Come out.' So Pamela did. Nory said, 'Hi, Pamela, come on, let's get our stuff.' Nory got her hurried away and waved to the French teacher who waved back. The French teacher probably didn't know much of what was going on, but that was good because Pamela did not want any teachers to know, because then they would have a word with Mrs. Thirm, and then she would have to have a word with Mrs. Thirm, and she thought Mrs. Thirm thought she'd done all those bad things last year.

Nory said, 'Pamela, you've got to go to Mr. Pears, because Mr. Pears is very nice. You've got to complaint to him. If you don't complaint to him nothing will get better. It'll just keep getting worse.' But Pamela said she couldn't find the time to complaint to him. The problem was that if you get bullied for a certain amount of time, you start thinking that it's average to be bullied and you end up stopping being able to fight back for yourself. It's like having a cold for so long that you start thinking its normal to have a stuffed-up nose. Nory didn't want to say that to Pamela because it wasn't the perfect thing to say. Pamela had the sound of almost-but-not-quite-crying in her voice when she said, 'I have to get my stuff,' and she went off.

The next thing that happened, not counting music, which was fairly anonymous, was that everyone was outside, waiting to be picked up. Nory was out with a bunch of other kids, including Kira. Pamela came out and sat down nearby with a big sigh and slumped her backpack down, and everyone froze and went dead quiet. Pamela concentrated on doing a strange thing, which was: taking off her shoe and sock and checking on an orange Band Aid that was on her toe. That was such an unexpected thing for Pamela to do that all the girls started to laugh at her, and then Nory couldn't help it and she laughed, too, although she felt it was mean. Jessica said to Nory, 'Can you please get her to go away?'

'Why should I?' said Nory. 'She's happy there. No, I can't get her to go away.'

Kira grabbed her arm and pulled her over and said, 'Nory! The more on her side you are the less popular you'll be.'

'Kira, is that all you can think about in this school?' said Nory. 'If you're my friend and Pamela's my friend I'm just fine in the area of being popular.'

'You're not thinking!' said Kira, in a whisper-shout, which is when you shout, but you do it in a whispering voice rather than a shouting voice.

'Oh, puff,' said Nory. She went to sit down next to Pamela and said, 'Hi, Pamela.' Pamela said 'Hello,' and kept checking away at her bandage, which had that old bandage look to it. Then she put her sock and shoe back on. Kira was waving to Nory very urgently, over and over, saying, 'Nory! Come *over* here!' with her mouth. Nory shook her head in refusion as if to mean 'Pardon me, but

I'm *sitting with Pamela.*' To Pamela, she said, 'You should tell the teacher about those girls.'

Pamela said, 'Girls? The girls are the least of my problems, it's the boys who are giving me a headache.' She pointed over at some of the boys who were in a little group on the steps pointing at her and pretending to throw up at the sight of her. But you could tell that it hurt Pamela that the girls had laughed at her when she looked at her Band Aid, including Nory, because you could hear the same crying in her voice, unless that was just the way she talked when she was angry, with a little sort of trembling. She'd wanted to be near the girls but she knew they wouldn't want her to be there, so she'd made up this idea of checking her Band Aid, maybe, which turned out to be so unexpected of a thing to do at that second that it worked out even less well than if she'd just walked over and said hello to everyone and nobody had answered. Pamela didn't understand that the girls were just as bad as the boys, not in shoving her into the boxes, but in just going along with this whole Porkinson Banger of an idea that Pamela was for no convinceable reason a kid who should be put into a state of misery every born day she went to school. Or probably Pamela did understand it, but didn't want to admit it, because obviously you don't want to think that everyone dislikes you. Nory told herself, 'Forget it, just forget it, don't talk to her about the other kids, just talk to her about something totally separate from the meanness that's going on, and show the other kids that Pamela is a kid like any other kid at the Junior School who can have a friend who will sit down next to her and talk to her normally.' So Nory told her a joke she remembered from Garfield. Garfield was her favorite comic strip, because it was really hilarious and really well drawn. Garfield went up in a tree to catch a bird in a nest. He had it clutched in his hand and was just about to eat it, when a mother bird the size of an eagle came in the back yard and glared at him with a vicious glare. Garfield looked up, still squeezing the bird in his hand, and said, 'Um—chirp? Chirp?' The eagle pecked at him wildly and Garfield got down from the tree and was all touseled and ruffled and bruised from the eagle. He said, 'Well, it was worth a try.'

Pamela nodded a little and managed a sad little grin of a smile. Then Nory asked her what books she was reading for Readathon. Pamela took a big breath and said, 'Well, I'm reading *The Call of the Wild.*' She started telling Nory the plot of the story, which was about a magnificent dog who gets stolen away, and then she hopped up and said, 'I've got to go, I'll miss my train.' Then she said, 'Thanks, Nory, bye,' and nodded at Nory a little, which made Nory happier and made her stop feeling the guiltiness she had been feeling about being magnetized into laughing at her when Pamela had first taken off her sock. Pamela seemed definitely more cheered up by the time she dashed off. Then Nory sat back down on the wall and waited to be picked up by her mother or her father. Kira didn't come over to sit next to her, but that wasn't too surprising, only a little saddening.

There was a humongous sign in one of the halls that said 'Bullies Are Banned' in balloon writing. Balloon writing was a very, very thick kind of puffy writing.

39. Reading Tintin to Her Babies

That night, after Nory's mother read to her and her father brought her up a glass of water, Nory bundled

Cooch and Samantha together in bed with her, with a plan of reading some *Tintin in Tibet* to them, because they were just about ready for that level of book now, as long as you explained some of the words. The difficult thing about reading to any of her dolls, as you may imagine, was that it was hard to keep both children sitting up so that they could see the book. They tended to slide down or over, and then Nory would have to tilt the book so that if Samantha was staring off toward a corner of the ceiling she could still have the chance to see the pictures, as long as Nory held the book right down over her head, and the same thing with Coochie. In the case of Tintin books you really had to be able to see the pictures—in fact if you were the one reading you had to point to each person's head in each square as you read what they said so that the person you were reading to would know who was talking. The pictures were very important to the story, because Hergé was such a good drawer, especially of mountains and people climbing mountains wearing backpacks. His dreams were very realistic. Captain Haddock dozes off while he's walking along and dreams a number of strange things that change from one picture to the next as he's walking. Nory had only sleptwalked a few times. One time she sleptwalked into the closet in Littleguy's room when she was eight and was under the general impression that it was the bathroom and so she peed carefully there, pulled up her pajama-bottoms, and went straight back to her bed.

The hard thing about holding the book so that Cooch and Samantha could see was that then it was not all that easy for Nory to see, and her arms and shoulders got so tired that they started to have a case of the sparklies, and couldn't hold the book up for one more second. Luckily

Cooch and Samantha both corked off in a very short time and she could relax the book and scoot down in her bed. Nory felt sleepy, too, but not quite enough to go to sleep herself. She didn't feel that there was any major bad dream getting itself ready to bother her—probably the last bad dream had been bad enough that she might not have any more for a month or two. So she wasn't bothered about that. But she wasn't completely sleepy, and she didn't want to start another Jill Murphy book about the Worst Witch, even though it was Readathon, because her brain was stuffed to the gizzard with reading for Readathon, and yes, by all means, leukemia was a horrible disease to strike a small innocent child but she would read more Jill Murphy books at another time, since they were very, very good books. Sometimes the problem with telling someone about a book was that the description you could make of it could just as easily be a description of a boring book. There's no proof that you can give the person that it's a really good book, unless they read it. But how are you going to convince them that they should read it unless they have a glint of what's so great about it by reading a little of it?

It was a challenge, but worth it because it was much better when somebody else has read a book you've read and you can talk about it, unless they try and be cool by saying something like, 'Oh sure, I read that ages ago, that was really easy and kind of stupid.' Kira had read all four of the Worst Witch books and about a hundred books besides that and she said she liked them but she didn't seem to want to talk about them too much, as usual. She sort of read a book, *bzzzzzzz,* as if she was sawing through it, and then on to the next. Nory felt a little jealous of how fast she could read. It was nice to talk to Roger Sharpless about

Tintin books because he had read them a lot and had them filed away in his brain, and you could play a game of describing a scene with five or six clues—say, falling out a trapdoor of an airplane into a wagon full of hay—and he would say, *King Ottakar's Scepter!* because he was so fast at identifying which book had which scene. You could say just three words, 'Acting the goat!' and he knew that you were talking about *Destination Moon.*

When Nory closed her eyes she saw the little red and yellow and orange dots that spread out on the computer screen to show that you've crashed the plane in I.T. If you forgot that they were the sign of a massive crash, the dots were as pretty as a screensaver. She lay there for a while, thinking about little snibbets of the day, I.T., playing with the conkers with Kira, then Kira helping her clean off the bird leisure, which had been very nice of her, and her smelling her hand, also very nice. But she didn't want to think about the day very much because in some ways it was such a dirty-clothes-heap of a day, all twisted around and garbled and wrinkled. She wanted to close her eyes peacefully and be told an unexpected story, but since she'd already been read to that wasn't much of a possibility, so she picked up the small Chinese doll on her bedside and looked at its eyes. They were painted with different colors than they used to paint Barbie's eyes, which are blue and purple. Then she imagined that maybe she could tell herself a story—maybe a short emotional story of the kind that Mariana, the girl who had been in the burning rain, would tell herself. So she did.

40. Amnezia and the Dragon

In ancient days, even before there were hot and cold faucets that can offer something of a problem in England because the hot comes storming out of one faucet and the cold comes freezing out of the other one that is about a foot and a half away from the hot, and they don't mix, and the hot is screamingly hot, hot enough to boil tea, so that if you want to wash your hands you have to move back and forth very fast, hot-cold-hot-cold-hot-cold-hot-cold, to imitate the sensation that it's warm water, which is by the way how the art of claymation works—you move one tiny pinch of clay and then walk over to the camera and take a picture and move another tiny movement, move-click-move-click-move-click—but long before there was any of that kind of advanced modern technology, there was a girl. Her name was Amnezia. Amnezia's mother told her when she was only very little that the Dragon of the Fourth Continent would come. There were seven huge pieces of land in those days, and are now, distributed around the world, and the Fourth Continent was good old Asia. The Seventh Continent is Antarctica, which is a landmass with a huge thing floating underneath it called Magnetic South which is made up of magnets and tons and tons of anonymous rock.

So the Dragon of the Fourth Continent would come, Amnezia's mother told her. 'Only to very special people like yourself,' whispered her mother, who was herself from the Western region of China a thousand miles from the Great Wall. This was when the child was two, one night, and she asked to be told a story. The story turned out to be true and about her own life in the future. 'We'll have to defeat the dragon,' her mother said. 'The dragon will try and come to get you. He will try and eat you. But you are strong, dear child, he cannot win.'

Then the mother whispered, even more quietly, 'I have experienced it, just like your grandmother, and her mother and her grandmother, and back and back.'

But there was one thing that the mother did not know: that her daughter would have to meet the dragon *two times*.

Many years later, when the child was about eight, it happened. Now she was a very pretty child. Her black hair was shinier than ever, and very, very long. It could almost touch her ankles. The experience happened at nighttime. She was doing her studying, she was learning what is now known as botany. It was very late at night and there were no sounds at all except the rustle of the dried plants she was looking at through what is now known as a microscope, but then was known as a Chenker-Pah and made of jade and mother-of-pearl. (A grain of sand is an orphan-of-pearl, because think about it: a pearl is made from a grain of sand held in the loving home of an oyster, and if it never gets a loving home, it will never get the mucousy stuff to harden around it and will never become a pearl.) Amnezia was sitting on her bed, writing on the little table on which she kept her face towel and the equipment she used for her late night studying. She stopped to dip her pen in the ink, for this was long before the days of cartridges, but just as she was about to take it out of the ink, everything changed.

Her bedside table disappeared, her room vanished. Her house, everything. She was on a black ground with millions of people, including her own parents and her. A huge dragon was coming. She touched her shoulder and fell back on her bed. Then in a split second she realized it was coming. All these grownups had come to watch her defeat the dragon. They were all holding candles, beautiful caramel-colored candles. She looked at her mother with pure fear, but her mother smiled at her, as if to say, 'Everything's all right.' It was then that she remembered the time when her mother said, 'It will happen, the dragon will come, but you will defeat him.'

She clutched her shoulder even harder. She thought to herself hard, 'Amnezia, gain up all your courage, just like your mother told you!' Now she could feel dust and hot air brushing against her face from the steps of the monster, it blew in every direction, but all the adults didn't seem to care one whiff. Now his hand was almost grabbing her. He grabbed tightly now, without her even being able to do as much as take a breath.

She was very smart. She decided she would scoot out from his hand. But it was not as easy as she thought it was. He clutched hard, and what would have been his thumb if he was a human had a very sharp nail. It was an inch away from her arm. She knew it would scrape her if she slithered down. But then she thought, 'No, it's better to be alive than not to have a long scrape across you.'

So she began to squirm. She bit the monster, she kicked and punched. But he did not move, he was looking around curiously at everyone else. And foolishly enough he was very preoccupied. She squirmed and squirmed. She managed to slither out. But now she started to turn this way and that. His thumb scraped her all the way down her chest to her hip. Finally only her head was caught in his hands. She pushed off his hands as hard as she could, and fell. It seemed like only five minutes that she fell, and then everything blacked out.

The next day, she woke up. Her mother came in. She spoke softly, just in the same voice she did when Amnezia was only two. 'You did it, you did it, Amnezia,' said her mother. She seemed very pleased. Amnezia was glad. She had been scared of that moment for ages.

Then she went off to a boarding school. She went there for five years. She came back when she was thirteen, a very learned girl now. She was ready to become what she had dreamed of for months, years, and what seemed like a decade to her. She was ready to be a professor. The day she came back, it happened again. She was thirteen now, and still just as pretty as she was when she was eight.

She stood taller than ever, her mother's eyes shined when she came back. She had never seen her mother look so happy in all her life. That night, she was washing, helping her mother wash, when it happened again. The basket in her hand did not disappear this time. She found herself in the black place she had been in before, kneeling down on the same flat blue pillow, holding a basket of clothes. There was her bed, behind her. She sat back on it, scared. But not as scared as the first time. Now many people were there. Thousands of them, not all adults, but also children. There was a woman holding a baby. Holding her tight. Amnezia had a shock. 'The baby is the only one here who is also supposed to defeat the dragon,' she thought to herself. 'The mother is scared. How could a baby do it?'

The mother set the baby down beside her and smiled at Amnezia. Then Amnezia thought, 'I am only brought here to protect the baby. I was chosen to protect her.' She looked around her. Now all the candles everybody was holding were not caramel-colored but a baby blue. 'It is a ceremony for an infant,' she thought. So they used blue.

Then she felt the dust from the monster's foot again. She put the baby behind her and lay with her body protecting her. She used all her chest-power to scream at the monster, 'Don't try and eat her, try and eat me. I am so much bigger than she is.' The monster got a strange look on his face, as if he understood. He picked up Amnezia and took her away.

And no one ever saw her again, because now she is in heaven.

That was what Mariana told to herself, as she sat on the big cozy bed. She sang softly, 'She'll be coming round the mountain when she comes.' She got up, picked up her two dolls Heleza and Releza, yawned and decided to read herself a book, the end.

41. In Real Life

'It was only pretend,' Nory said to reassure Samantha and Racooch when she was finished whispering herself the story—in case one of them had been only dozing lightly and caught some of it, or was only pretending to sleep, as Nory sometimes did herself, so she could hear a glimpse of things she wouldn't normally hear. 'In real life there are no dragons with long fingernails,' she said to her dear babies. 'There are, it is true, many terrible things in real life, but you two are young and you don't need to know about all of them yet. There will be plenty of time for that. You just need to try to do your best to be as good as I know you can. I will cradle you away from anything that might harm you, because I love you very much, as you know.' She kissed them in their sleep, and then it was unavoidably time for her to conk.

42. The Lady Chapel

Littleguy called the morning the good-morning time, because that was what Nory had called the morning when she was Littleguy's age, and Nory's parents still did. Nory didn't have the slightest memory of ever calling it that, though, because of how much you undoubtedly forget, she just knew about it from her grandmother telling it. One time their plane was cancelled and Nory and Nory's mother and her grandmother were all in a hotel room near the airport. They got in bed very late and turned out the light. The two grownups had just finally closed their eyes and dozed away when Nory stood up in her crib and said brightly, 'Dood morning!' Little children say 'dood' instead of 'good' and 'breaksiss' instead of 'breakfast' because some sounds are not all that easy for them to make and sometimes they give up trying to teach their tongue to make, for instance, a 'g' sound and think to themselves, that's dood enough for now. But later on they hear it so many times as 'g' they can't help it and they finally say 'good morning.'

A little kid calls it the good-morning time because you don't have the slightest idea of what time of day it is then, but you *do* know that at a certain particular time of day people always say 'Good morning' to you, so sensibly it's not just plain morning time, but good-morning time.

So in the next good-morning time Littleguy woke up very, very early, before Nory's mother and father were up, and Nory and he closed the door to their mother and father's bedroom and snuck into the Art Room together and closed that door. The Art Room was a true multi-purpose room. It was actually a tiny extra kitchen in the upstairs of the house where there were markers, and a stapler, and Scotch tape and scissors and all kinds of supplies like that, including a sink where you could do water projects. You could play egg-beater games in there or make things with clay or just be by yourself and do anything. 'Littleguy, what do you want to make?' Nory whispered, because again today the idea of doing some kind of project was burning a hole in her pocket, and since Littleguy was there and wanted to be involved, well, she would make a project with Littleguy.

'I want to make a auger driller,' said Littleguy.

So they made one, together, extremely early in the morning, out of an empty cracker box and a small empty Legos box and some paper rolled into a tube. They decorated it with drawings of all four of them, and put it in a shopping bag and when Nory's parents got up they said, 'Here's something for you.' When you give your parents a present and they are very appreciating of what you've done and say that it's the most beautiful thing they've ever seen, it can give you a undescribable feeling in your chest, a certain kind of opening feeling, as if your heart's a clock in a furniture museum with little doors that open up and a clockwork princess twirls out for a short time. While Nory and Littleguy had been working on the auger driller Littleguy stopped once and said, 'I'm sho happy!' So she did get to do a project and it turned out well.

But that day was a Saturday, which meant—because this was something that was very different between England and America, at least at this school—it meant, school in the morning. So, put on shirt and skirt and tie, tuck tie in skirt, brush hair and teeth, oatmeal, rush to school. While they were walking there, the swans came up hunching their shoulders in a threatening way, and Nory's mother asked, 'How's Pamela doing?'

'Not exactly perfect,' Nory said, and told some of the details. Her mother said Nory should tell the teacher that these bad things were going on, but just not use Pamela's name since Pamela didn't want to be mentioned. She could just say, 'I have a friend who keeps getting treated badly by other kids, and she doesn't want me to bring her up to you, but I really think someone has to know about it at the school because it's bad, and what should I do?'

Nory said okay, maybe that was a solution. They got there almost on time, and first there was R.S., then history class. In R.S. they were given the assignment of designing a piece of stained glass for the Lady Chapel, in a drawing. Nory drew the Virgin Mary in a blue dress with puffy sleeves and the golden thing over her head, holding up two fingers, but the fingers were quite stubby because Nory did the drawing in a cartoony style, since when she did her very precise style she often made mistakes from trying to do it too perfectly, like the painters you see in the Fitzwilliam. When she used her realistic style a lot of times she got into trouble with the eyes, making one of them too bulging, or the nose too nostrilly. A cartoon style was a set style she knew how to do, and when she used it she was pretty sure that the face would turn out all right and have a loving look which you need for the Virgin Mary and not have one side that looked like an off-kilter monster face or hands that looked like chicken claws or something like that.

There was a whole separate part of the Cathedral called the Lady Chapel that was dedicated to the Virgin Mary, but it had only a tiny bit of stained glass in it. That's why they talked about it in R.S.—what kinds of decoration would you want in a Lady Chapel? You could have the seasons of the year or other important nuns and lady saints, or do scenes from Mary's life. Long ago it had been painted rich colors, but right now the Lady Chapel definitely had problems, in Nory's opinion. It smelled very coldly of stone. Probably that was because the stone powder was always falling, since there were so many places that the stone was broken open, and over the years it kept falling from them, like pollen. It was a sad bare place, the exact opposite of what you would want in a church devoted to the Virgin Mary, since it was a place to honor the memory of the mother of the Lord Jesus Christ, Mary, and her job had been to shelter the baby Lord Jesus in her cradling arms. As we know, the stone had been broken up very tiresomely by the people in Threll who got out their hammers and started breaking things in the churches because they had a sudden powerful brainwash and came to the decision that they were totally against the monks.

Nowadays if you walked up to any statue in the whole Mary Chapel you saw that there were very few heads on them, so it was almost impossible to enjoy looking at them, since they were just pathetic little carved stone dolls about the size of Samantha dolls except not quite as plump, that stopped at the shoulders with no expressions whatever. The most important part of a doll, or a sculpture, or a drawing is, by all means, the face, because all your senses come from your face, except for your sense of touch, and even that is included on your face, if you think about it, since your skin can feel, and even your teeth can feel although it's not exactly touch when your teeth are very sensitive to the pain of having a huge ball of ice-cream in your mouth, but it's not taste either and it's not touch, it's another sense that only your teeth have, maybe, that dentists study. Sometimes you can have the feeling that your face is the only part of your body. Some people think there's another sense in your chest, though, in the oystery place around your heart, and maybe it would be possible for you to think with your heart.

Littleguy was a good example of how important faces were in art, Nory thought, since he was just starting to make his first really good drawings of people. Before he had drawn two big circles and connected them with a line he called the driving bar to make the two wheels of a steam engine and he would very happily say, 'That's a steam engine!' But now he was drawing the same two circles and the same line, but now they were the two eyes and the mouth and he would say, 'That's Juliana!' Juliana was a girl who he was best-friends with in Palo Alto that he missed very much, even though he was going to school here in Threll, too. He was even drawing the legs now, the way little kids do, with the feet poking off in one direction and capturing the movement and not the other aspects that you learn later, like the knees.

A sad thing to think about was all the little heads from all the little statues lying on the floor of the Mary Chapel at the end of the day, after the nitwitted men had finished slamming around with their hammers and gone away. Maybe then an old nun would have come in by a side door with a broom made of straw bundled up. Shaking her head sadly, she would have swept up all the little bumbling stone angel-heads very carefully into a cold little pile, like a pile of brussels sprouts, and maybe she would have scooped them into a velvet bag and taken them out into the Bishop's garden and planted them. Each little head would grow into a rare tulip or a lily or a conker tree in the spring, probably a lily since the lily was Mary's special plant, especially devoted to her. The passion-flower is a vine that was Jesus Christ's plant because you can see a cross inside it if you look at it close up. Someday Nory thought in a hundred years someone would go around the Bishop's garden with one of those wands with the little halos at the bottom that they use to find things underground—a sculpture-detector—and discover the heads and dig them up. They would wash them off very gently with certain chemicals they use to do that kind of work, and glue them back in place one by one, so carefully you couldn't even be able to tell where they had been broken off, and the whole place wouldn't seem so destroyed. UHU was the name of the glue people used most often in England, but they pronounced it as 'You-hoo,' not 'Uh-huh.'

If Nory grew up to be a stained-glass maker and not a dentist or a popup-book maker she would design each window in the Mary Chapel to tell the story not just of Mary's life but of the digging of the stone for the Mary Chapel and the whole construction of it and the story of the people who came around one Thursday afternoon for no reason smashing the stained glass and the statues, and she would illustrate her own story of the woman who saved the heads and the flowering of the heads and the gluing back on of the heads with UHU. Then the place would be filled with the colors of the stained glass again and not seem cold at all. The idea of the heads growing up out of the ground wasn't her own idea. It came from something they talked about in Classics class, the planting of an army out of teeth by Jason.

Now it was almost all clear glass in the Lady Chapel, in little square pieces going all the way up each window, and near the bottom of each window it said a name, like 'Lord Chinparm' or 'Lloyd's Bank' or 'Tesco.' Tesco was the name of one of the food stores in England. There was Tesco and Waitrose and Asda and Safeway. Safeway was exactly the same name as in America. It was a good name for a supermarket because it gave you the idea of very calm smooth aisles of food that were so wide that you would never have an accident with another shopping cart and would always be able to buy your groceries quickly and safely. Each window of the Mary Chapel had a name on it because that was who originally gave money to put up that piece of transparent stained glass, or rather unstained glass. So now it just said TESCO, plain and simple, with no picture of Mary, not of Adam and Eve, not of Solomon or the ark or Jonah or Jesus Christ going down into H-E-double-hockey-stick.

So this is what happened to a visitor now. You went in and looked around, and thought, 'Hmmm.' You might not want to look at the headless sculptures, because you didn't want to think about people doing that with hammers each by each, so you looked up at the glass, and then you saw LLOYDS BANK and you thought, 'Oh, right, that reminds me, I need to get some money at the cash machine,' and you turned around and walked out. Or you saw TESCO and you thought, 'Oh, right, I need to get some brussels sprouts and some dwarf cauliflower for dinner,' and you turned around and walked out. You didn't necessarily think of how the Virgin Mary protected her son because she loved him. She would have died for him, as any mother would. That's why she was so important! She would have died for her son just because she loved him so infinitely much, even if he hadn't been Jesus Christ but just simply her own child—but the way the Catholic religion had adjusted the story a little was that it had her son dying up on the cross out of love for the world, to save it, as if it was his dear child. His own personal dying was a symbol for the kind of love that Lady Mary had for him. Long ago it would have been a much, much more Mary-Mother-of-Goddish sort of building when the stained glass was there, because the colors would be red and blue and you might feel you were in a humongous stone kangaroo pouch. There is such a thing as warm colors and cold colors, so that even if a place is cold in a temperature sort of sense it can be quite heartwarming. Though your heart is always fairly warm anyway because think how much exercise it's getting.

Once at Christmastime when she was seven, Nory made a nativity scene using the miniature baby from Babysitter Barbie as the Baby Jesus and dressing one of her Barbies in a blue dress with a crown as the Virgin Mary and then arranging the Three Wise Barbies, one blond, one dark-haired, and one African-American, in front with pipe cleaners decorating their heads and show that they'd come from foreign lands. The Three Wise Barbies couldn't kneel, so they had to kind of lie there near the gifts they brought, which were in little Polly Pocket suitcases. But that was sensible because in Roman days people very often ate dinner lying on the couch.

43. A Talk with Mrs. Thirm

So that was what Nory did in Religious Studies, drew the Virgin Mary. This made a little bit of a strange comparison with History, where they were still busy discussing the Aztecs and investigating the way the Aztecs sacrificed their people in order to feed the blood-red sunsets. There was a picture of them sacrificing in the textbook. First of all—and Nory thought that it was good of them to do this, at least—they made the person who was going to be sacrificed very drunk, so drunk he almost fell asleep waiting in line to be killed. Then they held both his legs—two people holding his legs and one person holding his arms. In other words, one person holding one leg, the other person holding the other leg. There was one person in the middle, on one side, who had a spear and a skull on his outfit. His hand was all red from killing people and he held a sword that was all red, and his sleeves were soaked with blood to the elbows. There was a wooden block that they had the person lie on. Blood was dripping down the stairs they had to walk up, slobbed all over the place, because what they did in order to sacrifice them was to cut their heart out while it was still beating.

Nory thought that it was really nothing to be proud of, this type of behavior, nothing that should allow the Aztecs to have elaborate costumes and solid, proud faces. Of course it was a picture that was painted many years after the sacrifices happened, but still—they weren't smiling, so they didn't look totally wicked, neither did they look very very upset. And what they were doing was unspeakable. It was not just unspeakable. It was unsingable, it was unchattable, it was unsignlanguageable. It was way, way past the limit. However, maybe it was good to learn about at school because kids love gory things, especially boys and certain girls, like Bernice, and it wasn't something especially made up to scare your living dits off, like *Tales of the Crypt* or *Goosebumps,* it was something that was a part of real-life history, which was why it was being taught in Mr. Blithrenner's class. And, really, being sacrificed on a wooden block was not the worst way to die, if you had to die in some fancy way other than old age. There were three worst ways to die in this world. One was to be on one of those posts with a fire under you that trickles up your legs. The second was to be smuggled by surprise with a hand over your mouth. And the third was to drown.

At break Nory discussed this with Kira, who pretty much agreed, except that she said that the absolute worst-of-all-worsts way was: being buried alive. Pamela came over and said there were some fresh conkers under the tree, and this time, quite amazingly, when Nory said, 'Come on!' to Kira, Kira came along. She didn't play with Pamela, exactly, but Pamela and Kira both played with Nory, in a sort of separate way. Pamela said that she thought the worst way to die was probably to fall off a cliff onto needle-sharp rocks, and both Kira and Nory had to admit that, yes indeed, that was a pretty unattractive way to die, as well. So there was a tiny spark of Kira and Pamela maybe starting to get along. But meanwhile a few other kids came over for the conkers and Kira went over to them. So obviously she was still embarrassed to be with Pamela. And then, on the way to lunch, Kira asked Nory out of the clear blue sky if maybe Nory could come over to her house the next day and play, and Nory said she would check with her parents, because it couldn't hurt to ask.

Just before Nory left she had a horribly nervous moment of talking to Mrs. Thirm. She told her that there was a girl, a friend, who was having one bad experience after another with bullying. Not physically bullying so much as mental bullying. She told her about the time with the jacket and the time that day with the boys, and the girls not talking to Pamela and laughing at her, and a few other times, like the time one of the boys kept throwing Pamela's duffel coat down and hanging his duffel coat on her peg. 'This friend doesn't want me to say her name,' said Nory, 'but she is quite, quite bothered that this is going on day and day out, and I was just wondering if you might have a recommendation on what to do about it.'

'I suppose you mean Pamela,' said Mrs. Thirm.

'Well, I can't exactly—I mean—she's a friend,' said Nory.

'Thank you for mentioning it, Nory,' said Mrs. Thirm. 'We'll keep an eye on it.'

'Thank you, because it does really bother her,' said Nory. She breathed the hugest blast of a sigh of relief because she had been worried all day about saying something to Mrs. Thirm about Pamela, and lo and behold it turned out that the teachers already knew about the situation. And fortunately Nory hadn't had to give out Pamela's name, although it was a close call.

44. Six Extra Brains

Her mother picked her up from school at twelve-thirty, and Nory asked right on the spot if she could go over to Kira's house the next day. Nory's mother and father discussed it. The difficulty was that they were going to drive to Wimpole, which was a Stately Home, the next day. 'Couldn't Kira come with us?' Nory asked. Nory's mother and father looked at each other and made their 'I don't see why not' expressions. So Nory scrummaged around in her backpack and found Kira's phone number on a little folded piece of paper in her pencil case. She called the number: 'Hello, this is Eleanor, could I please speak to Kira?' Then Kira came to the phone and Nory invited her to come with them to Wimpole. Nory heard Kira shout, 'Can I go to Wimpole tomorrow afternoon?' Then she heard, 'Wimpole!' Then, 'WIMPOLE!' Then, 'With Nory.' Then she heard, 'A girl from school. Yes.' Then after a second Kira came back on and said, 'Yes, I can go, but my mother would like to talk to your mother to sort out the logistics.' So it was all settled that Kira was coming over an hour before they left so they could play a little, as well. And Wimpole was a good place to go because Nory's mother said it had a farm with a number of endangered species of cows and pigs and goats, which made it good for kids of all age groups. Nory was so happy to hear the good news that she cleaned up her room for Kira from the northeast corner to the southeast corner, like a hot butterknife. And what usually happened happened again as usual, which was that as she cleaned she began rearranging her dolls, and thinking of little events that could happen in their adventurous everlasting lives. So while Littleguy took a nap in a little clump on the couch she came down with two dolls and sat next to him and started to tell herself a story of Mariana. But she kept getting distracted by the idea that Kira was coming over, so she put it on the back of the stove.

Kira's mother dropped Kira off and Nory felt the surprise of 'Wow, this is very strange to have Kira in my house,' because of course she was used to seeing her at school. They were a tad-bit shy with each other for a few minutes, but then everything turned pleasantly chatty as can be, except for one very big hitch. Kira was being brought up, through her whole childhood, without any TV allowed in her house, so of course as soon as she came over to Nory's house she was desperately craving a long juicy watch of TV. She knew precisely what was on, and she knew what she wanted to see. It was an American cartoon called *Space KeBob 7*.

Space KeBob 7 was about a fifteen-year-old named Space KeBob with a huge skull that was built up using bone grafts. Six extra brains were stored inside his skull, which had little partitions in it sort of like the chambered nautilus, and he was able to connect up to each of the brains by unplugging a wire and connecting to the next brain, so that if he wanted to think like, for example, a wise old Native American man, he plugged into that plug and connected up to that brain, and if he wanted to think like a falcon, he connected up to a tiny little falcon brain. The six extra brains plus the boy's personal brain he was born with equals seven, which was why 'Space KeBob 7' was the most logical name for the show. Nory wasn't wild on seeing it, because she had seen plenty of the episodes and they usually had some sort of enormous space-dragon with a gargling voice. Also it didn't make sense because if you were the bad guy it would be quite easy to take a little dab of modeling clay and press it into a couple of the boy's brain plugs and Space KeBob 7 would immediately be Space KeBob 5, and a little more clay stuffed in a few more sockets, he'd be Space KeBob 3, then Space KeBob 2, and then he would be right back down to his own brain, with nothing else to rely on, and it wouldn't be a popular show anymore and would just be a shy little slip of a cartoon about an average kid in space.

But Kira was passionately interested in seeing it, since she almost never had an opportunity to, so they watched it from start to finish. Nory got very sleepy. She had woken up early that morning, and again gone right to the Art Room with Littleguy. Littleguy had seen some styrophone packing chips in a box and said, 'They look like tato chips.'

So Nory stapled together a bag of pretend potato chips out of them that said:

EVER LASTING
CRISPS

** Now Even Freasher **

Nory wasn't allowed to eat the kind of Prawn chips that Pamela usually brought in for break except on special occasions because they had an artificial fragrance of sugar in them and Nory's parents didn't want her to possibly get brain damage from a chemical molecule that dressed up in a sweet disguise as if it was sugar when really there was nothing sugary about it, so that your brain didn't know how to clean itself out after the feeling of sweetness was gone from your mind. Kira didn't care for Prawn chips—but they really were wonderful because they dissolved on your tongue almost as if they were that kind of super-sour candy that foams up on your tongue.

Finally *Space KeBob* 7 was over and Nory and Kira went up to Nory's room and Nory showed Kira her dolls. Kira was polite about them, but not as interested as she might have been. She did like the little metal cars on the edge of the bathtub that changed color depending on whether they were dipped in cold water or hot water. So they played with the color-changing cars for a while. Kira didn't seem to want to try to get a story going about them, though, the way Debbie probably would have.

45. Nogl Erylalg

Wimpole House was a long quease of a drive away. The farm was good. Some of the rare cows had huge heads and quite bulging eyes that looked as if they might plop out onto the hay. That might explain why they weren't as successful as the kinds of cows farmers used now. One black cow nipped Littleguy's finger when he was feeding it some green pellets and the finger turned red. Littleguy cried but then he bravely went on to feed the goats, which turned their heads to fit their horns under the bars of their cage—their lips were soft and speedy over your hand, taking the crumbles of food, and they stretched their necks out so far sometimes that they cut off their breathing a little against the bars and you heard them making choking noises, like a dog when he pulls at his collar. But because there were bars you didn't feel nervous the way you could feel with the beady-eyed swans by the river.

The house had a crunchy stone path going up to it. Crunchy paths were very important to this kind of fancy palace-house because then when you walked into the house the feeling of walking on a real floor or a real rug would feel unusually wealthy and very hush-hush. Also the gravel helped to clean off any dung or mud or other nonsense from your shoes, although there was much less anonymous dung nowadays than in the days of the wives of Henry the Eighth, for example.

While they were walking up, a little girl bumped her head on a place under the stairs up to the house and cried without any exaggeration, for it had been quite a sharp bump. Nory's father bought two children's guidebooks, so Nory and Kira could both have one. The Wimpole children's guidebook wasn't quite up to the snuff of the Ickworth children's guidebook, but what could you do? The main thing about the afternoon basically was that it was a totally different experience going around a Stately Home with Kira because Kira was infinitely competitive, so that if the guidebook said, 'Can you find such and such a teeny little bell-pull they used to attract the servants?' then Kira was off in a frantic dash and scrabble to find it before Nory did.

Tables and paintings and chairs and hidden doors went flittering by from room to room that Nory couldn't look at because she was trying to keep up with Kira. She didn't want to race, but then again she also didn't want to lose if Kira *did* want to race, and Kira definitely wanted to race. Not that they were running, either, just going as fast as they could while pretending to be very calm and smooth and angel-may-care. They came to a picture of a girl walking her dog. 'Oh, what a lovely painting,' said Kira, but Nory looked at her out of the corner of her eye because she wasn't so completely sure Kira actually liked the painting all that much. Kira was just pleased to have gotten there first, possibly, since it was mentioned in the children's guidebook and Kira was so competitive. Nory had wanted to arrive at the painting at least at the same time as Kira, so that she could admire it without a feeling of having lost a race, because she was a fan-and-a-half of dogs in things like paintings and statues, mainly because she so very much wanted a dog of her own, craved for one, and couldn't have one, and Kira did have one, a golden retriever, which was just exactly the kind of big, hairy, smelly dog that Nory desperately wanted and couldn't have because, for one thing, the English government locks up every single dog that comes into England for six months to make sure it doesn't have a plague.

So, because Nory felt a trifle cross, she said, when they were both in front of the painting of the girl walking her dog: 'Hmm. Her shoes aren't perfect, and the dress could go higher up.' Then she said, 'Let alone the strange pink sleeve floating out behind her. Also, her hat could be improved. It looks like it's about to jump the gun. The dog looks a bit vicious, too. He could be improved.'

'Well!' said Kira, with some chin in the air and some humphing in the voice. 'I guess you don't like that painting very much at all, do you?'

'I like the ground quite a bit,' said Nory, 'and the light catching on the rocks. The bush is good, and the houses, there's plenty I like, but it's true—the whole middle part of the picture, including the girl and her hat, is not exactly my taste.'

Kira went back to her guidebook. She was much, much better at the word-puzzles in the back than Nory was, because Kira was a wiz of a speller, and Nory was a speller from Mars, if not from the Big Dipper. Kira knew right on the spot that NGOL ERYLALG was a scramble of LONG GALLERY.

46. Some Chandeliers

On the stairs they passed by a painting of dead birds, which was called a still life because the birds are not moving or flying, but are just there, still as glass, which makes them easier to paint. 'Still deads' would be a more realistic name for them than 'still lifes.'

'Ulg, I think I just lost my appetite,' said Kira.

'Wouldn't they go a little rotten while they were being painted?' asked Nory. She was remembering something Mr. Blithrenner told them in History about the Aztecs, which was that once the priests were done with a sacrifice, they let the person's brains rot in his chopped-off head. That was somewhat like what they did to Oliver Cromwell for chopping off the king's head. They dug him up a few years after he was dead, then cut his head off of his by now totally disgusting body, and put it on a spike on a building so that any child passing by would point at it and say, 'Mom, what is that strange black lump with teeth?' Once again, nothing to be proud of.

The people who figured out Ickworth House had a better idea of what you would want to pass by on the stairway every day and instead of a big painting of dead birds they put up a woman holding a fan. The real-life fan that was painted in the picture was attached to the wall above the fireplace in one of the rooms upstairs, so you could compare the painted fan and the real fan and see how good a job the painter had done. He had done a fine job. Some fans used to be made from chicken skin, though, so they would qualify as being still lifes, too.

The Yellow Drawing Room of Wimpole House was quite reasonable, and it had a dome that was shaped like the Jasperium of the Cathedral, but with a chandelier hanging down from it that was slightly on the scrawny side. Ickworth had a humongous chandelier over the dining room table. A man there had explained that it used to be at a different house but it had suddenly plundered from the ceiling one day for some reason and they'd had to prune it down, like a huge bush that was run into by a tractor. They carefully saved all the good pieces, and threaded it with new string, and now you couldn't possibly tell that it wasn't the way it was meant to be when you looked at it, since it was an extravaganza of sparkles as it was. Kira found out from the children's guidebook that it wasn't actually a chandelier but a 'gasolier,' running on gas power.

'Is it a diesel?' Littleguy asked.

Nory suddenly remembered the bathrooms at the restaurant of the Ritz-Carlton hotel in San Francisco where she had gone to lunch one day with her parents. Each stall of the bathroom had a chandelier above it. She told Kira about it.

'Wow, your own personal chandelier,' said Kira. 'That's pretty incredible.'

Nory was quite content to have impressed her with a known fact about America.

45. The Bad Sister and the Good Sister

In the car home from Wimpole House, Kira licked Nory on her face, pretending to be one of the rare kinds of cow. Nory happened to be squeamish about being licked on the face and said, 'Kira, stop.'

'Let's not have any saliva games in the car, please,' called Nory's father from the front seat.

That made Kira stop, and instead she and Nory played a game in which you pass a little orange ball back and forth, and whoever has the ball has to tell the next part of the story. Kira started it off.

'Once,' she said, 'there was a good girl and a bad girl. They were identical sisters. One day the bad girl decided to play a trick on the good girl. This trick was . . .' And Kira passed the orange ball to Nory.

'Oh dear, I've come unbuckled,' said Nory, fixing her seatbelt. 'Okay, the trick was for the bad girl to put her foot down on the girl's dress in a very fancy party that she was going to suggest to her mom that they have. She was spoiled and knew as a matter of course that her mom would agree. If she stepped on her good sister's dress, her good sister would be embarrassed in front of everyone and be very upset. And so . . .' Nory passed the ball to Kira.

'So the mother let them do it,' said Kira, and gave the ball back to Nory.

'Let them have a big garden party,' said Nory, and passed the ball back to Kira.

'Have a huge garden party,' said Kira. 'But there was one desperate problem, and that problem was . . .'

'That it was raining on the day they were going to have the garden party,' said Nory.

'So they decided to have the party inside,' said Kira. 'But there was another problem as well. The bad little girl, whose name was . . .'

'Kuselda,' said Nory.

'Kuselda,' said Kira, 'was feeling rather sick. And the party went like this.'

'The first part was successful,' said Nory. 'The good little girl was fussed over, everyone was nice to her, she was superb. Everything went well, until the bad girl decided that she would stagger out and she would still carry out with her plan. She suggested a dance, saying, "Of course I have to be with my beloved sister." And the sister said . . .'

'The sister said, "All right," ' said Kira. 'And they had the dance. But when Krusella was just about to do it, something else happened.'

'What happened was,' said Nory, 'the bad girl felt horribly sick. She felt so sick and faint she was almost too weak to press down hard enough with her foot on the dress. And yet she still decided she would try. But the mother, thinking it wasn't intentional, called out, "Careful Kruselda, don't step on your sister's dress, you're about to." '

'So Kruselda had to not carry out her plan that night,' said Kira. 'But will she carry it out later? Find the answer.'

'She decided firmly she would,' said Nory. 'She had made a plan and she was going to carry it out. She was so angry that she didn't get to do it all that night she couldn't sleep, and she was so tired that . . .'

'She couldn't get up for a week,' said Kira. 'Her plan almost slipped out of her mind, but at the end of the week, constantly thinking about how she could get revenge, she decided to . . .'

'Not only step on her good sister's dress,' said Nory, 'but somehow make her good sister's hair come out of place and fluff up, in such a way that the good sister wouldn't know it happened, just before she went out, so she would look just dreadful, and it would be just as well as she stepped on her dress.'

Kira whispered to Nory, 'You still have to say *when* she would do this and *how* she would do this. Would she have another party, or what?'

'But she didn't know how to do carry out her plan,' said Nory. 'Then she finally thought of it. She'd have to . . .'

'Have another party,' said Kira. 'But this time everyone was supposed to come all dressed up so you couldn't guess who they were. If you guessed who a person was, the person had to . . .'

'Duck for apples!' said Nory. 'And that would be pretty embarrassing at such a fancy wonderful party . . .'

'Because you had to stick your head in the water,' said Kira.

'And because,' said Nory, 'the water would have food coloring in it, that made your face turn a awful color of pale green for a day, which would be extremely embarrassing, for this was a very rich and dignified family. So the bad girl asked her mom, who said sternly . . .'

' "Yes," ' said Kira.

'The bad girl sang a carol at the first part,' said Nory, 'just to make herself more popular. A goose could have sang it better than she did. She sang it like a wild chicken.'

'Then the dance was to begin,' said Kira. 'The two sisters, not knowing each other of course, because they had chosen different outfits deliberately and not telling each other what they were being and what they would look like, chose themselves. They danced with each other.' And then Kira whispered her advice to Nory: 'The bad girl has to fall.'

'First their steps went quickly,' said Nory, nodding. 'The good girl, Emmerine, had swift lovely steps. But the bad girl, Kruselda's steps were big and bulgy, slow and ugly steps. They danced on together for a long time, until Kruselda finally remembered what she was to do. She was just about to do it, but there was a corner of the rug that was flipped back. She tripped on the rug, fell on her chin, and made her nose be an awful shape, which looked so awful and swollen that no one wanted to look at her for the rest of the day, so she decided to sing . . .'

'But then decided no, she would not sing,' said Kira, quite strongly. 'Instead her mask and fake hair came off, and everyone knew who she was and she had to . . .'

'Duck for apples!' said Nory. 'She ducked and ducked and ducked, but her face was so dirty and ugly from the beginning that it turned an awful red, and . . .'

'No one would look at her and she was in disgrace,' said Kira. 'And she learned to be nicer. The . . .'

'The Dog was important to the story, too,' said Nory, because she didn't want to say, 'end,' which Kira of course wanted her to say.

'No, the end,' said Kira.

'The end!' sang Nory. 'The end—the end, the end, the end, oh way-ay-end! And then—and then—and then and then and then and then and THEN!'

'Then that was the end,' said Kira.

Nory's parents called out 'Nice story' from the front.

'I have a story to tell!' said Littleguy, waving his hands in his car seat. 'It's about two girls and it's the story you telled. There are two good girls. One's bad and one's good. They cide to to something. The end.'

'I like it, good,' said Nory.

'But it's not the end,' said Littleguy. 'There's something they had to make up, their momma said they can make marshmellons, they cide to make something, and it's something they made. They made two engines, the Flying Scotsman and the Mallard. Steam engines! And there was something in the party. It was a double-decker jelly cake, a double-decker bus, to eat. Like a double-decker bus. When it went in the sun, it rolled out, it drived, when it was on the grass it drove!'

'A double-decker jelly cake,' said Nory, 'Good story, Littleguy.'

'Not quite yet,' said Littleguy. 'It's a big digger, the scooper, scooper, it goes, kksssh, scooper, scooper, digger. And then there was a big thing there, a dumptruck, auger driller, a front loader.'

'Yay, good story,' said Nory.

'Not quite yet,' said Littleguy. 'And there was something in the story, once upon a time, I have another story, I have another story too! Another story!'

'Okay, just one more story,' called Nory's mother.

'Once upon a time were two flat holes, and there was a big digger truck came over and ran over they, and got dirty dirt on they. They washed their feeties and eyes and toesies and they were all clean, the end.'

They dropped Kira off at her house and the outing was over.

46. Marks

About a week later the Threll School stopped for a vacation. Nory and Pamela shook hands, as if to say, 'We made it.' Kira went with her family to a place nearby London, so they didn't see each other. Guy Fawkes Day happened during the break. There was a huge enormous bondfire and life-size models of Guy Fawkes were thrown into the bondfire. Nory was expecting the models to be little voodoo dolls of Guy Fawkes, not huge floppy heavy dolls the size of people, but life-size was how they did it. Guy Fawkes was a strongly Catholic man who had snuck barrel after barrel of gunpowder down into the basement, and he was just about to blow up the king when he was caught. So they burnt Guy Fawkes in a bondfire and now they have fireworks to celebrate that. Guy Fawkes Day is much more important a holiday in England than Halloween. Possibly they first chopped off Guy Fawkes's head then burned him in the bondfire, Nory wasn't clear on that, but that would certainly have been Nory's preference, because she was not attracted to the idea of being burned. In any case, he was severely punished, in a way the Aztecs would understand quite well. Nory burned her finger on a sparkler in the backyard after the fireworks were over, because the metal got remarkably hot. The skin turned white where it was singed but it felt better when she put an ice cube on it.

No letter from Debbie came in the mail during break, but something else did: Nory's marks. At International Chinese Montessori School they didn't have marks at all, just a special conference with Nory sitting there with her parents. The teachers always said this and that: 'Eleanor, oh, yes: bright, nice girl, talks too much, though, and she has to work harder on her spelling.' The principal, Xiao Zhang, translated for the Chinese teacher, since Nory's parents didn't understand Chinese. There was never a piece of paper with marks on it that said good or bad, the way there turned out to be at Threll school. Threll sent out a sheet of paper with a list of Nory's different classes and a set of boxes for either Excellent, or Good, or Satisfactory, or Weak, or Poor. Nory got all checkmarks for Satisfactory, except for one Good, in History. No Excellents whatever. She was a little disappointed not to get a Good in Classics because she had liked that class more than all the others and listened like a demon when Mr. Pears read to them. But she was relieved because she had been very worried that she was going to get a Weak in French because the French was completely refusing to stick in her head. Her goal for the year, she decided, was never ever to get a Weak or a Poor. But still, she was a tiny bit sad about English, because she thought her story about the girl and the dog wasn't just a drab old Satisfactory. It wasn't just the minimum you had to do, it was actually somewhat above the bare necessities and was possibly in the Good category.

But probably the objection for Mrs. Thirm was that Nory was supposed to write a shorter story that she would finish, and instead she'd written a longer one that ended with TO BE CONTINUED, and also of course her spelling was a disgrace-and-a-half, although Nory's father said Nory spelled better than anyone did a thousand or two thousand years ago, because back then they had about eight different ways to spell every English word, and people just chose whichever way they felt like. They would say, 'Today I think I'll spell *chair* as *chayer* and tomorrow *chayrre* and the day after that, hmm, *chaier* might be nice, and the day after that I think it will be *chere*.' Now it had to be *chair* every time, no matter what mood you were in.

47. Three Forbidden Words

One other reason Nory might have only gotten a Satisfactory and not a Good in English was that it turned out that Mrs. Thirm was not terribly fond of 'nice' and 'then' and 'said.' When they went back to school after break Mrs.

Thirm told them that from then on they had to try whenever they could not to use 'nice' or 'then' or 'said' in their assignments, because they were extremely overused and she was tired of seeing them in their books. Nory felt a little discombobbledied at hearing that, because she used 'nice' and 'then' and 'said' quite often. There were only so many different ways you could say, 'he laughed,' 'she giggled,' 'he answered,' 'they whispered,' and so forth and so on, before you suddenly felt, 'Okay, ladies and jellyfish, it's time to go back to good old *she said.*' And without 'then' Nory had to use 'the following day' or 'the next thing that happened was' or 'later that week' or 'Three days passed,' which were fine, but so was 'then.'

Also Mrs. Thirm turned out to not like rhymes in poems, and the poems Nory had written for her had a fair amount of rhymes. One of her poems was:

I Went to a Poor Man's House

I went to a poor man's House yes,
The First thing I did was to Look at the poor man's Dress yes,
The second thing I did was to look at the Horrible big mess yes,
The Third thing I Did was to stand up and confess yes
'What a Horrible Big Mess' yes.
The Poor man looked down at the Horrible big mess yes
And spoke up But did not confess but merely said 'yes'!

Another one was:

Please Don't Frighten Little Birdies Away

Proud people walk through
The little Birdies' Feast.

And make them fly away.
And make it so they
Can not come back to where
They could have played
All day So please don't
Frighten the little birdies
Away.

The poem she wrote most recently for Mrs. Thirm was:

I am trapped in a waterfall
And can hear the singing fishermen's call,
But through the waves and
In a dark and gloomy cave,
I am enjoying what the world gave.

Basically all of Nory's poems had rhymes in them somehow or other. And then Mrs. Thirm suddenly said: 'I particularly don't like poems that rhyme, but it's just a matter of opinion.' She told everyone, 'It's so difficult, there's really no point.' Nory raised her hand to suggest that one thing you could do would be to make a list of all the words that are rhyming words, which would make finding the rhymes a lot easier.

'Yes, yes,' said Mrs. Thirm, 'but it's such a waste of time to make the list, and then you're right back where you started, aren't you?' So Nory's poems were not exactly the poems Mrs. Thirm would have naturally preferred. She was still perfectly nice about them, though. She didn't gnaw her teeth and say 'Not more disgusting rhymes!' Teachers in England weren't like teachers in America writing 'Great Job!' and 'This is a gem of a story, Eleanor!' and whatnot, and stamping cat-chasing-a-ball-of-yarn stamps around on the page—they just made a quiet checkmark to prove that they'd seen what you did and sometimes corrected the spelling in the margin. Once in a great while they wrote 'Good' or 'Excellent prep.' They weren't as emotional.

The complete and total ban on 'said' and 'then' and 'nice' was hard for Nory, though, and it got harder. Poetry they didn't do that much of in class, but they did unquestionably do a fair amount of story-writing, and Nory would sit writing her story and come to a place where she needed to say, 'he said' and she would spend five minutes trying to figure out a way not to say it, and by then the thing she had in mind to write next had disappeared in a chuff of steam, as Littleguy would say. Sometimes she would even write the 's' of 'said' and then think, 'Oh, I'm too tired, I just can't possibly go through the effort of pulling the top off the ink eradicator at this moment,' and so she would try to imagine a word that began with 's' but wasn't 'said,' like 'he smiled' or 'he smirked' or 'he shouted.' But then whatever it was that 'he' did changed his personality totally and he became this very unaturally smiley or smirky and shouting person that didn't fit in with the story. Another thing you could do was change the comma to a period and change the 'h' into a capital 'h' and then go on with a new sentence about what he was doing. Say as an example you by mistake wrote:

'Mmm, this coliflower looks delishous,' he s

You're all the way to the 's' of 'said' and suddenly you remember, 'Oh no, I've done it again, Mrs. Thirm said no *he said*!' Well, then just go around and around the comma with the point of your pen, turning it into a big and very circular and very confident period, and then just change the lower-case 'h' to a capital 'H,' which is easy to do since you just have to straighten out the rounded part of the 'h' and make the short part long—and then have him doing something casually beginning with 's.' So it would become:

> 'Mmm, this coliflower looks delishous.' He spooned out a large amount for him self and breathed-in the steem.

That was just an example. But that way of solving it also could cause confusion in the story because often it worked out that when you read it out loud to people you couldn't tell who was talking and it sounded jerky. That was why it drove Nory totally bonkers to have the ban on 'said.'

As for 'nice,' well, yes, Nory did use 'nice' a lot, quite frankly. But 'nice' was a very, very important word for kids in fifth year, which is fourth grade in America, and it was important to the younger kids of Littleguy's age as well, and kids in general, because if you think about a kid's language, it can mean about eighty million different things. You can say a person is nice or a school is nice or a way of spending an afternoon is nice. It's not as definite as 'fun'—say a few things went wrong in your afternoon, so it wasn't completely and frolickingly 'fun' but it was still a very 'nice' afternoon. Or say Littleguy made a drawing of the Lord of the Isles, a distinguished steam engine, and gave it to Nory as a present. So basically two little circles and a big circle and some driving bars. If you said, 'Oh, Littleguy, that's very *kind* of you,' it could almost sound a little sarcastic, or too fancy, but if you said 'Oh, Littleguy, that's so nice of you,' you were saying what you intended to say. If you said a person at school was very kind, you could just mean that they were very kind to you, and yet maybe you wouldn't say they were very nice because for some reason you didn't want to be with them because they had a different set of interests or maybe they were not very kind to some other person, like Pamela. And furthermost, it was the exact word that kids used, and Nory was writing conversation that kids had, so she would come to a point in the sentence where obviously the word that the child would tend to use was 'nice' and she would suddenly remember, 'Alert, alert, no "nice" allowed' and she would be ready to tear her hair out by the roots.

Actually Nory wouldn't be ready to tear her hair out by the roots because it was almost impossible to tear out your hair, from Nory's point of view, either by the roots or by the bare tips, because you would pull on one big grab of hair, but only some of that would come out, since you never have quite as much of a grip on the whole thing. And besides you can't have the willpower to pull hard enough to make it all come ripping out like a plot of grass. You could of course cut your hair so that it looks like it's been teared out if you want to be included in a chapter in one of those books that include all the amazing, but luckily untrue, things in the world. That would be 'tearing your hair' to some extent. But the only time Nory ever pulled even one hair out was not when she was going crazy over something like having to not use 'nice' in her prep, but when she was thinking very very carefully about something, and as she was thinking she would anonymously take a tiny piece of hair in her fingers and pull at it ever so very slightly, testing how much pulling it could take. Sometimes possibly one hair would finally go *poink* and come out but that was it, nothing drastic.

48. Another Bad Thing That Happened to Pamela

Thomas Mottle's hair was cut straight as a pin in back, so that when he walked it moved with a bobbing motion. He was a chorister, like Roger Sharpless, and he looked like such a pearl of a boy, but really inside he was the kiss of the devil, basically. And one day, which wasn't the finest of days anyway, Thomas Mottle did something to Pamela that made Nory want to tear out some of *his* hair, it made her so steamingly angry. It began as a good day because Nory and Kira got into a state of herorious giggling by pretending to worship Nory's almighty ink eradicator, after Nory got it to balance upright on the table. Actually Nory laughed before Kira noticed, but quite quickly they were laughing the exact same amount, and the funny thing was that Kira hadn't seen Nory do the thing that was actually funny, she only heard Mrs. Thirm say 'Nory, what may I ask are you doing?' Nory had been bowing her head in worship before the ink eradicator and then she and Kira starting saying, 'No, no, no, no, you can only worship one god,' so they pretended to attack it and punch it without their hands touching it, because they didn't want to knock it over.

That was extremely fun, as you can imagine, but then the bad part of the day was that Mrs. Thirm gave them a Mental Maths test in which Nory got one answer right out of fifteen. Mrs. Thirm was saying the multiplication problems aloud very fast in a way Nory didn't understand, since English people say double-naught or triple-three sometimes when they mean 'zero zero' or 'oh oh' or 'three

three three'—let alone when they say 'M-I-double-S-I-double-P-I' for the spelling of Mississippi, which always tempted Nory to want to write a letter d for 'double' or a number two, depending on whether it was numbers or letters, that is. Mrs. Thirm was doing something similar, but not exactly that, and Nory couldn't conceivably figure out what in the Blue Blazers Mrs. Thirm was asking the class to do—so bingo, one right answer out of fifteen in Mental Maths, which is not a very good record. So that made it not the finest of days. And then after lunch along came Thomas Mottle.

The bothering of Pamela was continuing steadily anyway, and getting worse. It had progressed to the stage of barking Pamela's shins. But the kids who did it were clever kickers and never did anything when a teacher would catch sight. 'Barking your shin' is what it was called because it's as if the bark came off. In other words, the skin was scraped. Pamela told Nory about it but she only saw it with her own eyes a few times, because they didn't do it when Nory was there.

Then that afternoon Nory watched Thomas Mottle sneak up behind Pamela and kick her very viciously in the back of the leg and then try to dash off. He was probably thinking he would disappear as quick as lightning, which is what the boys would normally do. Naturally Pamela fell down and her books splattered out on the path. She turned bright red this time, and she cried a little, too. Nory was a ways away with some other kids so she only saw it off from a distance, and she was on her way over to help Pamela, when one eighth of a second after Thomas kicked, Mrs. Hoadley, the science teacher, appeared from out of somewhere, and stepped up to the plate. Thomas Mottle saw her and completely changed. He was a different child.

Very purely and simply he helped Pamela up and picked up her books, one by one. By the time Nory got there she heard Mrs. Hoadley saying, 'Thank you *very* much, Thomas.' That was they way they acted, these blasted bullies—not just kicking someone in the shins, but then as soon as the teacher was on the spot, pretending to be sweet as pie, nicely helping the person.

'You should have told Mrs. Hoadley that Thomas was the very one who made you trip!' said Nory to Pamela. 'Now she probably thinks you tripped on your own two feet! You have to tell them!' But Pamela was still thoroughly mum's-the-word. That's why she was having the absolute worst year of her life, while Nory was having the absolute best year of her life, just about. A few people teased Nory about her accent or said she was ugly, but nobody would ever possibly dare to sneak up on her and kick her, because if someone kicked her, oh boy, she would be off like a rocket and chase them down and kick right back just as hard, and if they hid her jacket she would wring whoever's neck who hid it, and if somebody tried to capture her duffel-coat peg with their duffel-coat she would scrummage fiercely for it and get her duffel-coat peg back, no questions asked. But Pamela never fought. It was not her personality to fight, or if it was, they'd changed her personality bit by bit since the beginning of the year by being constantly awful to her. When Nory said to two of the kids, 'You better stop being mean to Pamela or she's going to tell Mr. Pears,' they just laughed, they didn't bother to stop, because they knew that Pamela wasn't going to Mr. Pears. She never had and never would. Again and again Nory said, 'Pamela, it would really be much better if you told somebody,' but she didn't want to at all. So no matter how much Nory wanted to take one of them by the scroll of the neck to Mr. Pears, she couldn't, since Mr. Pears would have a word with Mrs. Thirm, and so on and so on. So the bullying went its merry way.

Nory planned out things she could say to the people who were doing it, but words didn't really help because the boys kicked and then disappeared, and whatever insulting thing you wanted to say couldn't be said in time for the person you wanted to insult to be insulted. Nory did try to fight back at Thomas Mottle by calling him Cinderella's stepsister a few times, since one time in drama class Thomas had played the part of one of Cinderella's stepsisters, wearing a big blond wig. 'Just the sort of thing Cinderella's ugly stepsister would do,' Nory said to him.

'Hardly!' he said. And that was that.

49. Word-Fighting

Even Julia Sollen was a little shocked and a little bit nice to Pamela after she saw her being kicked by the revolting Thomas. If you hear that somebody took a kick at somebody, you just think, 'Oh, I see, that's bad.' But if you see it eye to eye, the sneakiness of it, the pure meanness of it, it is something quite else besides. Nory was furious to think that a kid could have a basic urge to kick in his impudent mind and then get away with doing it, just because he knew from his observations that Pamela wouldn't be the type of person to kick him back, so he was safe from punishment. Maybe there was so much constant kicking of shins in England because all the boys wanted to be footballers when they grew up. That was what they said that they wanted to be in class, anyway, except for a few kids like Roger Sharpless, who said that he wanted to go to

Durham and learn to make barometers. In football, which is actually soccer, you use your feet more than your hands, so you have all this practiced ability with your feet that you could easily use for barking up the wrong shin.

So a few of the kids were beginning to go over to Nory's side and be a little nicer to Pamela. And Roger Sharpless always had been nice to Pamela. However, Kira was still trying her hardest to get Nory to stop being Pamela's friend. She'd say things like, 'Nory, you do know, don't you, that you're the only person in the whole school who likes her.'

'I don't know if that's quite true,' said Nory.

'Yes, it is true,' said Kira. 'Nobody else is her friend, nobody.'

But Pamela did definitely have other friends from time to time. One time she waited a very long time to meet one of her friends who was in sixth year. Nory waited with her—Pamela said it was just a quarter of an hour they waited but Nory thought it was more like fifteen minutes. And even if Nory was the only one in the whole Junior School who was steadily Pamela's friend, that wasn't necessarily a *bad* thing, she thought. What in the world was so bad about being Pamela's one and only real friend?

Also, Nory liked being Pamela's friend, because she liked planning out with Pamela what kind of vicious attacks she could use to fight back for Pamela, and she admired that Pamela was good at maths, since if you were good at maths it allowed you to go on and do so many different things in science or dentistry, and she liked that Pamela had unusual aspects about herself, such as being double-jointed. Pamela couldn't use certain kinds of pens, she told Nory, because she was extremely double-jointed. Her thumb was a whole level further of being exposable than most normal people. She had to use a special other kind of pen. It looked like a simple everyday kind of medium-nib fountain pen to Nory, but she didn't say so. So there were surprising things like that about Pamela that Nory liked, and she also just liked Pamela's very hush-hush way of talking to you—Pamela always spoke very softly and had quite a lot to say but you had to listen very carefully because she only spoke to one person at a time and she was very particular about who she told things to, which in this old day and age is probably a good thing.

Nory's parents got extremely upset when they heard the news from Nory that Pamela was having an even worse time of it now than ever. They said that things had gotten utterly untolerable and something just had to be done. The mistreatment of Pamela was something that they personally had to go to Mr. Pears about, they said, or straight to Pamela's parents, because it simply couldn't be allowed to go on. Nory cried at the dinner table and said that it was Pamela's choice and nobody else's, and Pamela absolutely, definitely did *not* want the teachers or her parents to know, and she had made Nory promise, so please, please, please not yet. But Nory did promise to go to the teacher again herself, at least, and announce that physical shin-kicking was now going on. And her parents promised Nory, not exactly as a trade (since they wanted her to get one, too), but sort of as a trade, that she could have a gum-guarder. A gum-guarder was a thing you use to keep your teeth from getting knocked out. If a hockey stick whams into your mouth and you have a gum-guarder on you would get a fat lip, but no particular tooth would fall out. Nory wanted the gum-guarder because other kids had them and she thought it would make her feel stronger and more able to stop the bigger kids from being bad to Pamela, even when she wasn't wearing it. She could think, 'Aha, I have a powerful gum-guarder, nobody can bother me now!' Also she wanted to be sure that none of her teeth tumbled out onto the Astroturf. If you want to be a dentist your own teeth are kind of an advertisement of your work, and it's important that there is nothing strange about them, or people will say, 'Oh no, I won't go to that dentist to have my teeth fixed, because take a gander at hers.'

Nory went ahead and told Mrs. Thirm that she had a friend—a friend who was quite possibly the same friend as she had talked to her about before, who was now being—no question about it—bullied. Nory had promised her friend not to say what the exact bullying was, but 'Let's put it this way,' she said. 'It involves a boy's foot, and a shoe, and a shin, pure and simple.' Mrs. Thirm said, 'Thank you, Nory, it's good of you to let us know.'

Sometimes it was quite efficient to tell two boys, say, who were being bad to Pamela that they were 'imbecile-idiot-numbskull-nitwits,' saying the words super-fast, or tell them, 'Gee, I hope you don't sleep on your side at night, because your pea-brain might tumble out your ear.' But some of the older kids had a style of word-fighting that Nory couldn't do anything against, because it was just too confident. Pamela asked Nory one time to help fight back against an older girl named Janet who was constantly saying mean things about Pamela's cheeks. Nory said to the girl, 'Excuse me, would you please do me a favor and stop being mean to Pamela or take a long deep dip in a dump?'

The girl looked at Nory for about a minute and a half and said, 'Turn around, I don't like looking at your face.'

'Well,' said Nory, 'I don't like looking at your face!'

'If you don't like it, don't look at it,' said the girl.

'Well, if you don't like looking at my face *don't look at my face either*!' said Nory. The girl laughed and flossed off to the library because she fancied one of the librarians, a boy in seventh year, and the next time Pamela asked Nory to fight back with words against that girl Nory said, Gee, she could try, but she just didn't think she could do all that much against her, because the girl was so sure of herself and so able to think quickly in those kinds of tense moments.

50. The Core of the Friendship

In Geography they began doing the countries of Europe—in other words, Sweden, Denmark, Norway, Holland, Finland, Greenland, Iceland, Ireland, Scotland, Lapland, the UK or United Kingdom, and of course, not to be forgotten, England itself. Land after land. There were an amazing number of big and little lands all fitting nicely tucked together, and when you concentrated in on one, you tended to forget about the others, although there was just as much going on in them, too, every day of the week. And when you concentrated on all of them, the low countries and the high countries and the medium or 'mixed-traffic' countries, as Littleguy would call them (if he knew clearly what a country was), since he called a plain donut with chocolate frosting on top a 'mixed-traffic donut' on the idea that an engine like James the Red Engine that can pull either passenger cars or freight cars is a 'mixed-traffic engine'—when you concentrated on Belgium and Barcelona and whatnot (those are just examples), you forgot about America, something that you would think would not be all that easy to forget. One day Nory almost lost her geography book and had to take out everything from her backpack, looking for it. She found it, finally, but she also found, way down at the bottom, some Flake 99 wrappers and six old conkers. They were turning rotten. They were black in some places and white in other places and they were wet soggy things that when you touched them you wished you hadn't. They smelled extremely good, though, because they were becoming peat.

Nory missed playing with Kira under the conker tree, all those weeks ago—or not that many weeks, actually—and she had a feeling that she and Kira were not such good friends now as they had been then. Kira had something of an idea of being friends, true, but not the whole idea. A friendship was like the core of something, not a conker but something really basic like an apple, and there were all these things around it—the peel and the leaves and the wax they put on the peel to make it shiny, and whatnot. The shiny peel is a fun part, but the friendship has to go down and down into the very core, and Kira didn't seem to understand what that core should be. Or maybe she just had a different opinion of what it should be than Nory did. Nory believed that the core was not just to stick together and be friendly from time to time, as the case may be, and *definitely* not always to be in a competition every second, and not to just be tomboyishly friendly, but also to be able to empty your heart out to the person. Say, for instance, you had the horribly embarrassing secret that you were keeping inside that you really loved playing with Barbies, and you were afraid to tell anyone because boys, especially, not to mention some girls, are vicious about instantly making fun of anybody who likes Barbies and they laugh at you for liking them. To a real friend you could casually empty your heart out by saying, 'You know what? *I really like Barbies.*' And there would be no problem. They would be able to be trusted not only not to tell anybody but not to laugh at you, either. And a real friend, if you had another friend that people were being awful to, wouldn't say 'Stop being friends with that person, nobody else is friends with her, stay away from her.'

Mostly it was connected with Pamela. Kira was never directly mean to Pamela the way the other kids were. Then again, she was never directly nice to her either. But Pamela still didn't know how strict Kira was about things like not eating at the same table with her. It was probably a good thing she didn't know. When Pamela steered toward a table where Kira was sitting, Nory would say, 'Oh, er, Pamela, that table looks a little full, um, why don't we go to that other table over there?' And of course Kira when that happened would be furious that Nory would prefer to eat with Pamela at a separate table and not with her. But really it was Kira's choice, not Nory's, since Nory would have been happy as a horse to eat with them both if they got along together. One time Kira and Nory were walking to lunch together and Pamela came up to walk with them, and Kira said, 'Oh, Pamela, your backpack! You forgot to put away your backpack, better hurry back! Nory, we'll go on ahead! Hurry and put away your backpack, Pamela!'

'I don't absolutely *have* to put it away,' said Pamela.

'But you really ought to,' said Kira. 'It's so clumsy, really you shouldn't take it along. Go on and put it away, Pamela! Go on!'

'She doesn't have to if she doesn't want to, Kira,' said Nory, because she could see that Pamela's feelings were a ways down the path toward getting hurt.

Kira then grabbed Nory's arm and said, 'Come on, let's go.' But Pamela grabbed Nory's other arm and said, 'Stay, Nory, stay.' Both pulled, Pamela on one arm and Kira on the other arm, and they started circling around. It was almost fun. Then Kira gave up and asked Nory if she could borrow two p. Nory gave her the two p and Kira went off to be with Shelly and Daniella, and Nory went to lunch with Pamela.

'Does Kira secretly hate me as much as the others do?' asked Pamela.

Nory decided it wouldn't be such a smart idea to admit straight out that Kira didn't like Pamela, since she'd already made that mistake once before, and after all there was still plenty of ways Pamela could be hurt, even now. Even if Pamela basically knew something was true she didn't have to have it rubbed in her nose. So Nory said, 'You know, I don't understand Kira one bit. Sometimes she's as nice as a friend can be, and then sometimes she's so competitive about who is friends with who and who walks with who and who sits with who and bup bup bup bup bup bup bup bup bup. From how she reacts to me being friends with you I would say that she likes her friends to be only her friends and nobody else's, like she's got the copyright on that particular friend. She is so marvelously in awe of how other kids act that she can't think privately what would be the obviously right thing and draw her own conclusions.'

'I'll be very glad when we reach the end of term,' said Pamela.

Nory was suddenly reminded of something she had thought of in the mirror brushing her teeth. 'You know what we should do?' she said. 'Okay, you don't want to tell the teachers or your parents. But we could still write a book about your whole experience, every good or bad thing that somebody did, Thomas kicking you in the shin, hogging your duffel peg, every single thing. We could make a timeline, first this happened, then that happened.'

Pamela shook her head fiercely. 'It isn't something that I want to think about any more than I have to.'

'Oh, but think about it: you would be thinking about it not in the unhappy way of having it just anonymously happen to you, but in the way of telling it,' Nory said. 'And then other kids could read it and know what happened, the story of one girl, or two friends. We could do it together.'

'I can't imagine that it would interest people, and I wouldn't dream of doing it,' said Pamela. 'I like to write about nice things.'

'Okay,' said Nory, 'how about—not a book about the present, but a book about the future. Say when we're both eighteen and we go off to college and have adventures.'

Pamela gave it a second of thought and nodded. 'Okay,' she said, 'but I can only come up with the adventures because I'm double-jointed and don't particularly like writing as it hurts my thumb. But I'll give you hints for some of the adventures. For instance, we could visit a live volcano together and have an adventure. I once visited a live volcano.'

'That's perfect!' said Nory. 'What name do you want for yourself?'

'Claudia,' said Pamela.

Before bed Nory wrote the first page of the book, which was called 'The Adventures of Sally and Claudia.'

The Adventures of Sally and Claudia

'Mom I'll need my file as well,' Claudia screamed up the stairs. In her freshly washed uniform, she looked as if she was going to a disco rather than Oxford University. She was 18 very smart, and especially keen on maths and the study of vulcanos. She had only just left Threll Senior School and missed it alot and so she might as she had started there when she was in year six and never missed a year. One of the reasons she missed it so much was because of her best friend Sally who had been her friend from her first day at Threll School to her last.

Sally was a very tall girl who was extreamely interested in dentestry and was American. She was know going to Stanford University while her brother borded at Threll School and was a prephect. He was taking a class in model bildiung, where he was bilding a large balsa wood model of the Mallard, which as many are aware is a preticular kind of high speed steam traine. For this whol life he had been interested in everything about traines and it looked as if that woud continue into his double-digets.

If Claudia only knew that Sally was sitting at a table even now and thinking about her, while she did her studying! Claudia was still thinking about Sally as she set off for school on the wet path with her hair sopping wet because of the rain.

As she reached school she could almost see Sally as she had been in Year Six in her school, she felt she could give anything to see Sally agin. So did Sally, who was now hard at work writing a letter to Claudia It went like this:

Dear Claudia,

I miss you so much and think about you every day. I had a maths exam today and I did all right but I could have done better if I hade seen you befor. How are things in England?

Love,
Sally, your friend

TO BE CONTINUED. . . .

Nory showed the page to Pamela the next day, and Pamela read it over twice carefully. 'One very important thing you should know is that here we don't say *Mom,* we say *Mum,* and we spell it with a *u,*' Pamela said. 'And I think you shouldn't describe Claudia by her interests, but by how she looks. You probably should rewrite the beginning including a bit more about her appearance.' That was Pamela's complete reaction. She didn't say 'Good,' or 'Nice try,' or 'Well done,' or anything like that. (If you fell or dropped something, sometimes the boys would call out, 'Well done!')

Nory thought to herself, 'If you don't want to write it, Pamela, fine, but don't refuse to help write it and then tell *me* to rewrite it. I did the best I could.' But maybe Pamela was a little embarrassed by the mention of the two of them being best friends, since they'd never actually talked about being best friends.

They chatted about the book quite a number of times after that, but the first page was the one and only page that got written down. Oh well.

51. The Wind

Mostly Nory and Pamela spent more and more time together at school as friends. Actually at times there were four friends total, since Pamela had an I.F. named Leyla (I.F. stands for Imaginary Friend), and Nory thought it would be a friendly gesture to have an I.F. herself, too. She thought for a long time and came up with Penny Beckinsworth as her new I.F. She liked the name Penny, and Beckinsworth sort of sounded like a person you would think was worth beckoning for. She made up a song that she sang to the rhythm of 'She'll be coming round the mountain': *Penny Beckinsworth I reckon is a friend. Penny Beckinsworth I reckon is a friend. Penny Beckinsworth I reckon. Penny Beckinsworth I reckon. Penny Beckinsworth I reckon is a friend.* But Nory had never been too good at keeping up with imaginary friends. For example, if you write an I.F. a letter, you never get one back, unless you write it, too, which takes some of the fun out of it. On weekends in particular, Nory sometimes missed having someone real over to play with. Just simply to play with, period, end of discussion. It hadn't happened very much this year, strangely enough. Her parents were happy to watch her perform a play in which she dressed up Littleguy as a dog or a swan or an airplane engineer, and they were happy to listen to a story she had made up or play Battleship with her, and Battleship was quite fun, even when you were hit, because you could think up a new way to say you were hit, such as 'Ouch, I seem to have developed a yawning hole in my forecastle,' or 'Yikes, hoist out the rubber dinkies, she's a-going down!' But it wasn't the same as having your very own friend over to play. Littleguy also missed his best friend from school in Palo Alto. His new friend Jack spit onto the steam engines and that was not good to do, he said. But he had a different friend, Oliver, who he said was 'a very nice shy boy.' Littleguy had gotten into the usual habit of walking up to a stranger in the toystore and saying, 'Hello, I'm shy.'

Nory played some with her dolls but she was desperate just to have another nice girl her age in her room. Pamela refused to give Nory her phone number because she said she wasn't supposed to give out vital information such as her phone number unless her parents said it was okay, and she kept forgetting to ask them if it was okay. Her number was ex-directional, which means that you can't get it by calling 192. 192 sounds like it would be the same as 911 in America but actually it's the same as 411. Nory had Kira's number but she and Nory were not getting along all too well. They had just enough of a shred of friendship left to want the other person to act the way they wanted them to, rather than just not caring.

On Sunday afternoon Nory's mother took Nory and Littleguy to a playground near the Cathedral. There was a nice little child who was Littleguy's age for him to play with, but as usual, no child Nory's age. Nory's mother went over to supervise Littleguy on the slide, and Nory swang on the swings, which always made her feel lonely feelings unless there were tons of other people swinging on them, and then she sat anonymously on the bench. She started flipping through a catalog that her mother had brought along. There was a wind that day, and Nory liked the wind. Whenever she had a chance in a drawing or a painting, she included a tree with long flexible branches being blown by the wind, because it was one of her favorite things to paint or draw in all art. She noticed the pages of the catalog rustling and thought, 'I know, I can try being friends with the wind!'

She held the catalog open on her lap. She asked the wind, 'So what do you think, do you think I'd look good in this dress?' And the wind would either turn the page or not turn the page, or rattle the page a little without completely turning it. If the wind didn't turn the page, it meant yes, it liked the dress. If the wind only rattled the page, it meant that it still hadn't reached a decision. And if it did turn the page, Nory would look at the new page and say, 'Oh, so you think I'd look good in that dress? How interesting. I'm not so sure, but maybe.' The wind was not all that chatty, but it seemed nice and it had definite ideas about the fashions Nory should wear. That was kind of fun, although it had something of a lonely feeling to it, too.

That night Nory had a bad dream, not horrible, but not exactly enjoyable. It came to her probably because the light in her bathroom had burnt out again and it was windy, which meant that squeakings kept coming from outside. She dreamed her winding way through old dark and deserted buildings and found a room where there was a giant ring of black metal, with black metal hooks all the way around it. She knew they were the hooks you use in a slaughterhouse, where you would hang up the meat. The ring was turning, slowly, but it looked as if nobody was in the building except Nory. That was the frightening thing.

She got up and paddled into her parents' bedroom and asked them if it was morning, or if it wasn't morning could she possibly read because she'd had a scary dream. They lifted their heads and croaked out that they were sorry she'd had a scary dream but everything was all right and yes, she could read. She went back into her room and turned on the light to read some of *Puppies in the Pantry.* Then she stopped reading and remembered a really good speech at Cathedral service. Mary, Jesus's mother, had been frightened and someone told her, Do not be frightened, the Lord is using you as his servant, and we all must do as Mary did and strive to serve the Lord and be helpful to him. 'I will strive to serve the Lord, I will strive to serve the Lord,' Nory said to herself, and when she had said it she felt infinitely happier and smiled her way deep down into the pillow and closed her eyes. Before she went back to sleep, she had a strong wish to tell a quick story to herself about a girl who met a princess. Nobody had anything else for her to do, since it was plum in the middle of the night, so that's what she did.

52. A Story About a Girl Who Meets a Princess

It was a bright, sunny day in May. A girl, by the side of a large creek, sang. She was happy and playing. She was totally content. She was an orphan; she lived on the street, or places like that. She ate wheat straight from the kernel, and whatever she could find in her wanderings. Except meat, which she did not care for.

She was not very big for her age. She was what's known as a small, young girl, to most people. To herself, she was not young at all. She was very smart and had lived awhile. She had no recollection of what had happened in her younger days, but when she was ten years old, she got her dog, a big golden retriever. He was the person she looked after, and he looked after her. He was the person she knew best in the world. She loved him. He came along wherever she went. They were content.

Now she was in her thirteenth year, with jet black hair that hung in huge sausage curls down her back, which were tied up at night with long grass peels, and were wetted by pure lake water. Her hair was as gleamy and fresh-looking as ever. And when she tied it up with grass, she was careful to put basil in it, that would take the odors from the wet lake away from it, and make it smell so good you would want to just take one of the locks and eat it—maybe. She had never thought of doing that, but other people must have.

And now, she was playing. Playing, singing, and finding conkers, throwing them across the country to her beloved dog, Flame. He would jump and collect them, and run back with them. It was wonderful. He would be very careful not to miss the conker, for if he did, it could fall into the lake, and then he would not be able to have a conker, or a horse chestnut. We'll call them conkers. Real chestnuts were harder to get, for though the horse chestnuts came in spikey shells, they were not so spikey that you couldn't get them out. The chestnut shell was so spikey that you had to stamp on it. And when you tried to get the chestnut out after the shell was cracked open, it still could prick your finger. So the dog was being very careful not to lose them in the lake. And indeed he was good at jumping and catching them. He caught them almost every time.

Suddenly something awful happened. She threw the conker and it hit a tree, which rumbled and shook. Tons of conkers fell on the poor dog. She'd hit the largest conker in the largest conker tree, so that it had made the branch shake and all the fresh conkers in it fall all over poor Flame. Oh, how it bruised him, for they were huge ripe conkers. The girl picked up every single one. 'Oh, I'm so sorry,' she said. 'I'm so sorry.' Then Flame rolled over and they laughed together. That would be a good dinner for them, all those conkers. They were not very tasty on their own, but she found that if she let them sit in the sun all day, then put some parsley in, which grew very near by, mixed it with corn, and then added a bit of pepper in, it made a good dinner for them. Pepper was hard to buy, but she could get a job, whenever she wanted, and work, and buy some. As soon as she had enough to get the pepper she would say, 'Thank you very much,' keep on working for a while, and then go off.

As she picked the conkers up under the tree, she noticed something. There in the grass was a large purse of blue silk, with ruffles on it. Inside it were a number of precious things like a silver brush, and a tiny sewing kit, with scissors in the shape of a bird, and spools of gold and silver thread, and thimbles and needles so bright you could see them a mile away. She wanted to confiscate that purse, but she knew she could not. Just then, a ringing bell charmed in her ear. She looked up. What she saw was nothing but a lovely princess about her age.

The princess had neatly, neatly brushed hair. Her hair was in thick curls, and it was yellow. Shiny yellow hair. The girl loved the sight of that hair. The princess's shoes were fancy and her dress, oh her dress, it was the most beautiful lavishing color of blue—turquoise blue. It was a lovely blue. Puffy sleeves, so gorgeous, and it reached down at her ankles. And little roses at the end. It was puffy beyond belief!

'Hello,' the princess said quietly. 'What's your name?'

'Oh, ah, um, uh—' The girl was speechless. She was dressed thoroughly in rags and did not think it was a good idea to talk to this distinctive person. But then she thought she must answer. She didn't have a name, though, she'd never had one. What *was* her name? she wondered. 'Ah, mm, I don't have one,' she said finally, stuttering. 'Um, your majesty,' she said. For the princess was obviously of royal vintage.

'Hah, don't bother about it,' the princess laughed. 'Don't bother. I'm not very much a relative of the Queen, you see. My dad's brother was related to the Queen so I trace back from the Queen, yes, it's true, but not really closely . . .' she said.

'Oh wow,' said the girl. 'But, please—your name?'

'Oh, um, just call me, um, just call me—' The princess seemed to be thinking, too. 'Just call me, well, most people call me Mademoiselle Saram Shi-Kah, but just call me Shee, for Shee-Kah.'

'All right, Shee,' the girl said. 'Shee, how is it spelled?'

'Oh, Shee,' she said, 'well, it's spelled as She is normally spelled.'

'And, and how is that?' The girl looked a little scared.

'Well, to be quite honest,' the Princess said, 'it could be spelled "she" but that's probably not how it's spelled. To be quite honest, I've never thought of it. I think I'd like it if you'd spell it, S-h-e-e. Notice the doubled e.'

'Oh, right,' the girl said, 'Of course. And—what does an "e" look like?'

The Princess took the ruffled purse that the girl handed her and opened it up. In it she found the most beautiful notepad, with lovely marbled silk outside, and if you lifted the silk off there was beautiful Chinese paper, embroidered. 'Do you like it?'

'Oh yes,' the girl said.

The princess wrote down a lovely 'e'—the kind of 'e' that only princesses would learn how to write. It was a gorgeous letter. 'That's how I write it. But you know some people write it this way.' She gripped her pen; it was a lovely quill pen, too—a blue one to match her outfit—and wrote a smaller 'e,' not as fancy.

It seemed ordinary to the girl. 'Yes, yes, that's the one I'd be able to write,' she said.

'Right,' the princess nodded. 'That's the one that most people write. But impress people with this one,' she said, pointing to the one that she'd drawn first. 'It's really fun. It makes you seem so royal,' she said. 'What would you like me to call you?'

'Well, um, well, I think my last name is . . .'

'Oh, come on, don't tease me,' the princess said laughing, with a whiff of her hand. 'You have to have a name.'

'Well, I, er, don't,' she said. 'You see, I'm, um, er, call me, um, Sorsumpon . . .' She tried to make up a name. 'That's what you should call me.'

'Where does that name come from?' the princess asked.

'Um—my brain,' the girl said nodding. 'I don't have a name. I'm a servant, I'm a peasant girl, an orphan,' she said. 'And, well, I don't have a name at all. I wish I did, though. If you'd like, I'll tell you what I'd like to be—actually, I think what I'd like is, call me Sally. It's a nice name, I like it. It's the only one I know,' she confessed.

Then she talked the grownup way, the way she loved to talk, the way that she didn't talk when she was scared. The more mature way, not the scared, childish way, but the grownup way—she spoke: 'Now would you care to have some fresh conkers cooked in the heat of the sun?' she asked.

'Oh,' said the princess nodding. 'I, I'd love to. But I must return to the castle. Please come with me. Oh, but wait, I can't go in the dining room with my hair like this.' She touched one of her beautiful curls. 'I just can't, I can't go in with my hair curled. Oh, why can't mine be straight like yours?'

'I was just thinking why can't mine be curly like yours?' the girl said.

'Oh, you wouldn't want curly hair,' the princess said. 'You'd be too embarrassed to go into a dining room with it.'

'I'll switch hairstyles with you,' said the girl. 'I'll tell you how I keep it down—because I used to have somewhat frilly hair—and you tell me how you keep it up.'

'All right,' said the princes. 'I just tie it up every day with silk bows. Oh, but you wouldn't have any, would you?' And she handed the girl five silk bows, one blue, one red, and one TO BE CONTINUED.

53. Good Result

The very next day two unusually wonderful things happened. First, Nory was the lucky getter of a letter. The mail in Threll was delivered by men on bicycles with big red packs strapped to their handlebars, and it came early in the morning, before breakfast-time. Littleguy brought the envelopes into the kitchen, saying 'Mail livery! Mail livery!' Nory's father stopped singing to the microwave and said, 'Something for you, Nory.' She read it:

> Dear Eleanor,
>
> How are you? Ive been making lots of strange things with FIMO latley, including tarts pies and cakes. I miss you too. I wish I could pay a visit but that's not even a possibilility. So when are you coming back? Ms. Beryl is moving away so Ms. Fisker is coming back, maybe!!! I won second place in the soccer turnemint. Love from your friend, Deborah.

'Aw, that's so nice,' Nory said, folding the letter to herself. It made her suddenly strongly love Debbie and miss her, and made her think, 'How could I be letting such a good friend trickle away from my thinking just because there's so much going on here in England?' She hummed Ji Gong, the song about the crazy monk, on the way to school, looking down at her feet and remembering every detail about Debbie and her panda collection, and she thought about going back to school at the International Chinese Montessori School, and of how fun it was to know Chinese and to be able to point out to her parents some Chinese characters on the sidewalk in Chinatown that said something like 'Warning, telephone here' in orange paint.

Then, Wonderful Event Number Two, at school: towards the end of the day, Mrs. Thirm came up to Nory outside and said, 'I'd like to give you this.' It was a small piece of paper with a seal on it and a signature.

'Thank you,' said Nory, not by any means grasping what it was all about.

'It's a Good Result for being kind to Pamela,' Mrs. Thirm said.

Nory's face got a totally flabbledigastered look of complete amazement on it. She said, 'Wow, you're kidding, thank you, thank you!'

Nory only knew a little bit about Good Results. A Good Result was one of the best possible things you could ever get at the Junior School, higher than getting an Excellent, and if you got five of them in a row, you got a gift certificate to buy a special book of your choice. Good Results weren't too unusual, though, since quite a few of the girls had gotten them for different things, like for music or science projects or maths or handwriting. But still, Nory had never even come close to getting one, and she never knew that it was possible to get one for something like being nice to Pamela. She was standing in some mud in a dazzle-and-a-half of pure delight, when Mr. Pears came up to her and pointed to the piece of paper and sort of gave her a wink and said, 'That's my favorite kind of Good Result, for kindness.'

'Thank you,' Nory said. She was in a state of triumph, pleased out of her gourd, and she hopped up and down and told everyone who was nearby her, 'I got my first Good Result, I got my first Good Result!'

'Really?' said Shelly Quettner. 'What for?'

'For being kind to Pamela,' Nory said. But then she thought, 'Oops,' because it didn't feel quite right to tell. On the other hand, she wanted to tell everyone, because it proved without a doubt that if you went against the bad things that kids were doing a good thing could unexpectedly happen to you when you least expect it. She ran over to Kira.

'Kira, I got a Good Result for being nice to Pamela!' she said.

'You didn't,' said Kira.

'Yes, I did,' said Nory. 'If you don't believe me, look at this.'

Kira looked at the paper and got angry and said, 'It's not as good a Good Result as if you'd got one for a particular subject. Many people get those.'

'No,' said Nory. 'Mr. Pears said that this was his favorite kind of Good Result. He seemed to think it was somewhat unusual. You're jealous.'

'I am not!' said Kira.

'You most certainly are!' said Nory.

'I most certainly am not!' said Kira.

'Okay, I'll take your word for it, Kira,' said Nory. 'You're not jealous.'

Later Roger Sharpless came over. Usually what he did was to pretend to kick Nory in the shins, so that Nory could get back at him by pretending to kick him: onk, *conk,* onk, *conk*. Or they would do a strange kind of punching in which they would punch at each other's fists and then say, 'Ow!' and walk around making a huge production of their injured hand, flapping it around, even though it wasn't injured the least bit. But this time Roger just said: 'I think you ought to know that Pamela is unhappy because Shelly Quettner told her that the reason you've been being nice to her is that you've been trying to get a Good Result, and according to Shelly you've finally got what you wanted.'

Nory turned as red as a piece of origami paper. 'That's not true!' she said. 'Yes, I did get a Good Result, but I didn't plan on it, I didn't even know you could get a Good Result for something like that!'

'I told Shelly she was a nitwit,' said Roger. 'But you should have a word with Pamela.'

Nory tried to find Pamela but she couldn't find her anywhere. The next day she sat with her at lunch but Pamela was quiet. 'What Shelly said is totally, totally not true,' said Nory.

'You have been very nice to me,' said Pamela.

'But do you believe me?' Nory asked.

'Believe you about what?'

'That it's totally untrue?'

'I believe you,' said Pamela, 'but I'd prefer to talk about something else.'

'What do you want to talk about?' Nory asked.

'I have no idea,' said Pamela.

'Well, what's your favorite color?' Nory asked.

'Turquoise,' said Pamela.

'Ah yes, turquoise, good.' Nory pretended to note it down in an imaginary notebook. 'And what's your favorite vegetable?'

'Spinach.'

'Spinach, ah yes, very interesting.' Then there was a long silence. Finally Nory said, 'Okay, what's your favorite piece of potato chip on this plate?'

'That bit,' said Pamela, and ate it.

'That was chip number 1306B, yes, yes. I have that noted down. Now, what's your favorite water molecule?'

'What do you mean what's my favorite water molecule?' said Pamela. 'What's your favorite water molecule?'

Nory put her eye close to Pamela's glass of water and peered in. She said, 'It's a difficult case, but I believe my very favorite is that particular one there, sort of near the top. See it? A little to the side of the tiny air bubble. That one. What's yours?'

Pamela poked her finger straight into Nory's glass of water. 'That one,' she said.

Nory laughed. 'Which one?' said Nory.

Pamela pulled her finger out of the water and flicked it so that a drop or two splashed on Nory's face. 'That one,' she said.

'Ah yes, that one,' said Nory.

54. End of Term

The day before the last full day before the End of Term, everybody in the school was told to pack up everything in their backpacks and kits and take it all home. Every book, every notebook, every pen, every pencil case, every netball outfit and pair of shoes—home. The next day, the science teacher passed out strange dull little pencils, since of course their pens were no longer available, and told them to spend the class finding as many words as they could in *scientific* and *cathedral*. This was the kind of thing that Nory was never good at, and in 'scientific' she only found words like 'in' and 'it' and 'sit.' For 'cathedral' Roger Sharpless gave her the very useful hint of starting at the end and going backwards, and she luckily found 'lard' right off the bat, which was a more important word in England than in America, and 'death.' Roger said afterward that you could easily have gotten 'teach' from the word, too, but her brain unfortunately didn't work that way. During break Nory and Roger were pretending to chop off each other's heads with their bare hands when a boy came up and blurted out, 'You like Pamela, don't you?'

'My, you are slow,' said Nory. 'I've already answered that question about four separate times.'

'Of course Nory likes Pamela,' said Roger to the boy. 'Pamela is a hundred times nicer than you are. You are a sorry bowl of soup.'

The boy made a delighted expression and skipped off. Soon after that, when Nory was walking to I.T., a few people came up and smirked wildly at Nory. They said, 'You fancy Roger Sharpless! You fancy Roger Sharpless!'

Nory thought of saying 'I certainly do not!' But she didn't want to lie. So she said, 'Well, I do like him, yes.'

When they were gone Nory was quite relieved to remember to herself, 'I've got this secret that's burning a hole in my pocket and I need to talk about it with someone, and I can't talk about it with Shelly or even Kira, but I can with Pamela, because she's a friend and she can be trusted with the situation.' So later she went ahead and told Pamela, 'You know what? I used to fancy Jacob Lewes, because I'm attracted to boys who are my height or taller than me and highly intelligent and a tiny bit mean and kind of ugly in a particular way. But now, guess what? I fancy Roger Sharpless.'

'Oh, yes, Roger Sharpless is beautiful,' said Pamela. 'I fancy him too.'

'No way!' said Nory. 'I'm quite shocked!'

'Just kidding,' said Pamela. 'I think.'

On the very last day of term, all they had was house meetings and then Cathedral. Then each kid was supposed to meet their parents. Nory gave cards to Mr. Blithrenner and Mr. Stone and Mrs. Hoadley and Mrs. Hant and all her teachers, and to Mrs. Thirm she gave chocolates that she and Littleguy had made the night before. They made the chocolates by melting down a big chocolate bar and pouring it into little plastic molds. One of the molds had turned out to be of an owl. 'But not a scary owl,' Littleguy said, when he saw what it was. 'A chocolate owl. A chocolate owl is not a scary owl.'

In return Mrs. Thirm gave all the kids in class chocolates each, or caramel candies each, from a box, whichever they wanted. Someone said, 'Let's say thanks to Mrs. Thirm!' Everyone shouted, 'Hip hip hooray! Hip hip hooray! Hip hip hooray! Hip hip hooray!' Then everyone put their chairs up on the tables for the last, last, last time that term, and while Nory was lining up the little metal sliders on the legs of her chair on the tabletop so that it was perfectly straight, since that was how it would sit, in just that precise position, until she came back after Christmas, she had a strange feeling of never wanting that term of school to be over but wanting it to go on and on to an endless limit. She slipped Pamela a little present of a pop-up card, homemade, which had a cutout of herself and Pamela in their school clothes standing on top of a little volcano, and she made it so the volcano leaned forward a slight extent when the card opened, which you can do fairly easily by cutting two little slices in the folded-over edge so that the place where you cut can be folded outward the opposite way as a little ledge for something to be attached to. The Pamela pop-up and the Nory pop-up each had one flexible arm that waved back and forth when you pulled the two louvers at the bottom that ran all the way up the back of the card as two strips of paper and sometimes got completely out of whack. They both were saying, 'We made it!' and a bird was tucked conveniently halfway in a pocket of paper that was shaped as a cloud.

A little while later Nory remembered something Mr. Pears quite sternly said about not enough people saying thank you personally to the parents who organized the party before the fireworks on Guy Fawkes Day, so she personally said, 'Thank you for the chocolate,' to Mrs. Thirm. But she said it quietly, while Mrs. Thirm's back was turned, because sometimes it makes you shy to say thank you in person before anyone else has cleared the path by saying thank you. Shelly Quettner heard her say it and spun around and said much more loudly, *'Thank you for the chocolate, Mrs. Thirm!'* Mrs. Thirm turned and smiled at Shelly and said, 'You're welcome.' But that was quite all right because it isn't the giving, it's the thought that counts. 'On the other hand, if the other person doesn't know that you've thought the thought, how *can* it count?' Nory wondered.

Everyone streamed up the path toward the Cathedral and Nory looked at them walking. Each kid had their own particular personality, good or bad or mezzo mezzo, and each personality, no matter what it was, was interesting in some way. Sometimes a kid lost their personality for Nory when all they seemed to want to do was to be cruel to Pamela—then they just became a dull, boring idiot, shuffling through the day—but just lately some kids were getting more preoccupied in other things and losing interest in being cruel to Pamela, to a certain extent, though not totally. Maybe a little bit of the reason was because they saw that Nory was persistently going to be Pamela's friend, and so they began to notice that it wasn't necessarily the absolute end of the world to be Pamela's friend as well or at least not be her vicious enemy.

Inside, since it was a very bright cold day, the green light blasted in through the Jasperium and onto quite a few kids, including Nory. She didn't exactly think God's thoughts, but she thought: 'Frankly, I love school.' 'Love' was one of the most important of all the words that seemed to be spelled wrong on purpose, just to confuse you. It should be spelled 'lov' because the rule is that an *e* makes things long, and there is no long *l* or long *o* or long *v*. For example, it's not 'I loave school,' it's 'I lov school.' But however it was spelled, it was true. The best thing about school was that there were so many teachers teaching different things, so that you learned about how to get stabbed in drama, or about the Aztecs, or the Virgin Mary, or how to type or how to not cry when your plane crashes six times in a row, or about Achilles being dipped into the water, or the friction in a brick, or any amount of things, and there were so many hundreds of kids, and each kid was given quite a bit of responsibility. They were treated as if they were hundreds and hundreds of adults pouring in to work at a factory, wearing a jacket and tie, with that level of independence. You walked to and from Cathedral and to and from lunch, and during break you could choose to go to the art room or the library or back to your classroom or stay outside, whatever you wanted, and you would run into all of the people you knew, and each time you saw someone you had a particular thought, like 'Ah yes, Colin, who is always asking to borrow my eraser,' or 'Ah, Kira, how are you? Haven't seen you in a while!'

A sad thing was that Kira and Nory had stopped being very, very good friends because of Pamela. But it wasn't really Kira's fault or Pamela's fault. It was the fault of all the people who had decided not to like Pamela. If they hadn't been at the Junior School, then there would have been no problem. Of course you could say that there wouldn't have been much of a Junior School, either, since almost everyone was part of the meanness from time to time. But now that some of the kids had decided that they liked Pamela better, or weren't going to bother to hate her, presto, Kira was liking Nory better again.

While Nory was by the South Door of the Cathedral waiting for her parents to pick her up, Pamela came by to give her a note. She didn't want to leave but she had to because her parents said they had to go or they would miss their train. The note said, 'Dear Nory, Thanks for being my best friend, Love Pamela.' And it had her phone number on it, for once. So things were working out rather well. Not to mention that for the first time in a very long time Nory had a wonderful loose tooth. If she bent it past a certain position, she could feel the sharp edge of it that was usually hidden under the gums, and there was a distinct salty taste of blood in her mouth.

The End.

About the Author

NICHOLSON BAKER was born in 1957 and attended the Eastman School of Music and Haverford College. He has published four novels—*The Mezzanine* (1988), *Room Temperature* (1990), *Vox* (1992), and *The Fermata* (1994)—and two works of nonfiction, *U and I* (1991) and *The Size of Thoughts* (1996). He lives in Berkeley, California, with his wife and two children.